Who She Is
Diane Byington

Always dream big!!
Best,
Diane Byington

Who She Is
Red Adept Publishing, LLC
104 Bugenfield Court
Garner, NC 27529
http://RedAdeptPublishing.com/
Copyright © 2018 by Diane Byington. All rights reserved.
First Print Edition: March 2018
Cover Art by Streetlight Graphics

For my grandchildren

Chapter 1
"A Change Is Gonna Come"

October 4, 1967

My first day at Valencia High started with a bloody nose. I had physical education class right after homeroom, and I wandered around the sprawling school, looking for the gym, for ten minutes. When I finally found it and changed into my PE uniform, I saw that the other girls were playing volleyball. I groaned. I loved nearly all sports, but I had always loathed volleyball. Something about spiking the ball and charging the net never worked for me. But of course, I didn't have a choice. The teacher assigned me to a group with another white girl and two black girls, who eyed me with suspicion. That kind of thing happened in every school. I was the perpetual new girl, the one nobody trusted.

Sure enough, as soon as we started playing, one of the black girls elbowed me in the nose. Immediately, blood spurted all over my clothes. I lay on the floor and tried not to cry. The girl apologized and helped me up, and the teacher gave me a towel to hold over my nose. She told the white girl from my team to take me to the nurse's clinic.

"Thanks," I said to the girl when we were on our way. "I don't think I could have found the clinic on my own."

"Sure. Not a problem. I hate volleyball."

I glanced at her to see if she'd read my mind and was making fun of me, but she seemed serious. I tried to remember her name, but pain and embarrassment drove out that information.

"Me, too," I said, sniffing back blood. "It's my first day here."

"Not a great way to start at a new school. But your mom will probably come and take you home or at least bring you clean clothes."

"Not likely."

"Really? Why not?"

I sighed. There was no way I was going to get into my family's weirdness with a girl whose name I couldn't even remember. I held the towel more tightly on my nose and mumbled from beneath it, "She's really busy."

"That's too bad. Your nose isn't great."

That was cold comfort, but I nodded, trying to be polite.

She guided me through a maze of hallways to a door marked Nurse's Clinic. Smiling, she said, "See you around," before turning away.

UNSURPRISINGLY, MOM said she was too busy to come to the school. Luckily, the nurse helped me clean myself up enough to attend the rest of my classes. My nose looked like a balloon and felt like a hammer was pounding into it, but I held my head down and tried to cover my face with my hair.

Just before the end of the last class, the principal gave announcements for the next day over the intercom. I listened with half an ear and thought about my crummy life. Moving all the time, new schools every few months, walking into classrooms and having everyone stare at me—I could go on and on about my woes, but it did absolutely no good. Nobody cared how I felt.

"Should meet at the track tomorrow..."

Wait. Had the principal said something about the track team? I tapped the guy in front of me on the shoulder, and he turned to look at me. "What did he say about track?" I asked.

He glanced at my nose then quickly looked away. "They're looking for some new kids to be on the track team. Tryouts are tomorrow."

"Do they take girls?"

"I don't know. I guess so." He shrugged, nodded, and turned back around.

Suddenly, my nose didn't hurt so much. I loved to run. I ran around all the time on the farms where we lived, just for the fun of it. Being on the track team would give me something to do other than go right home after school and start on my chores. And it might also give me a life of my own, for however long it lasted.

THAT EVENING DURING supper, I gave it a shot. I hadn't asked to do anything after school since I'd played basketball in Ohio, two moves back, and Mom owed me this. Glancing between Mom and Dad, I said, "They're looking for new people on the track team. I'd like to try out. Mom, will you pick me up at four thirty tomorrow?"

She stared at me for a moment before saying, "After what happened to you today, you want to do something athletic? I can't believe you."

"It was just an elbow in the nose. I guess I got too close to that girl when she was trying to spike the ball. That won't happen when I'm running."

"It wasn't just an elbow in the nose. You could have fallen down and hit your head, and that might have triggered a seizure. You're too fragile to take risks like that. In fact, I'm going to write a note so that you won't have to take PE at all."

I fought the urge to roll my eyes. She only brought up my epilepsy when she didn't want me to do something. It never stopped her from making me do heavy work around the house, like washing windows or moving furniture. No matter what my mom said, I knew running wasn't bad for me, because I'd run long and hard playing basketball without the slightest problem.

Mom always kept me from doing what I wanted. I was tired of it. "But, Mom, I like PE, except for volleyball. I'll be more careful. Don't write a note. It'll make me stand out even more than I already do."

She bit her lip and glanced at Dad, who shrugged. Then she shook her head in defeat. "All right, I won't. This time. But if it happens again, I will write that note. Now, eat your supper."

I took a few bites and tried again. "I really want to try out for the track team. I'd play basketball if I could, but the gym teacher said they don't have a girls' team here. Besides, I haven't had a seizure for as long as I can remember."

"Which is exactly why you shouldn't join the track team. Running is harder on your body than basketball, Faye. I don't want to risk it."

That made no sense. "You wouldn't be risking it. I would."

Dad slammed his hand on the table. "Don't sass your mother," he said, raising his voice and giving me a stern look.

Dad mostly ignored me, but things didn't go well when he paid attention.

I looked down at my food. "Sorry."

Arguing was getting me nowhere, so I needed to change my strategy. Mom got weird sometimes, and when that happened, lying was my best bet.

After I washed the dishes, I asked Mom, in my most innocent voice, if I could stay after school the next day and go to the library. "The math teacher's going to tutor people who need it, and I'm really behind." I tried to keep the sarcasm out of my voice when I continued. "It's not running, so it shouldn't harm me."

She grunted then folded and shook out the dish towel several times. "All right, you can do that as long as you keep your medicine with you."

I headed to my room and managed to maintain a straight face until I'd closed my bedroom door. Then the smile broke through. Success!

AFTER SCHOOL THE NEXT afternoon, I sat on the bleachers and watched as six boys in maroon-and-orange T-shirts ran around the track. A slim man in shorts stood on the infield grass, a whistle around his neck, tapping his foot. The coach, I presumed. He glanced at his watch and frowned. Eventually, a boy came out from the school and wandered over. After a short conversation, he joined the others on the track.

I waited, but nobody else showed. Finally, leaving my books on the bench, I made my way over to the coach. He was writing something on a clipboard but looked up when I stopped a few feet away. The eagerness in his eyes turned to disappointment when he saw me. He asked in a strong accent, "Can I help you, young lady?"

I couldn't think of how to begin, so I just stood there, tongue nailed to the roof of my mouth. He tapped his foot and waited.

I cleared my throat and said in as strong a voice as I could muster, "I'd like to try out for the track team."

The corners of his mouth twitched as he stared at me. "Back home in Cuba, girls were involved in all aspects of sports. But in Valencia, only boys are allowed to join the track team. I'm sorry. I wish I could help you, young lady, but I can't." He turned his attention back to his clipboard.

I stood rooted to my spot, getting more annoyed by the second. He obviously needed to add people to the team, and from what I could tell, only one new boy had shown up. After all I'd gone through to be there, the coach wouldn't even let me try out for the piddly high school track team just because I was a girl?

I cleared my throat. When he looked up again, I said, "Uh, how far is one lap around the track?"

"A quarter mile. Four laps make a mile." He smiled at me. "You can run for fun if you want to. Just stay in the outside lanes. But if you're going to run, let me give you a tip: start slow."

I walked back to my seat and untied the wraparound skirt I'd worn to school over my shorts. I would run a mile that day if I had to crawl. And I would run it as fast as my feet would carry me.

I joined the boys and began to jog on the track's soft surface. The rubber gave a little with each step. I felt like I was running on a trampoline or a cloud. I stretched out my legs and swung my arms and watched the world whiz by. My mind settled into a peaceful hum, my breath slow and easy.

The first curve arrived quickly. I sped up. The jog turned into a flat-out sprint, with my feet kicking up high behind me and my arms pumping. As I ran, I lifted my arms out to shoulder height, feeling about three years old. I pretended to be an airplane, for no other reason than that it was fun, and laughed for sheer joy.

The boys on the track team glanced at me curiously, but nobody said anything, so I kept running. Some of them were faster than I was, but I didn't care. I was running like the wind, and I felt light and free.

Before long, the Central Florida heat and humidity got to me, and I started breathing faster. I slowed down just a little. Then I noticed that a girl had joined me on the track. She was running slowly, as though it hurt.

I caught up to her and matched her pace. "Hi, I'm Faye."

She looked at me and said in a snotty tone, "Yeah, I know. You told me when I took you to the clinic yesterday. In case you don't remember, I'm Francie."

I could feel my face flush. "I'm sorry I didn't recognize you. I was in a lot of pain yesterday." Because we moved so often, I had an iron-clad rule to not make close friends so I wouldn't be sad or miss people when we moved. Mostly, I didn't even bother to learn people's names. Francie would just have to get over being mad. Or not. I really didn't care. Running was one of those things a person could do alone, and I was used to being alone.

I sprinted off and ran around the track as fast as I could. When I lapped her, I slowed down and waited for her to accept my apology. But she didn't even look at me. *All right, then.* I was done trying to make up.

But after half a lap of running at her pace and not talking, I couldn't help myself. "So, *Francie*, do you run a lot?" I knew I should follow the ironclad rule, but she was a girl, and she was out running. We didn't have to be friends to run together.

"Today's my first day. I read in a magazine about this girl who got attacked by the race director when she ran the Boston Marathon last spring. Can you believe that? It pissed me off so much I decided to try running."

The Boston Marathon. Something about it sounded familiar, but I couldn't place it. I shook my head and looked over at Francie. She seemed to be waiting for me to say something.

"So how do you like it? Running, I mean."

She panted as she said, "I'm not sure. It's harder than I thought it would be."

I didn't think running was hard. I liked the rhythm of my feet hitting the ground and the way the wind dried the sweat from my face. I wasn't sure what else to say, so I ran ahead, gradually speeding up until I was flying. After my fourth lap, I collapsed onto the grass, huffing and puffing. I'd run hard, and except for being tired, I felt fine. Mom had been wrong about running causing a seizure.

The coach walked over to me, a big smile on his face. "I timed you, and you were faster than most of the boys. You didn't tell me you were such a good runner."

I laughed. "You didn't ask. You just turned me down."

"I'm sorry about before. You know, I don't think the rules specifically exclude girls. I guess it's just a custom here. Anyway, I'd like to have you on the team. I can't say for sure, but you're fast enough that you might even get a track scholarship to college."

A track scholarship? Really? I couldn't keep the grin from my face.

Convincing him to change his mind about me hadn't been too hard. Maybe Mom would be just as easy to win over. I'd give it another try when I got home.

He leaned over to shake my hand. "I'm Coach Lopez. Welcome to the team."

Francie joined us, panting and flushed. Coach Lopez asked her if she wanted to be on the track team, too. "You're not fast, but I can tell you've got endurance. I can train you to go faster, and you might be good in the two-mile race."

"No, thanks. I do want to go far, but fast doesn't interest me."

"All right." He turned to me. "See you tomorrow after school." Glancing at Francie, he said, "I'll still coach you, if you want, even without you being on the team."

Francie shrugged and waved to me as she ran toward a woman who was standing in the doorway of the school. I picked up my books and headed for my locker. Not only had I made the team, but I might even get a scholarship to college. Suddenly, my world was bright with possibilities.

Then I spotted Mom walking toward me, an angry scowl pulling down the corners of her mouth. *Uh-oh. Trouble.*

I trudged to meet her, my mind spinning with thoughts of how I could get out of this situation.

Mom looked like a thundercloud. "You were supposed to be in the library," she said, spitting out the words like bullets.

"Uh, it turns out I got the day wrong. So I ran instead."

"I've been watching you for the last ten minutes, missy. You stayed after school to run, after I specifically told you not to last night."

She'd caught me, so I faced her and tried to keep the excitement out of my voice. "I wanted to try it, and I like it, Mom. I ran a mile today, and nothing bad happened. And I got on the track team."

Mom glanced around. The coach was staring at us as if he wanted to come over and introduce himself but was waiting for an invitation. Mom ignored him, took a deep breath, then turned to me and said in a low, tight voice, "Where are your books? We'll continue this when your father gets home."

WHEN MY DAD CAME IN from the orange groves, I heard Mom talking to him in a hushed voice. I tensed and waited for him to call me into the living room. Hopefully, he wouldn't be too mad.

"Faye, get in here." I winced at his tone. Apparently, he was.

When I went in, he was standing in the center of the room, an angry scowl on his face. "I understand you lied to your mama."

"Well..." I sat down on the couch and crossed my legs, trying to keep the one on top from jiggling.

"What have we told you before about lying?" He wasn't yelling, at least not yet, but his words were clipped and careful, like he was holding himself back. I knew not to sass him when he sounded like that.

"That I shouldn't do it." Of course I knew it was wrong. But what choice did I have if I wanted to run?

His eyes bored into me. "That's right. So why did you?"

I stood up and faced him, quivering all over. "Because I feel like I can be good at running, and I'm not good at much else. You move me all over creation and expect me to be okay with it, but I'm not." In spite of my best effort, a whine crept into my voice. "Running doesn't hurt anybody. Why is it such a big deal?"

He took a breath and glanced toward Mom, who shook her head and marched into their bedroom, slamming the door behind her. Dad sighed and shrugged then went to the refrigerator and took out a bottle of Mountain Dew. After he took a drink, he said over his shoulder, "Go to your room. We'll let you know when you can come out."

I stomped to my room and turned the radio up loud. Aretha Franklin was belting out, "Respect," and I sang along as loudly as I dared.

Mom and Dad talked in their bedroom. I couldn't hear their words, but Mom sounded really upset. Eventually, Dad came out and called me back into the living room. In his most no-nonsense voice, he said, "Your mama thinks that even if other girls could run without harming themselves, which is doubtful, it's bad for your health. So you need to come home on the bus, and you can use your extra energy to weed Mr. Barrett's vegetable garden. You can only run on the track if it's during a class when you're supervised."

"But Coach Lopez will be..."

"I don't want to hear it. Maybe next time you'll think twice before you lie to your mama. Now, go and apologize to her."

I trudged to their closed bedroom door and called out, "Sorry. I won't do it again." Another lie. I would run again as soon as I could.

"All right," came the muffled voice from within. "Go do your homework."

FOR A WEEK, I STAYED in my room as much as possible after school and barely made any headway in weeding the Barretts' vegetable garden. Ordinarily, I wouldn't have minded helping out the old people who owned the farm where we were tenants, but I was on strike, and I wanted it to show.

By Wednesday, I started to wonder if my strike was pointless. I had my heart set on being a PE teacher when I grew up. About the only thing I was good at was sports, so it made sense that I would be a good PE teacher. But to reach my goal, I would have to go to college. The truth was that farm workers like the people in my family didn't go to college. They started working in the fields as soon as they left high school and then worked until they dropped. Picking fruits and vegetables, all day every day, wasn't my idea of living. If my parents forced me to do that, I might as well be dead.

As I wallowed in my misery, I thought I must have been insane to even hope that I could accomplish something so... huge. The problem was that I didn't have another dream to replace that one. Still, a little voice deep inside told me that if I could do something big like get a scholarship to college, maybe I could make a different, happier future for myself.

By Friday, I'd decided that I wasn't quite ready to give up on this dream, even if it was pointless. Maybe a miracle would happen.

Only two and a half more years until I was eighteen, and then I would be free.

Chapter 2
"Sound of Silence"

Every day when I went into the cafeteria to each lunch, I faced the dilemma of where to sit. The school system had recently been desegregated, and the black and white kids sat with their friends on opposite sides of the room. Even though I was white, I didn't have any friends, so I usually sat by myself at an empty table in the middle and pretended to enjoy munching on cheese crackers and reading whatever I'd checked out from the library.

One day I was reading a story about Sherlock Holmes when somebody pulled out the chair across from me. I glanced up, prepared to move if a group of kids wanted the table. Fortunately, it was just one girl, smiling at me. Francie. I recognized her this time. I could tell by her rumpled jean skirt, straggly brown hair, and minimal makeup that she wasn't one of the popular girls. I gave her the tiniest smile I could manage. The ironclad rule was firmly in place.

She asked, "How come you haven't been out at the track again?"

"My parents won't let me stay after school anymore." I tried not to sound resentful, but it was hard. I hesitated. "You been running?"

"Yeah, I have. Most days, anyway. I'm training for the Boston Marathon, and I'm up to two miles now. The coach asked about you."

I shrugged and stared down at the book while I waited for her to go somewhere else.

After a few seconds, she asked, "Where do you live, anyway?"

"Way out on Wolf Branch Road, at the Barretts' farm."

"Hey, you're my next-door neighbor. I knew somebody had moved into that little cottage, but I didn't know who."

"Huh," I said, interested in spite of myself. "Do you live in that yellow farm house about half a mile toward town?"

"Yep. My parents and my brother—Kyle—and me. Kyle's a freshman at the University of Florida, so it's just me now." She leaned toward me, smiling. "My mom's the school nurse, so we have to stay after school in case any of the athletes gets hurt. Maybe you could ride home with us, and then we could run together. I'm sure Mom wouldn't mind dropping you off."

Excitement rushed through me as I considered her offer. Maybe this was my miracle. Then I remembered Dad's tone when he told me I couldn't run anymore. I shook my head. "That was your mom in the clinic?" When she nodded, I said, "No wonder you knew where it was." I hesitated. "Thanks for the offer, but my parents want me to come home and do chores." I paused. Then I burst out, "Why are you being so nice to me?"

She chuckled. "You're not making it easy, that's for sure. I don't like running by myself, and you're the only other girl in this entire school who wants to run."

Even without the ironclad rule, there was no point in trying to be friends if I couldn't run with her. "I wish I could, but I can't. Sorry. Enjoy your running." I took a bite of cracker and looked down at my book.

We sat in silence for a few minutes, and then Francie asked, "Where did you move from, anyway?"

Sighing, I gave up and closed the book. She had been rude to me at first on the track, but today she was like a puppy, all enthusiastic about everything. I wasn't sure how to discourage her without bopping her on the nose.

"Illinois."

"Wow. It sounds exotic. The farthest I've ever been from Valencia is Miami. We went there once when I was little."

That was only four or five hours away. What a strange life, to be so rooted. I'd have given my left arm to be her. "I've lived in twelve different states and gone to seventeen different schools. It's not so great, believe me."

"Huh. Why do you move so often?"

I gave my stock answer for when somebody asked that question. "Mainly because my dad does farm work, and it's seasonal. But also he likes to do different things. He says he's got itchy feet." That wasn't a lie, but there was more to it. My dad liked to flirt with the ladies, for one thing, and that didn't turn out well. He had a bad temper, too. He sometimes got into fights with other workers or told off the boss, and then he'd get fired and we'd have to move. But I wasn't going to get into that. People already thought I was weird because I was the new girl, and I didn't want Francie to think I was even weirder.

"Huh. How long do you think you'll stay here?"

I sighed. "We usually move every three or four months." I hesitated, and then, trying not to sound too hopeful, I added, "But my mom promised that we would stay here until I graduated. I don't know whether to believe her or not."

"That would be cool. I hope you do." She paused. "Listen, we're in the same geometry class, and... uh, I've noticed that you're struggling. I can help you catch up during study hall if you want."

I didn't know how to respond. It was true I would likely fail the class without help, and no one else was offering to tutor me. But I couldn't break my ironclad rule. "No, thanks. I'm fine."

She finally got it. "Suit yourself," she said in a strained voice and concentrated on finishing her salad.

AFTER SCHOOL, I USUALLY helped Mom with cooking and cleaning, but on Saturdays, I was Dad's teenage slave. He was toughening me up so I could work with him full-time when I graduated from high school, and he didn't care whether I liked it or not.

That Saturday, at Mr. Barrett's suggestion, we were raking up the oak leaves that covered the lawn in front of our house. Our landlord liked to watch us from his picture window. He was lonely, I thought, since his wife was losing her mind and his daughter rarely visited. It was why we were there—so Dad could help Mr. Barrett in the orange groves and Mom could take care of Mrs. Barrett, who wasn't allowed near the stove anymore. I saw Mr. Barrett watching us and waved. He waved back but stayed inside.

The day was muggy and still, and puffy clouds were building for the usual afternoon storm. Scents were stronger in Florida than anywhere else I'd lived. I could already smell my sweat when I lifted my arms. But that odor was overwhelmed by something wonderfully sweet wafting through the air that Dad said was orange blossoms.

I jumped when Dad whistled. "Well, looky here." He leaned on his rake and stared down the two-lane road that meandered between New Smyrna Beach on Florida's east coast and Valencia, which was smack in the center of the state. Francie and her mom were running—or rather, slowly jogging—toward us. I recognized Mrs. Ivey from my visit to the clinic a couple of weeks before. Sweat dripped off her face and made her T-shirt cling to her breasts. Francie, who was much slimmer, looked like a preteen boy. Still, with their straight brown hair and fair skin, they were clearly mother and daughter.

They stopped when they were even with us. Dad's eyes twinkled. "Well, hello there. Do you pretty ladies need rescuing?"

Mrs. Ivey laughed. "Believe it or not, I'm not running from anybody. I actually chose to do this, although right now, I'm not sure why. My daughter has started running, and I thought I'd join her." She rubbed sweat off her face with her forearm. "I'm Laney Ivey, by the way. And this is my daughter, Frances. She prefers to be called Francie. We live down the road, sort of next door. Welcome to Valencia." She nodded toward me. "Hi, Faye."

Francie looked up the road, back down it, and then at her feet. Anywhere but at me. She stayed silent.

"Hi," I said, smiling at Mrs. Ivey.

My dad grinned. "I'm Bud Smith. Looks like you know my daughter. Sue, my wife, is in the house." He glanced my way. "Punkin, go inside and get these two ladies some ice water. They look hot."

"That would be nice. It's not that far between our houses, but I'm roasting." Mrs. Ivey moved into the shade and wiped her face with a handkerchief she'd pulled from the pocket of her shorts. Francie stood beside her, face bright red, staring at the cows in the field across the road.

I threw down the rake and headed for the house. Mom stopped vacuuming to ask, "Who's that talking to your dad?" By the time I explained and returned with aluminum glasses filled with ice water, a couple of minutes had passed.

Everybody was right where I'd left them, and Dad and Mrs. Ivey were clearly having a good talk. I heard him say in a friendly tone, "I don't know. We need her in the afternoons for chores."

Oh no. They were talking about me. Even worse, they were staring into each other's eyes while they talked. Flirting, I thought. I felt my face flush, but I knew better than to interrupt when adults were talking, so I handed the glasses to Mrs. Ivey and Francie and then stood beside my dad.

"I'm sorry to hear that," Mrs. Ivey said. "We'd have her back by four thirty. There's still a lot of daylight left after that."

Dad thought a minute. He glanced back at the house and over to Mrs. Ivey. Then he winked at me. "Punkin, this lady says you want to run with her daughter after school. Is that right? You didn't get enough last week?" His voice was light and teasing, totally different from the voice that had told me on Thursday night that I could never run again.

I glanced at Francie, and she looked away. I didn't understand why Mrs. Ivey was doing this for me, but I wasn't going to turn her down. "Uh, yes, sir. I mean, no, I didn't get enough. I'd like to do it."

Mrs. Ivey asked Dad, "Have you seen her run? She's amazing."

He laughed. "She runs away from chores all the time. And I agree, she's pretty fast."

They chuckled. I wanted to sink into the earth, but I stood there, rooted. There was a long pause while we all waited for his decision. Finally, Dad shrugged. "I guess we could try it for a week or two." He turned to Mrs. Ivey. "I hate to put you out, but she needs to be home by four thirty."

Mrs. Ivey finished her water and handed the glass back to me. "We've got a date, then. See you on Monday, Faye. And please call me Laney, at least outside of school. Nice meeting you, Bud."

Francie handed me her glass without a word, and she and her mom ran back toward their house. Dad took off his new Florida Gators cap and fanned himself. A few seconds later, he shook his head and gave me a sharp look. "Wipe that smug look off your face. We've got work to do."

BEFORE SUPPER, I HEARD Dad tell Mom in a casual tone, "By the way, our neighbor Laney Ivey came by this afternoon. She asked if Faye could stay after school and run with her daughter, and she'll bring her home by four thirty. I told her we'd try it for a week or two."

There was a long silence. Finally, Mom said, "Why did you do that? We talked about this, and we agreed. It's not healthy for her."

His voice hardened. "Mrs. Ivey's the school nurse. She'll look out for her." He cleared his throat. "Besides, the bus doesn't come by here much earlier than that, anyway."

I could tell that Mom was trying to speak softly so I wouldn't hear, but her loud whisper carried easily into the bathroom, where I was washing my hands. "I saw her from the window, you know, with her tight T-shirt. You'll do anything a pretty woman asks you to."

His voice lowered in pitch, and it sounded harsh and dangerous. "Yeah, well, I'm still here, aren't I? And the last I checked, I was still wearing the pants in the family." He'd never hit Mom, as far as I knew, but I thought he might if things went any further. Mom probably didn't want to test his restraint. She didn't say another word, and he stomped outside, slamming the door behind him.

I'd won, at least for the moment. But things in my family tended to change pretty quickly, so I didn't count on it lasting. I had no idea what Mrs. Ivey was up to, but I'd make sure to have her drop me off at the road instead of coming up the driveway. That way, there'd be less of a chance that Dad would be able to flirt with her again.

ON MONDAY AFTERNOON, I walked out to the track, nervous about how things would go with Francie. She was sitting in the bleachers, reading *To Kill a Mockingbird*, which I had already finished. She came down, stood in front of me, and spoke in a rush as though she'd memorized the words. "Look, you don't have to run with me. My mom saw us running together the other day and thought we were friends. But you've made it clear you don't want to be my friend, so I won't bother you."

Uh-oh. She was really mad. The ironclad rule was designed to protect me, not to make enemies. I bit my lip and looked away until I had myself under control. Finally, I said in a shaky voice, "I don't mind running with you." I headed toward the track.

Running was as much fun as I remembered. Unfortunately, my big toes hit the end of my old Keds with every step. My toenails would likely turn blue the next day, and Mom might have to stick a needle in them to let the blood out, but for the moment, I didn't care. I just enjoyed the thrill of running.

Francie and I ran together at her slow pace, but she didn't talk to me. After a couple of laps, I couldn't stand the silence any longer. I waited for a group of sprinters to pass us, and then the words fell out of my mouth like hot coals. "I'm sorry I was rude to you. Could we start over? I haven't had a friend in a long time."

There. I'd said it, and I wasn't struck by lightning. The seconds before she answered seemed like an eternity. Then she said, "That's cool."

Just like that, the ironclad rule was history. The weight of carrying it around all the time was lifted from my shoulders, and I laughed. "Why did your mom try so hard to get Dad to let me run with you? You didn't even like me then."

Francie shook her head. "I don't have many friends, so I guess she was trying to help me. She knows how to twist men around her little finger to get what she wants. She embarrasses me sometimes."

"Geez, my dad embarrasses me, too." I hoped things wouldn't get out of hand and force us to move, but it was nice to have something in common with my new friend.

Coach Lopez appeared as we were walking off the track after running eight long laps. "Good to see you out here again," he said to me. "Have you given any thought to running in a race? There's a meet here in two weeks, and I need at least one more runner for the mile." He glanced toward Francie. "Either of you interested?"

Francie shook her head. "No. I just like doing my own thing. Sorry."

I considered. "Do you think I'm fast enough?"

"Sure. And competition will make you even faster. Why don't you give it a try?"

"I'll think about it." It sounded like fun, but I knew Mom wouldn't let me run in a race. She was still mad that Dad had agreed to let me run with Francie. Before I'd left for school that morning, she'd warned me again that running might bring on a seizure. She told me to run really slowly and keep my pills in my pocket. And take breaks every few minutes. And don't blame her if I fall down, foaming at the mouth, and conk my head.

I knew I would have to kiss running goodbye if my parents found out I'd run in a race without their permission. But if I didn't run in any races, how would I manage to get a college scholarship? It was a puzzle. I was pretty good at figuring out puzzles, so I'd give this one some thought.

FRANCIE AND I SAT IN the back seat of her mother's car on the way home so we could talk. She went on and on about the Boston Marathon. "It happens every April, and you run for 26.2 miles around Boston. Even though the race is officially limited to men, two women ran it last year. Bobbi Gibb did it just for fun, but Kathrine Switzer managed to register using her initials. The race director saw her running and flipped out. He jumped on her and tried to pull the bib off her shirt."

"Bib? Like babies wear?" I frowned and shook my head. *Why would anyone, male or female, want to run twenty-six miles? Wearing a bib?*

"No, silly. It has a number on it so the judges can track how fast you run. It's what makes your time official. Anyway, her boyfriend pulled him off her, and she finished the race."

"Okay. That's interesting. But why do you care?"

"Because it's wrong for women to not be allowed to do anything they can."

Laney said, "Some people say that running a long distance will cause women's female organs to fall out. But that's simply not true."

I cleared my throat. "Uh, what about running causing seizures?"

She thought a minute. "A lot of things can trigger a seizure. It's different for different people." She glanced at me in the rearview mirror. "Faye, is this a concern for you?"

"I've got epilepsy, but I take medicine for it. Besides, I feel better when I run."

"Hmm. I don't know what to tell you. What kind of seizures do you have?"

"Kind? I didn't know there was a specific kind."

"You know, like grand mal, where you lose consciousness and your whole body jerks, or petit mal, where you might just stare into space for a few seconds. There are lots of other kinds, too, depending on where the brain is affected. I'm surprised you don't know this."

"I... I don't know what kind I have. My mom's never told me."

She paused. "Well, anyway, you should probably get a doctor's approval before you run too hard or too far."

"You sound like my mom."

"Maybe you should listen to her."

I hated when people told me to listen to my mom. If I listened to her, I'd never do anything but chores. I tried to keep my voice even. "But I told you, I take medicine, and it works. Besides, the coach said I might be good enough to get a track scholarship to college."

She was quiet for a minute. "Yes, I see the problem. I would definitely take it up with your doctor, though."

My mom would make me quit running if I told her I needed to talk to a doctor. We didn't have a personal doctor in Valencia or anywhere else. The only time I ever saw one was at a clinic when I got my school physical.

After a few minutes, Francie said, "So do you want to run the marathon with me next April?"

I forgot all about my mom and epilepsy. Turning to Francie, I said, "Are you crazy? That's way too far to run. Twenty-six *miles*?"

"If those two women can do it, so can I," Francie said. "I might not be able to run fast, but I can keep going. You're faster than me, but you can keep going, too. We can do it together. Wouldn't that be a blast?"

"That's six months from now. I... I don't think I could run that far. Besides, I doubt if we'll even be living here next April."

"I know you move a lot, but didn't you tell me your mom said you could stay here until you graduated? Maybe running Boston would help you get a scholarship."

Huh. She had a point. But the whole thing was a long, long shot. I didn't want to disappoint the first friend I'd had in years, so I gave my stock answer. "I'll think about it."

I PUSHED MY FOOD AROUND on the dinner plate that evening as I tried to figure out a way to convince Mom that it would be fine for me to run in the marathon. Even though running that far seemed next to impossible, I wanted to give it a try. I bit into my hamburger and talked as I chewed. "Francie told me there's a road race called the Boston Marathon. It's more than twenty-six miles long. It's usually only for men, but two women ran it last year. The race director saw one of them and tried to stop her from running. Can you believe that?"

"Faye, don't talk with your mouth full," said Mom.

Dad shrugged. "I can't imagine wanting to run that far to begin with. When I was in the army, I had to run ten miles with a pack on my back, and it nearly killed me. Running for pleasure doesn't make sense to me, whether you're male or female."

I laughed. "Francie wants me to run it with her next year. Do you think I could if I earn enough money to pay my expenses?"

Mom glanced at Dad then shook her head. "The Boston Marathon is in Boston. That's too far for you to go by yourself. And we will not go with you, so don't ask. I don't want you trying to run that far anyway. How many times do I have to tell you it's not good for your health?"

As she talked, neon strings of lights started to dance in front of my eyes. I tried to see past them, but I couldn't. I closed my eyes.

"Faye, are you all right?" Mom's voice was sharp.

The neon strings started to fade, and I opened my eyes.

"What's happening?" she asked, her voice filled with concern.

"There was something..." But I couldn't continue. I had no words to describe the overall blankness that consumed me. I covered my face with my hands and sat there, mind and stomach churning.

"Here." Mom got up and went to the counter, where she kept my pills. She plunked a pill down on the table. "Take this. Now."

I drank a sip of tea and swallowed the pill. Slowly, my nausea faded. The strings gradually disappeared, and the room came back into focus.

Every few months, I had a *spell*. Most of them were similar to this one. I hadn't thought of them as seizures, because I didn't jerk or fall down or anything. But according to Mrs. Ivey, I might be having a different kind of seizure. *What did Mrs. Ivey call it—petty mall?* Mom had always just called them spells.

My head still felt strange, like something inside it was loose, but I was finally able to speak. "May I be excused?"

"Yes, of course. Go lie down. I'll take care of the dishes."

I walked slowly to my room and lay down on my bed. I usually felt bad for hours after a spell. Could running have been responsible for this one?

I hoped Mom wouldn't think of that possibility, because I didn't want to stop running. It was the only way out of my crummy life, and I wasn't going to give it up unless I fell down, foaming at the mouth, and conked my head.

Chapter 3
"Groovin'"

The phone rang later that evening. By that time, I felt better and was sitting in the living room with my parents, watching television and doing homework. Hardly anybody ever called us, except Mr. Barrett, who occasionally asked Mom to sit with his wife while he went into town.

Mom answered. "Hi there," she said in a strained voice. "I'm sorry I wasn't able to meet you the other day. Thanks for bringing Faye home from school... yes, I think we can make it. What shall we bring?"

She hung up, looking flustered, and turned to Dad. "Your *friend*, Laney Ivey, just invited us all to a party on Saturday night. It's a potluck with a few neighbors and friends." She glanced at me. "And there will be kids your age there." She scrunched up her face. "I didn't see how I could turn her down."

Dad closed the newspaper and grabbed his guitar from the corner of the room. He banged a chord and sang a line from some old song about rocking around the clock. I rolled my eyes. Mom and Dad were so completely different that it seemed unbelievable that they'd ever gotten together. Mom was a preacher's kid from some small town in Kansas. She'd gone to a dance and met Dad, who was nine years older and playing in the band. He worked on a neighboring farm during the day, but mostly, he was bumming around after returning from World War II and joining fellows to make music when he could. He fell in love with the red dress Mom wore that night, and she fell in love with his easy smile. Three months later, they were married, and her parents disowned her for marrying outside their fundamentalist faith. She joined him on the road, and they had been traveling ever since.

Mom had married at seventeen. I was fifteen—only two years younger—and hadn't even had a date. Or a kiss. And I didn't own a red dress. I didn't care if I never got married, though. My parents weren't exactly an advertisement for marital bliss. I hoped their regular fighting wouldn't keep us from going to Mrs. Ivey's party. I hadn't been invited to many parties in my life, and I couldn't wait to go to that one. It was curious that Francie hadn't mentioned it to me. I'd ask her about it the next day.

When Dad put down his guitar, Mom said in her no-nonsense tone, "Listen, you two. This is our first time getting to know our neighbors, so I want all of us to be on our best behavior." She gave Dad a hard look. "You especially. I'll be watching."

"Sure, baby. You worry too much." He winked at me.

MOM SPENT SATURDAY afternoon making her trademark carousel cake. A devil's food cake started it, followed by fudge frosting, topped by animal crackers and peppermint sticks, then red-and-white tinsel paper to make a roof for the carousel. It was a sight to behold.

We drove to the Iveys' house because Mom was afraid the cake would melt in the heat if we walked. It was nice to sit in the truck seat. I had gone for a two-mile run up and down the road that morning then pruned the azalea bushes around the Barretts' house and helped Mom cook supper for the old people before I took a shower and slipped into my new used jeans.

The Iveys' home was similar to the Barretts'—a rambling yellow frame house, two stories, with a porch on the front and big windows.

Upstairs, two dormer windows peered outward. I'd always longed for a bedroom with a dormer window. I wondered if Francie slept there.

A friendly dog greeted us with a tail wag and led us around back, where a bunch of adults were packed into a screened porch that ran along the length of the house. I didn't see any other teenagers. Mom stood as stiff as a corpse when Laney welcomed us, but Dad grinned as if he expected a special hug or a kiss from the hostess.

Laney barely gave him a second glance before introducing us to a man standing behind her. "This is my husband. Richard, these are our new neighbors, Bud and Sue—and Faye, who is Francie's friend."

Dad's smile changed to icy politeness as he shook hands with Mr. Ivey. Mom's shoulders dropped, and she gave Laney a grateful smile. Then Laney took our cake and offered Mom and Dad a drink.

"I'm afraid we don't drink," said Mom.

"Well, there's sweet iced tea in a pitcher on the sideboard. You can help yourselves when you're ready."

Laney introduced us to a horde of adults then took me into the living room, introduced me to her son, and left. I could hardly keep my mouth from falling open when I met Kyle. He was the cutest boy I'd ever seen—tall and slim with short brown hair and piercing blue eyes. He looked a little like Paul Newman, whose picture I'd seen in *Seventeen* magazine. Apparently, Kyle was home from college for the weekend.

"Hey, I've heard about you," he said, flashing a heartthrob smile. "You're Francie's friend. She's here somewhere." He glanced around at the rest of the kids in the room, but Francie wasn't with them. He nodded toward a pretty blond girl. "That's Linda, my girlfriend. Can I get you a Coke?"

"Sure."

Kyle headed toward the kitchen.

Some kids were dancing to a fast song by the Young Rascals. I couldn't keep my feet from tapping. And then I was dancing for the first time in my life, other than in my bedroom. The dancers made space for me to join them. My heart beat in time with the bass notes, and my feet had a mind of their own. When the song ended, Kyle handed me a bottle of Coke. Another song came on, and I kept dancing, holding the bottle as still as I could so it wouldn't spill.

Eventually, we got called to the back porch for supper. Francie came in the front door with a boy I didn't recognize. She threw me a smile, but she was clearly more interested in flirting than talking to me. I was okay with that. We could talk on Monday during our run.

A long table was covered with food: barbeque pork, fried chicken, potato salad, green bean casserole, and much, much more. I filled my plate and walked back into the house. A boy who looked vaguely familiar made space for me at the kitchen table.

He smiled. "Hi, Faye, it's good to see you. I'm Reese." He had a huge pimple on his forehead that was about to burst, and I struggled not to stare at it. I'd have worn a bag over my head if my face looked like his. "I hope you run the mile at the meet. Joe and I are running it, too, but we need a third."

Ah. So he was on the track team. "The coach told you he'd asked me? I didn't know that."

He took a bite of hamburger and talked as he chewed. "He asked us what we thought. We all thought it was cool. You and Francie are both good runners, but especially you. A natural."

I could only muster a feeble "Thanks." I was sure my face was flaming and my freckles were standing out like pencil erasers. I let my shoulder-length red hair fall over my face while I took a bite of something that tasted like a mushroom stuffed with fish. I nearly gagged then set down my fork.

"So are you going to do it?" he asked.

"I don't think so." I'd considered it, but my parents would never give me permission to run in a race, and it was too risky to participate without their permission. They might find out some way. No, I'd have to find another way to get a track scholarship. I didn't tell him all that. Instead I said, "I just want to do my own thing." It had sounded good when Francie said it, although it wasn't true for me.

"Too bad."

We went back outside for dessert. Mom's cake had already been scarfed up, so I filled my plate with brownies and apple pie. I looked around for my parents. Mom was sitting at the picnic table, talking to some other women, and Dad had joined a group of men in the backyard. They were all laughing, but his laugh was the loudest of all. Several of the women glanced over at him.

Oh no. He must be telling a joke. His jokes had gotten him into trouble in the past. *Should I do something?*

"Did you hear the one about the priest, the minister, and the rabbi who went into a bar?" His voice carried throughout the backyard. Before he could get any further, though, Mom hurried up to him and said in a low voice, "Hush, Bud. You're out of line."

Everyone got quiet then, and I went back into the house. I didn't need to hear them arguing, especially in front of strangers. About two minutes later, Mom came into the living room and told me it was time to leave. I'd just finished eating and was eager to dance some more.

"How about if I walk home in an hour?"

She shook her head and gave me a look. We glared at each other.

Then Reese was by my side. "I can drive her home later, Mrs. Smith. It's no trouble."

For a minute, she seemed to be weakening, but then her eyes squinched up. "No, thank you. Faye, it's time to go. Don't make me tell you again."

I took a deep breath and hesitated, wondering what would happen if I refused. I didn't quite have the courage to defy her, but it was building.

Reese shrugged. "See you at school, Faye."

I nodded then leaned over and whispered, "Tell the coach I'll run at the meet." I grabbed my pocketbook, nodded to Francie, who was watching us with big eyes, and left.

On the way home, I considered how I felt. On the one hand, I wanted to scream at Mom for making me leave the party when I was having so much fun. And Dad had been such a jerk that I never wanted to be in the same room with him again. I didn't know how that joke ended, but I suspected it was either dirty or offensive in some way. It was probably a good thing Mom had stopped him before he finished it. At least he'd stopped flirting with Laney, and I could relax about that.

My parents were ruining any chance I might have of getting a social life in Valencia. They were the most uncaring, despicable parents in the world. On the other hand, I'd met two interesting boys and had a great time dancing. I knew nothing would ever happen with Kyle, because he was older and had a girlfriend, but I loved his movie-star smile. Reese was only average looking, but he'd actually stood up to my mom and offered to drive me home. I daydreamed about which one I would pick if I had to make a choice.

AS SOON AS WE GOT HOME, Mom sent me to my room. I knew what was coming: she would yell at Dad for telling off-color jokes, then she'd rush to their bedroom, crying, while he stormed off in the truck. I trudged to my room and turned on the Beatles' *Help!* album, trying to make a point by setting the volume as high as it would go. The record was scratchy from so many playings, but hopefully, the loud music would blot out the fight.

After a few minutes, though, I couldn't help but wonder what was happening on the other side of the wall. Part of me didn't want to hear whatever it was, but I also didn't want to miss anything. I held an empty water glass up to the wall between our bedrooms and listened. Silence. Opening my bedroom door, I was prepared to say I had to use the bathroom, but the house was deserted.

A row of tall azalea bushes surrounded the front of the cottage, and I squeezed behind them. Mom and Dad sat next to each other at the picnic table in the yard, talking quietly. They weren't yelling, at least not yet. A bright security light on a telephone pole illuminated them, so they probably couldn't see me hunched in the shadows. I edged around to where I could listen.

Mom said, "What on earth were you thinking? Do you have to embarrass me everywhere we go?"

"Oh, babe. You take everything too seriously. It was just a little joke. Nobody complained."

"You and I both know that joke offends people. Look, you've got to behave. You promised when we moved here that we would stay until Faye graduated. You can*not* get in trouble again." Mom's voice rose to something like a wail.

"All right, all right. It was just a joke. I won't do it again. Now, can we change the subject?" He slapped a mosquito on his forearm and flicked it away. "I think everybody liked your cake. It got slurped up before I even got a piece."

Mom leaned back and stared at him. After a moment, she asked, her voice stern, "What did you take? I know you weren't drinking, because I'd smell it on your breath. What was it?"

Giggling like a child who'd gotten away with stealing a nickel from his mother's pocketbook, he reached into his jeans pocket and pulled something out.

"Pain pills. Here, see? The prescription is for Richard Ivey. He got shrapnel in his leg at Omaha Beach, and I could tell he was in pain. So"—he shook the small bottle—"I had to go to the bathroom. And in the medicine cabinet were six bottles of the stuff. I helped myself to the one with the least amount. He'll never miss it." He giggled

again. "Want one? They're great. You need something to help you relax, baby."

He put his arm around her and pulled her to him. She jerked
away. "Of course I don't want one. And you shouldn't have taken
those."

"He won't miss one bottle. And even if he does, he won't know
who took it." He leaned around to caress her cheek. "I don't want to
fight. I'm sorry I embarrassed you. Now, come here."

"You are such an idiot." I could hear in her voice that she was going to forgive him. The next thing I knew, they were kissing. I wasn't
happy seeing them fight, but I *really* didn't want to watch them make
out. I couldn't believe my mom was taken in by his excuses, but she
was. As usual. It wouldn't be long before they came into the house
and went to their bedroom.

I sneaked back to my room, wondering how Dad's actions would
affect me. The off-color joke was a minor problem. The bigger problem was whether Mr. Ivey would find out about Dad stealing his
medicine and stop Francie from running with me, or worse yet, if he
would call the police. Worst of all, would we have to move? I was
starting to like Valencia, and I was sick to death of moving.

And then I remembered that I had agreed to run in the race in
two weeks. Geez, I was as bad as Dad sometimes with getting myself
into hot water.

Chapter 4
"Can't Help Myself"

Coach Lopez greeted me with a thumbs-up on Monday afternoon. "Glad you decided to do it. You're a fine runner."

"Thanks, Coach." I'd worried all weekend about what would happen if I got caught lying to my parents again. They'd make me stop running, for sure, and I wasn't certain what else. It wouldn't be good—I knew that. Running in the race would be a huge risk. Or maybe it wasn't so huge. They rarely left the farm, so how would they find out? I definitely wasn't going to tell them.

After going back and forth a dozen times, in the end, I had decided I'd have to take risks if I wanted to change my life. I would run the race, and I'd do what I could to keep Mom and Dad from finding out. Mainly, that would involve not mentioning running at home, and praying that one of their rare trips to town didn't coincide with the track meet. Coach gave me a permission slip for my parents to sign. I'd forge their signatures, of course, just as I'd use the last of my lunch money to buy a uniform and a new pair of shoes.

Francie and I usually warmed up together at a slow pace for the first couple of laps. After that, we were supposed to run intervals—one minute of sprinting followed by three minutes of running slowly and steadily. Because she liked to run slowly, Francie enjoyed intervals, but I hated them. Usually, I did them for a couple of laps and then ran as fast as I could until I got tired. But I enjoyed running at Francie's pace for a while so we could talk.

"Nice party," I said after our third lap.

She grunted. "I'm sorry I wasn't around much. But you seemed to have a good time."

"I did. It was great."

"My brother thinks you're pretty," she said. We were on our fifth lap, and both of us were starting to pant.

My whole body tingled for a second until I remembered the reality of the situation. "But he's got a girlfriend."

"I know, but watch out for him. He's got some good points, but mostly, he's a jerk."

He hadn't seemed like a jerk to me. "I wish I had a brother. Or a sister. I hate being an only child."

"Huh. I think I'd like it." We ran without talking for a while. Then she asked, "How come you've got red hair and your parents don't?"

"Oh, my mom's hair has some red in it. Maybe you didn't notice. And my grandma had really red hair, like mine. She died before I was born, but that's what my mom says."

She laughed. "I wish I had your hair. It's gorgeous."

Warmth spread through my chest, and it didn't have anything to do with the Florida sun.

After nine laps, we stopped and collapsed in the shade of a magnolia tree, where we drank water from bottles we'd brought from home. The slight breeze felt heavenly on my sweaty skin.

Staring up at the magnolia blossoms, Francie said in a quiet voice, "I know it's a crazy dream to want to run the Boston Marathon. But I really do want to do it. And I'd like for us to train together. Have you decided yet?"

I sighed. "Why does it mean so much to you?"

"I've thought about that a lot. The main reason is that I really like to run, and it's not fair that girls aren't allowed into the marathon. But also, I want to do it for my dad. He was a runner in high school, but he hurt his leg in the war. Now he can't run. He can barely walk." She frowned. "It's complicated."

We drank some water and watched the cheerleaders wave their pom-poms.

"Well, what do you think?" She sounded slightly irritated.

"I don't know. I've got other things on my mind. The way I see it, if I win the mile race, some college coach might notice me. I'm sorry, but getting into college is more important to me than running a marathon."

"I get that, but don't you think college coaches will notice you if you can run 26.2 miles?"

"Yeah, I guess. But honestly, it's not the running part that worries me. We have five months to train, and that should be enough with Coach Lopez helping us." I laughed, embarrassed to admit the truth. "The big problem is that even if my parents would let me go, which I doubt, they wouldn't pay for it, and I don't have any money."

She rolled onto her side and stared at me, eyes glittering. "That's a different problem. I think it's solvable. From what I can tell, we'd each need about two hundred fifty dollars for expenses. I get an allowance and have half of that saved up for a car, but I'd rather use it for the race." She was quiet for a while then asked, "Do you get an allowance?"

"Sometimes." The answer really was no. My parents gave me lunch money, and mostly I didn't use it except to buy a package of cheese crackers and a Coke, so I managed to save enough for a record album every now and then. Money was tight at our house, and I didn't like to ask for more than I absolutely needed. But the thought of admitting that to Francie made me want to hide in a corner and cry. From what I could tell, her family might as well have been the Rockefellers compared to mine.

"But don't you work for the Barretts sometimes?"

"Sure, but I don't get paid for it."

"They ought to pay you for your work. They've got the money. I'll have my mom talk to Mr. Barrett. Would fifty cents an hour work for you? It's what girls make babysitting, so that sounds about right." She paused. "Could you put in five hundred hours before next April?"

Five hundred hours divided by about five months. That would be one hundred hours a month, or twenty-five hours a week, in addition to the work I already did. "No, I'm too busy with chores. But I could maybe do half that."

"Well, it's a start. I'll try to think of some other ways for you to make money. What do you think? If we can get the money, do you want to do it?"

I wiped sweat off my face with my forearm. "I know you want me to say yes, but I need to get past the mile race before I can think about anything else."

Francie looked away and took a breath. After a couple of minutes, she said, "Okay. We'll talk about it again after the race."

TWO DAYS LATER, I WAS more tired than usual when I got home from school. We'd upped our distance to three miles. Also, my period had started, and I had a bad headache. Actually, everything ached, from my head all the way down to my feet. All I wanted to do was take a nap.

But when I walked up to the house, my dad and Mr. Barrett were standing in the driveway with a boy about my age. He was kind of overweight but strong looking, as if he worked out before eating three or four hamburgers and a bucket of fries. My stomach turned over at the thought of food, and I made a face. The boy saw it and pointed at me, saying something I couldn't make out.

My dad laughed. "Come here, Faye. I want you to meet somebody."

I trudged over to them, holding my books in front of me like a shield. Dad introduced me to Benny Maxwell, Mr. Barrett's grandson. "He's the heir to this property, so be nice to him." They chuckled when I rolled my eyes. "Benny's going to be here some afternoons, helping out. I expect you to do your best to make his experience fun."

The boy had a sour expression on his face, like this wasn't his idea of fun. Well, I wasn't crazy about it, either.

"I'm going to let the two of you weed the garden today. Faye, show him what to do."

I nodded, holding back a groan. Dad had told me more than once to weed the garden, and I hadn't gotten very far. The weeds were almost up to my knees. Weeding was the last thing I wanted to do right then. But since I was hoping Mr. Barrett would start paying me when Francie's mom talked to him, I needed to show him I was worth the money.

We worked for two hours in the afternoon sun as cucumber plants gradually appeared through the weeds. At first, Benny worked close to me. He was so slow that I wondered if he'd ever weeded before.

As he poked along, he said, "Man, this is hard. Almost as hard as playing football. I'm a running back on the JV football team. Probably make varsity next year." He looked at me as if he expected me to be impressed.

I wasn't. Football was a stupid game as far as I was concerned. I said, "Huh," and beat my hoe into the earth as hard as I could.

A couple of minutes later, he tried again. "My girlfriend is a cheerleader. You ever thought about trying out for the squad?"

"Not a chance," I said, standing up and stretching my back. "I'd rather weed cucumbers than jump up and down when some football player makes a goal."

He gave me a disgusted look. "Touchdown, not goal." He moved farther down the row. Other than muttering, "Bitch," which I was sure he wanted me to hear, he didn't speak to me again.

I was kind of sorry that I'd taken out my bad mood on him, and thanked him for helping me when we were done. He didn't answer, just turned his back, stomped over to his old Cadillac, and peeled out. As I watched him leave, a voice inside told me that I really should have been nicer to him.

Chapter 5
"You Better Run"

The track meet took place on a Friday afternoon at our school. As the runners gathered, I lingered at the edge of my school's team, trying to convince myself I didn't stand out. I knew it wasn't true, because my ponytail and breasts, as small as they were, gave me away, but it calmed me to think of myself as one of the guys.

It wasn't a major meet, so Coach Lopez had said there'd just be a few students and a couple of parents watching in the stands. But he was wrong. A few minutes after school let out, the bleachers started filling up. Then I saw the cameras—at least three of them, with the call letters of television stations on the sides. The local channels made some sense. I could believe they might cover high school sports. But then I recognized a slick-looking male reporter from the national news.

I threw a questioning look at Francie, who was sitting in the first row of bleachers. She shook her head, as confused as I was.

Coach Lopez edged closer to the reporters, who were moving as a clump in my direction. "What's going on, guys?"

The reporter laughed and answered that he was here to cover "the first girl runner in high school track in Florida."

I couldn't believe that was true. Even if it was true, I couldn't see why it was newsworthy. Before I could say anything, one of the reporters shoved a microphone in my face. I was too shocked to understand what he was asking, so I just stood there like a store dummy. Reese came over and stood beside me. He whispered, "You look a little wobbly," and grabbed my arm. The warmth of his hand steadied me, and I concentrated on that instead of the microphone.

Coach Lopez rushed over and pushed the microphone away. Then he pulled me back and asked in a low voice, "Are you willing to talk to the reporters just a little?"

I'd told my parents I'd be late because Mrs. Ivey had a meeting. I wasn't sure what would make them madder—me running in a race or me lying to them about it. Either way, they'd probably ground me for life or something worse. Even though they watched the news nearly every night, I could only hope they would miss it that night.

Spots formed in front of my eyes, and my stomach churned. I might throw up any second. I caught hold of Coach Lopez's arm and willed myself to stay upright.

"Give her some room, please." He whispered to me, "Maybe if you tell them something, anything, they'll go away."

Eventually, my vision cleared and my stomach calmed down. I looked around. The cameras were rolling. I had a choice: I could walk away, or I could say something. Either way, I would probably be on the evening news. "Okay, here goes." The coach stood on one side of me with Reese on the other. I spoke to the reporters in a trembling voice. "Look, I don't see why it's news that a girl is in a race. I just like to run." I gave them a tight smile and turned away.

"Are you trying to change the sport? You know that girls can't run long distances without harming themselves, don't you? Did someone put you up to this?"

That got to me. Heat rose up in my face, and I whirled around. This time, my voice was solid and strong. "No one 'put me up to this,' like it's something bad. Girls can run just as well as boys if they train for it."

Breathing hard, I stalked into the cluster of athletes from my school, and they closed ranks around me. The meet began.

The mile race was one of the last events. I moved to the starting position, along with Reese and four other runners, and waited for the gun. *Bang!* We were off. My jitters disappeared. Ignoring the spectators, I focused on moving into the inner lanes. Almost immediately, in spite of how hard I tried, I fell slightly behind the leaders. I ran smoothly, but most of the boys were faster. Dimly, I heard cheers, and a few boos, too.

By the half-mile mark, some of the boys were flagging. I ran in the middle of the pack, trying not to get elbowed off to the side or tripped. By the last lap, I was panting, and my hair had fallen out of its rubber band and hung down below my shoulders.

Finally, I saw the finish line. Gasping, I stretched my legs to their full length and kicked it out as hard as I could. But it wasn't enough. Some guy from another school won, and Reese came in second. I was third. After I caught my breath, I pasted a fake smile on my face. Reese and I high-fived, and he gave me a big hug.

Third place was good, but I had hoped to win. I was pretty sure that third place wouldn't get me a college scholarship. I leaned over and put my head down between my knees, trying not to cry. And then I had to go to the front to receive my ribbon from the principal, who plunked it into my hand instead of pinning it on my shirt. It was the first award of any kind I'd won, but it wasn't good enough. And if my parents saw me on TV, I'd probably never be allowed to set foot on a track again. Goodbye, college scholarship. I had gambled and lost. The only good part of coming in third was that I might not be on the news.

As the crowd melted away, Coach Lopez came over to me with a tall, blond woman beside him. "Faye, I can see you're upset. But you don't need to be. I didn't expect you to win against the fast boys. You did great," he said, patting me on the shoulder. "I want you to meet Coach Peters. She's an assistant track coach at the University of Florida."

Even though I'd only lived in Florida for a month, I knew that the University of Florida was the state's big school for running. My mouth went dry, and my heart did a flip-flop.

Both adults look at me, waiting for me to speak. I licked my lips and croaked out, "Wow. Uh... hello."

Coach Lopez said, "And this is our new star runner, Faye Smith."

Coach Peters stuck out her hand, and I rubbed my sweaty palm on my shorts before shaking hands with her.

"You ran a good race, Faye," said Coach Peters. "I think you might have won if you were racing against other girls." She paused, giving me time to say something. I didn't know if she was right or just being nice. I shrugged, and Coach Peters continued. "I understand you might be interested in running track in college."

I nodded.

"I'd like to talk to you about that." She gestured to the bleachers. "Why don't we sit down?"

Francie must have thought I was talking to a reporter and it was okay to interrupt, so she came over and gave me a hug. "Congratulations. You did great."

Coach Lopez said, "Coach Peters, this is another of our runners, Francie Ivey. Francie, Coach Peters is with the University of Florida track team."

I could hear Francie suck in her breath. We all sat down on the bleachers.

"Here's the deal," Coach Peters said, looking at me. "We're planning on starting a women's track team soon. It's in the planning stages now, so we're scouting talent. You're a junior, right? In two years, the team will probably be up and running. Judging from what I saw here today, you would be a good addition. You're fast and strong, and you didn't give up."

"Uh, thanks. I didn't win, though." As soon as I said it, I wanted to kick myself. We all knew I didn't win. I looked down at the ground for a few seconds before glancing back at her.

She smiled as though she knew what I was going through. "Yes, I know. But your coach tells me you just started working with him. You did well for having had so little training. Most people consider track and field to be a boys' sport, so we aren't sure what times we can expect from girls who've had good training. You're at the beginning of a new sport. I expect that, before long, there'll be lots of track programs, and even marathons, just for women."

"Marathons?" asked Francie, sounding hopeful.

"Yep." Coach Peters looked hard at Francie. "Are you interested in marathons?"

"Faye and I are planning on running the Boston Marathon next spring."

I wanted to punch her for including me in her plans, but I didn't dare.

Coach Peters said, "Well, now, that puts a different spin on things." She looked at me. "If you're interested, you can probably earn a spot on our new team, especially if you improve your time on the mile." Then she looked back and forth between Francie and me. "On the other hand, if you run the Boston Marathon and finish in, say, no more than four and a half hours, the publicity you would get would be great for our program. I'm making no promises, mind you, but in that case, I might be able to talk to you about full scholarships."

I sat there with my mouth open. Francie said in her most polite tone, "Thank you, ma'am, but I just want to run the Boston Marathon, not be on a track team. My parents have already saved up for my college tuition. But I think Faye would love to take you up on your offer."

Coach Peters turned to me. "Is that right?"

I nodded. I must have fallen into a sweet dream or something. This couldn't be my life. Nothing ever went right in my life. I almost didn't dare breathe, for fear I would wake up.

"I'm sure she can do it," said Coach Lopez. "She just needs a little training, is all."

"All right then," said Coach Peters. "Would you like to be a Florida Gator, Faye?"

"Really? I mean, yes, ma'am, I'd like that. But my grades aren't so great."

"Ah. You've got a little time to improve them. And we have tutors to help you once you get to Gainesville. So your work is cut out for you. Keep at it, and you'll be running for me in a couple of years." She held out her hand again, and I was in such a daze that I just stared at it. She laughed. "I'll stay in touch with your coach, all right?"

It was a defining moment of my life, and all I could say was, "Yes, ma'am." I wanted to thank her for the confidence she had in me and tell her I would do my best to prove myself worthy. But the words wouldn't come.

The coaches walked away, and Francie and her mom congratulated me. We walked together into the school. I leaned against my locker, and my daydream fell apart. Tears coursed down my cheeks as I cried my heart out. Laney and Francie exchanged a strange look, but Laney gave me a handkerchief and waited for me to calm myself.

Between sobs, I blurted out, "God, my parents are going to kill me. I told them I had to stay late because of you, and now they'll find out that was a lie." The tears started again.

Laney blinked and lifted her eyebrows. Maybe she'd thought I was crying for some other reason. "Not necessarily. It might not even make the news, since you didn't win. But I'm disappointed you didn't tell them the truth." Her eyes bored into mine. "Faye, is everything all right at home?"

It had been drilled into me not to talk about my family's business to outsiders, but I managed to say, "My parents really don't want me to do anything except stay home and do chores. So if I'm going to do anything at all, I have to lie." I started crying again.

Laney waited until I stopped. "Listen, sweetie, I don't want to get mixed up in your family situation. You shouldn't have lied to your parents. But if they give you any grief, why don't you have them call me, and hopefully I can straighten things out." She looked questioningly at me. "Most parents would be proud to have such a talented daughter. Maybe yours will be, too, once they get used to having a celebrity in the family. A college scholarship. That's wonderful!" She reached out, tucked my hair behind my ear, and waited for me to explain myself.

I shook my head, as confused as she seemed to be. "I think they'd be proud if I did something else, like get a ribbon for typing or spelling or geography. But not for running. Not even if I'd won. My mom thinks it's not healthy for me to run, and she won't listen when I tell her I'm fine."

Laney said, "Uh, did you ever talk to your doctor about it?"

I grabbed my books and headed for the car. "Please, can we just leave?"

Laney didn't say anything else, and we drove home in silence until something occurred to me. "How did those reporters find out about me, anyway?"

Laney thought for a second. "Oh, I imagine it was Reese's father. He owns the Valencia newspaper. Maybe he sent out a press release or something. But Faye, really, don't make too much of this. Tomorrow there'll be another story, and nobody will remember this one."

She didn't know my parents, but I didn't bother to correct her.

As I got out of the car, Francie patted my hand and said, "Call me later, and let me know if you survive."

"I will. And I want to talk to you about something, too." I gave her a hard look and slammed the car door behind me.

UH-OH. The expression on Mom and Dad's faces told me they'd seen the news, and I was on it. Mom slammed the dishes around so hard I was afraid they might break.

I had decided to do my best to act like this was a normal day. "Hi," I said, dropping my books on the couch.

"Sit down. We've been waiting supper for you," Mom said.

We ate in silence. The news was over, so I didn't even have the newscaster's droning voice to ease the tension. Afterward, Dad pushed back his chair and banged his hand on the table. "We've finished eating, like your mama wanted, and now it's my turn. Dana Faye, you have disobeyed us at every turn ever since we moved here. Your behavior is out of control. Am I going to have to whip you to make you behave?"

I wasn't sure why what I'd done was so horrible, but it wasn't the time to ask. "I'm sorry, Dad. I won't do it again."

"You damned sure won't do it again. You lied to us, you went against our wishes, and you ran on national television with boys. I want to know why you did it, girl."

Dad didn't seem to be proud of me, so I quickly said, "I just love to run, Dad." I hated how thin and tentative the words sounded. "It makes me feel better than anything I've ever done."

"You've got no business being on TV. You looked like a hussy out there, flaunting your body."

"Dad, I just wore the same uniform everybody else on the team did—shorts and a T-shirt. It wasn't indecent." I struggled to hold back the tears. "I'm not a hussy. I'm just a runner."

Mom and Dad exchanged a mystified look. She sniffed away tears, and he grunted. There was silence for a few minutes.

Dad said, "Well, you'll have to find something else to do. You've run your last race. Do you hear me?"

Something about his wording gave me hope. "Yes, sir. I promise not to race anymore in any track meets. But"—I hoped I wasn't pushing him too far—"would it be all right if I keep running with Francie? She needs me to run with her so she won't be all alone."

"No," Mom said. "Definitely not. No more running."

"Now, Sue, maybe we ought to give that one some time. The Iveys are our neighbors, and they've been very kind to us. And it's nice for Faye to have a friend." He looked at me hard. "You're grounded for a week while we consider what's next. To and from school on the bus, and no extracurricular activities. You hear me?"

"Okay. I'm sorry again. I won't run in any more track meets."

In my room, I breathed a sigh of relief. That wasn't as bad as it could have been. Being grounded for a week was better than for life.

AFTER I HAD CALMED down, I called Francie. As soon as she answered, I asked, "Why did you do that to me?"

"What?" she asked, trying to sound innocent.

"You know what. Getting me involved in running the Boston Marathon with you. You know my parents won't let me go, but you set me up. Why did you do it?"

She took a few breaths. "I did it for you. The coach only talked about giving you a scholarship after I mentioned the Boston Marathon. You know that's true."

"Yeah, but it's not going to happen. I already told you we don't have the money for the marathon."

"But you said if you *did* have the money, you'd like to do it."

My mouth was open to tell her that wasn't exactly what I'd said. Then I realized she really had done me a favor. I should be grateful.

We lived in such different worlds, Francie and I. Her parents would never have dreamed of grounding her for running in a race and almost winning. Instead, they would have been proud. It was assumed she would go to college, even without a scholarship. How I wanted to be from her family instead of my own.

But I wasn't quite ready to give up on being mad at her. "I'll have to think about it. Since you got me into this, would you still be willing to tutor me in geometry?"

"Sure. We can start tomorrow during study hall."

When we hung up, I heard a tentative knock at my bedroom door. I opened it, and Mom was standing there. She was crying.

Chapter 6
"(I Can't Get No) Satisfaction"

Mom sat on the edge of my bed and looked at her hands, which were tightly clasped in her lap. After a while, she stopped crying. "Honey, I need to tell you something. I'd hoped never to have to do this, but I guess you're old enough to know."

Oh jeez, what did I do now? I sat up straight and waited.

She looked at me, and I could see the tracks that tears had made running down her cheeks. "Do you remember when we lived in Harlan, Kentucky? I think you were in the third grade."

"It was second grade." It was really supposed to be first grade, but I'd been promoted because I'd taught myself to read. They hadn't done me a favor, though, because I'd gotten so far behind in math that I'd probably never catch up. Still, I'd liked Harlan. That was the last time I'd allowed myself to have a friend until we moved to Valencia. Her name was Sally. I pictured her freckled face and blond hair, and a wave of sadness flowed through me. But I didn't bother mentioning her. Mom was building toward something, and I couldn't imagine what it was.

"Well, something happened that explains why we're so upset about you being on television." She pulled a handkerchief out of her apron pocket and folded it into tiny squares then flicked it open and started over. "Your dad was accused of doing something illegal when we lived there. He didn't do it, of course, but we don't like to call attention to ourselves."

I closed my eyes, and Harlan rushed back. A tarpaper shack that smelled musty because the roof leaked. Dad coming home from the mines, black all over from coal dust. Playing jacks with Sally, who lived across the street.

"What was he was accused of doing?"

She sighed. "Stealing money from the miners' strike fund. But nobody could prove it, and they didn't find the money on him."

"Is that why we left town in the middle of the night?"

"It wasn't in the middle of the night, Faye. Don't exaggerate." She paused. "But yes, we did leave in kind of a hurry. The miners were about to swear out a warrant against him. He got the blame because he was the newest miner and not from around there. We didn't think there would be justice in those hollers if the sheriff got him."

Something felt wrong about what she was saying. "That was nine years ago. Surely they can't still be mad about that. How much money was it, anyway?"

"Around a thousand dollars, I think."

"Oh." That was a lot of money. "Are you sure he didn't do it?"

Her face tightened. "Yes, honey, I'm sure. We'd have been a whole lot richer if he'd stolen it, and anyway, your dad isn't that kind of man."

I wasn't so sure about that. I could imagine him stealing money if it was in somebody's coat pocket and easy to get to. Just as he'd stolen drugs from Mr. Ivey's medicine closet. But I didn't dare say that to Mom. I just nodded.

"So you see, you getting on television makes us nervous. Some reporter might say you're Faye Smith, daughter of Bud and Sue Smith, and the sheriff up there might hear it and come and arrest your dad, or at least call the local police so they could do it. I don't know how it works, but I need your father's income. I don't see how I could support us alone. Do you understand now why we're upset?"

I didn't really. It had all happened a long time ago. Besides, I couldn't imagine a sheriff from Kentucky coming all the way to Florida to arrest Dad for stealing. Murder, maybe, but not theft. But I didn't dare question her anymore. Instead, I changed the subject. "But, Mom, they say I made history today. Aren't you at all proud of me?"

She sat with her mouth open, confusion in her eyes. "Honey, I'm proud of you every day. You're a beautiful girl with lots of talents. I just wish you were using other talents instead of running."

"But the coach said I might get a scholarship to the University of Florida if I keep running and get my grades up." I left out the part about the Boston Marathon. That could wait until later.

Mom looked sad. "Honey, we don't have the money to send you to college. Even with a scholarship, there are other expenses. And we're planning on you working with us full-time after you graduate. You know that. We've talked about it before."

I couldn't let it go. I just couldn't. If I did, I'd be stuck for the rest of my life. "But, Mom, I want to go to college. Don't you see? After I graduate, I can make lots more money."

She pressed her lips together and gave me a look that said I didn't understand anything. "Honey, college isn't for people like us. We're blue-collar workers. I never even graduated from high school, and I've done all right. Besides, we need your income sooner rather than later."

I had thought she'd be excited for me to get out of the terrible life we lived. The fact that she wanted me to stay in it made my head feel ready to explode.

Mom said, "I know you don't like outside work. What about if you think about being a secretary? You can take typing and shorthand classes next year, and then you can get an indoor job right out of school. How's that for a compromise?" She smiled as if she were offering me a prize.

But this was no prize. "Uh, I'll think about it." Why did I have to compromise when I'd just been offered a scholarship? Secretarial work was slightly better than picking fruit and vegetables all day in the hot sun but nowhere as good as college. Maybe I was too stupid to make it through, but at least I could try.

I gave her a tight-lipped smile. I wasn't going to give her the satisfaction of arguing anymore. She knew what I wanted to do.

Mom sighed. "For now, your dad and I will let you keep running with Francie, but no more track meets. Ever. Don't let us find out that you're doing it behind our backs, or I won't be able to keep your dad from getting out his belt. You need to keep in mind that your actions could get us into a lot of trouble. And think about secretarial classes." She kissed me on my forehead. "All right. Enough of that. Bedtime in twenty minutes."

She went out and shut my door. I could tell by the lightness of her steps that she was relieved. But I felt heavy, like I was made of lead. I'd just found out my dad was probably a thief, and maybe even worse. Whatever he had done, evidently it was bad enough that it could get him arrested or even put in prison.

It really wasn't my problem, though. If Mom thought that telling me about Dad's legal troubles was going to make me feel so guilty that I would stop running, she was wrong. Even if the law found him and arrested him because of me, if he was innocent, he'd be fine.

After talking to Mom, I decided that I definitely wanted to run the Boston Marathon with Francie. It wasn't a track meet, at least not technically, so I wouldn't be breaking their rules. But even if I did break their rules, that was less important than running that race. I was going to give it everything I had, and I'd come up with the money somehow. Mom was not going to make me be a farm worker or a secretary—not if I had anything to say about it.

AT SCHOOL ON MONDAY, I was a minor celebrity. Kids I didn't even know passed me in the halls and said, "Hi," or "Way to go." My homeroom teacher announced that I'd been on the news, and everybody clapped. I'd never been the center of attention before, and my face heated up as I smiled and looked down at the desk.

At lunch, I told Francie I would run the marathon with her. "I don't know how I'll make it happen, but I'll do it somehow."

"Hooray!" She gave me a big hug, and we laughed together at the sheer audacity of our decision.

Reese brought his tray over and joined us. We told him about our plan. "That's great," he said, smiling broadly. "I'm sure you can do it. You're both fine runners."

We were deep in conversation when some cheerleader in a uniform and big hair leaned over me as she was returning her tray. It tipped, spilling half a plate of spaghetti into my lap. I yelled and jumped up. "Hey!"

She just sneered, directing a satisfied look at the mess on my skirt. "Don't even think that acting like a boy will make you popular." She smirked and walked away, her friends giggling as I swiped at the gooey mess.

Reese ran to get napkins, and he and Francie helped me clean off the spaghetti. I had a feeling that my best skirt was ruined.

"I don't even know her name," I said, holding back tears.

"Amy," Francie said. "I've gone to school with her all my life, and she's the world's biggest bitch."

"Why would she do that to me?"

Francie shook her head. "Who knows why somebody like that does anything? She's dating Benny, so maybe that explains it a little." It didn't make sense that he was holding a grudge because I was a little mean to him the day we weeded together, but it was the best explanation we could come up with. He hadn't come back to work on his grandfather's farm, so I figured he'd forgotten all about our little tiff. But some people couldn't stand it if another person got even a smidgen of the attention they thought was theirs by right.

Having spaghetti dumped on me made me even more determined to run the marathon. I was going to be famous some day, and that cheerleader was just going to be fat and lazy.

THAT AFTERNOON, I TOLD Coach Lopez that my parents wouldn't let me run in any more track meets.

He said, "I'm sorry to hear that. But I'll still train you for the marathon." He licked his lips and looked embarrassed then mumbled, "You still got that ribbon?"

I started to tell him it was in my locker, but something about the way he spoke stopped me. "Why?"

"I'm sorry, Faye, but I'm going to need to take it back. The Athletic Association decided a girl can't win or place in a track meet. It'll go instead to the boy who came in fourth."

After all the trouble I'd gotten into at home, I couldn't keep the stupid ribbon? I glared at him. It wasn't his fault, but I was not giving that ribbon back, no matter how many times he asked. I said, "Uh, it's at home. I'll bring it tomorrow."

"I'm sorry to have to ask you for it. I know you won it fair and square."

"Yeah."

The funny thing was, I didn't bring that ribbon back the next day or any other day over the next week, and Coach didn't ask for it again.

Chapter 7
"Paint It Black"

A week later, on Tuesday evening, I decided to push myself and run six miles on the road by our house. Unfortunately, Mom kept finding chores for me to do, so it was late when I headed out and almost dark by the time I turned toward home.

A mile or so from the house, I heard a vehicle roaring toward me from behind. It was the only one I'd encountered during my run. There weren't many houses out our way, so I assumed a neighbor was headed to town. I moved to the left side of the road and waited for whoever it was to pass.

I kept pounding my feet as a car came closer and slowed quickly, its brakes squealing. Glancing back, I thought I recognized the car, but I couldn't place it. And I couldn't see the driver because of the glare from the headlights.

The car slowed to a crawl.

Its headlights blinked off.

The hair on my arms prickled. I didn't dare look back again.

The track team boys had warned me that crazy drivers regularly ran them off the road. If this was somebody's idea of a joke, it wasn't funny. But maybe it wasn't a joke.

My mind raced as I considered what to do. There was a barbed-wire fence on my left, so running across the field wasn't an option—I might get caught in the barbed wire, and the driver might stop the car and... I didn't want to think about what might happen. I couldn't dart to the right for fear of getting hit. And turning around and running back to the last house I'd passed probably wouldn't help. The best I could remember, its windows had been dark. So I decided to continue moving forward in the hope that whoever was in that car would get tired of scaring me and drive on.

The car rolled along at my pace. I sped up. It matched me. I slowed down. It did, too.

My teeth were chattering, and my heart was beating so fast I thought it might jump out of my chest. I moved off the asphalt and onto the sandy shoulder, watching as carefully as possible where I put my feet. But one foot stepped into a hole, and I went down, scraping both knees. As I started to get up, the car roared off, male laughter drifting behind like smoke.

I lay on the ground for a few seconds, breathing hard. Then I felt something wriggling on my legs. All of a sudden, I lit up with pain. Some creatures were on me, stinging and biting. I scrambled to my feet and brushed whatever it was off my legs. My skin felt like somebody was holding a burning cigarette to it in a thousand places.

Another car drove up, and it stopped. I knew I couldn't run fast enough to get away, so I turned toward it. An old man with a kind face got out. "Are you hurt, miss?"

"Something's biting me."

He reached into his car and pulled out a flashlight then ran the light over my body and down to the ground. "It's a fire-ant hill." He looked at me, confused. "And you're bleeding. What were you doing on an anthill?"

I moved away as I said, "I tripped and fell."

"You shouldn't be out on the road by yourself in the dark. Can I take you home?"

I wasn't about to get into a stranger's car after what had just happened, no matter how safe he appeared. "No, sir. I'll be fine now."

He drove off. I walked home, shaking all over and hobbling because of the pain. Now I knew why those demons were called fire ants. Before, I'd thought it was just because they were red.

When I turned into our driveway, I noticed the car parked in front of the Barretts' house. And I realized where I'd seen it before. It was Benny's rusty old Cadillac. He must have been going to visit his grandparents and had terrorized me on the way just for fun. What a jerk.

I considered knocking on the Barretts' door and yelling at him, but something stopped me. For one thing, Benny was a football player, and I was essentially a nobody, even if I had made history in a small way. He could make my life at school even more miserable than he already had. Second, Mr. Barrett might side with him and make us move. After all, Benny was blood kin, and we were just tenant farmers. The one thing I didn't want to do was move again when I was finally beginning to have a life.

Still, something about that car gave me the creeps.

In the house, Mom saw my bleeding knees and the red welts and ran for a cold washrag. She cleaned me up and dabbed baking soda on my many bites. We stopped counting after fifteen. After an hour or so, the stinging lessened.

When the crisis was past, Mom asked, "Why did you fall?"

I knew what she was really asking. "I tripped. There was a hole I didn't see." That was the truth, although only part of it. "I didn't have any weird feelings or anything, if that's what you're wondering."

I wasn't sure she believed me, but she let it go. "All right. I don't want you running alone at night anymore."

She seemed a little surprised when I didn't argue. I tried to hide my shock from Mom, but I couldn't stop shaking. My mind felt frozen—stuck out there on that spooky road with that awful car following me. I knew I was more upset than I should have been, considering that nothing terrible had happened other than that I fell. Well, that and the ant bites, of course. The track team boys would say it was basically an ordinary day out running on the road. But my imagination was going wild, thinking about what might have happened, and I couldn't control it. I went to bed early.

I WAS IN A SMALL DARK space, alone, and I couldn't get out. The smell of pee was so strong it gagged me. I screamed and screamed, but nobody heard me. I was sure I was going to die.

Then Mom was shaking me. "Faye, wake up. You're having a bad dream."

The dream slowly faded. After a few minutes, I didn't smell pee anymore, so I must not have wet the bed. My pillow was damp, though—probably from tears—and I was tangled in the sheet. Mom shook me again. "Wake up, honey. You're safe. Calm down."

I opened my eyes. "It was so real."

"Was it the dark dream?"

I nodded. When I was little, I used to have that dream nearly every night, but it had been years since it had shown up. I'd thought it was gone for good. But on this night, it had seemed so real that I could feel and smell everything, although I couldn't see a thing. My voice was hoarse from screaming.

Mom gave me one of my pills and lay beside me for a few minutes until I stopped shaking. When she left, I asked her to keep the light on. My dad had a thing about not leaving lights on when they weren't needed, and he usually made me turn off my overhead light at ten o'clock. She gave me a look, but she did it.

I was too afraid to close my eyes for the rest of the night and too exhausted to go to school the next day. There was no way I was ever going to go running at night again. At least, not alone.

Chapter 8
"Eight Miles High"

I hadn't seen Kyle for weeks, not since Laney's party. I had a hard time keeping the shock off my face when I answered a knock at our door on Saturday afternoon and saw him standing there, carrying a basket covered by a cloth.

"Hey, Faye. I'm home for the weekend, and Mom sent me over to see if y'all are interested in taking one of Lady's puppies. They're almost old enough to be adopted." He gestured toward the basket, which I now saw was shifting around on its own.

"Really? Let's go outside." I knew Mom wouldn't let us get a dog, but I wanted to look at the puppies before Kyle took them away. He set the basket on the picnic table and lifted the cloth. Inside were two bundles of fur that waddled from one side of the basket to the other. They looked up at us and barked in sharp, shrill voices.

I reached in and grabbed one and held it up to my chest. It nestled against me. "Aw, they're so cute. How old are they?"

"Four weeks today. Lady had four, but two have been spoken for, so there's just these two I'm trying to find homes for. Do you want that one? It's a female. We've been calling it Ginger, but you can give it whatever name you want."

She was brown-gold with long hair. Yes, *Ginger* fit. I was in love. "What kind are they?"

"Mutt, I guess. Somebody dropped Lady off in front of our house a couple of years ago, and we kept her. She's a nice dog. We keep meaning to get her spayed, but she always gets pregnant before we manage it. This is her third litter. Mom's definitely taking her to the vet soon. She says this is the last time we're going through this." He laughed. "It's always my job to find homes for the puppies. What do you think?"

"I'll give it a try. Wait here." I went inside, still carrying the puppy. Mom was in the kitchen, cleaning up from lunch. "Kyle brought over some adorable puppies that he's trying to give away." I held Ginger up for her to see. "Can we take her? I'll feed her and take care of her." Seeing the look in Mom's eyes, I tried one last time. "Please, Mom? I've never had a pet."

She glanced at the puppy and shook her head. "No. We move too much to take care of a dog."

"But, Mom, you said we're going to stay here until I graduate. That's long enough." I knew how this was going to end, but I played it out anyway.

"Take that dog outside, Faye. We can barely feed the mouths we've got now. We can't afford to add another one."

I heard the edge in her voice, so I gave up. It had been a useless effort, anyway, and continuing to argue wasn't worth making her mad.

I took the puppy back outside and set it gently into the basket. "Mom says no. Sorry. Good luck finding homes for them."

"Sure," he said. "I always manage it. They're good dogs." Inside the basket, the puppies curled up together and went to sleep. He shrugged. "Mind if I hang out for a while?"

He wanted to hang out with me? I bent over the basket and let my hair hang over my face to hide the laughter that bubbled up. And I was sure that my face was beet red. When I had control of myself, I stood up and tried to act casual, as if it were an everyday occurrence that the boy of my dreams asked if he could hang out with me.

"Okay. I can take a break between chores." We sat at the picnic table and watched the puppies sleep for a while. Was I supposed to start the conversation? Apparently. I had no idea what to say. "Uh, how's college?"

He grinned and started in, talking a mile a minute. "I hate my roommate. He's in bed by nine thirty every night, so I have to go somewhere else to study. Not that I do that much studying. I've been really involved in ROTC. I'm learning how to march and use a gun." He looked at my face and quickly said, "There aren't any bullets in the guns. At least, not now. When I join the army or the marines, there'll be real bullets."

"Wait a minute," I said, alarmed. "You're in college. Don't you have a deferment?"

"Yeah, but it feels wrong. Why do the guys who aren't in college have to fight in Vietnam, and I get a pass just because my parents have some money?"

I thought about that. "I'd give anything to go to college. Why is going into the military so important to you?"

"Because I hate all those Vietnam protesters. It seems like there's a protest march every night, people marching down the streets, yelling for us to bring our boys home. They've got no patriotism, and it drives me crazy."

I could see by his scowl that he thought I would agree with him, but I didn't. "Just because you disagree with them doesn't make them unpatriotic. If I was there, I'd be marching with them." I was breathing fast and hard. It was the first time I'd ever argued with someone my age. It felt good. Lots better than arguing with my parents, who always won even if they were wrong.

He laughed. "I can see that we've got a lot to talk about."

And we did. We talked and argued for a couple of hours, until the puppies' little voices pierced the afternoon heat.

"Oops, I stayed too long. I need to get these little fellas home to their mama." He paused and gave me a look I couldn't decipher. "Really good talking to you, Faye."

"Same here."

After he left, I ran around and around the orange groves like a puppy with a fresh bone.

THE NEXT DAY, KYLE visited again, and this time he was without the puppies. He smiled when I opened the door. "Hi, Faye. Have you got a few minutes?"

My stomach lurched when I saw him being so friendly. I'd figured I would never see him again, after disagreeing with him so strongly the day before. I was in the middle of vacuuming, but I could take a few minutes. "Sure," I said, wondering if I was reading him right.

"Why don't we go out to the orange groves? I've got something for you."

"What is it?"

He grinned. "Wait and see."

"Uh, okay." I told Mom I'd be back in a little while, and we meandered back into the orange groves until we were out of sight of the house. He held out a thin, funny-looking cigarette.

I'd sneaked a couple of Dad's cigarettes in the past, but this didn't look like that. "What is it?"

"A joint. You looked pretty stressed yesterday. I thought you could use something to relax."

I'd heard of pot, of course, but I was surprised that anybody I knew would actually smoke the stuff. In health class, the teacher had lectured us about the dangers of pot and how it could lead to stronger drugs.

"No, thanks."

"Why not?" He ran his fingers down the joint and stuck it in his mouth. After digging a lighter out of his pocket, he lit the thing and inhaled deeply. Smoke wreathed his face, and a soft smile curled his lips. When he finally exhaled, his eyes were a little glassy.

Kyle held the joint out to me again.

I shrugged. "I don't know. I don't want to get addicted to drugs."

His laughter was kind, but he was still laughing at me, and I felt my face flush. "You won't get addicted," he said. "It's not like they say. Just try it. You'll see."

Confused, I walked away from him, toward a white ibis that was pecking at something in the grass. I tried to sneak up to it, but it squawked and flew off when I was a few feet away.

I stood with my back to Kyle, considering. It felt like an angel was standing on my left shoulder, shouting that this wasn't a good idea, and a devil stood on my right shoulder, whispering that I should try the pot if for no other reason than that Kyle, the coolest boy I'd ever met, was offering it to me. If I refused to do this, I'd probably never see him again.

Taking a deep breath, I turned around and walked toward him. Kyle handed me the burning joint and told me to take a big puff and hold it in my lungs for as long as possible. I did that, but then I started coughing so hard my lungs burned as though I'd swallowed fire. A few minutes later, after a few more puffs, I noticed that Kyle was right—I did feel more relaxed.

We sat on the grass, careful to avoid the sandy cones of anthills, and smoked the entire joint together. For the rest of the afternoon, we lay back and watched the clouds gather and change into animals that flitted across the sky. Just before he left, Kyle leaned over and brushed his lips against mine. It was my first kiss, soft and gentle. His lips lingered, and I wondered whether he could tell that I didn't know what I was doing. He didn't seem to notice, so I relaxed into the kiss. But when his hand started to caress my stomach, I tensed. He removed his hand and apologized, but the spell was broken.

He left immediately, saying, "I've got to go. See you later." He flashed me his heartthrob smile as he walked away.

Confused about what had just happened, I stumbled inside, gobbled three chocolate chip cookies, then took a nap. It was the best sleep I'd had since Benny had run me off the road. Not a single nightmare.

Mom woke me before supper. She sniffed and gave me a hard look, but she didn't say anything. She must have been relieved that I'd finally gotten some sleep. Later that evening, just before bedtime, she said, "I don't want Kyle over here again. He's too old for you. If he asks again, tell him you can't see him anymore." Her tone hardened. "Either you do it, or I will."

Outrage erupted in every fiber of my being. "Aw, Mom, why not? He's just a friend."

"Dana Faye, you are not allowed to date until you're sixteen, and that won't be for another two months. And even then, you can only go out with boys in your school. Kyle's a college man now, and he's too old for you."

She'd probably snuck up on Kyle and me while we were out in the orange grove, stoned. Maybe she had even seen the kiss. *Eww!* I didn't dare ask her what she'd seen, and she didn't say anything more.

Mom might have been right about Kyle being too old and too experienced for me, because later that evening, he called. She gave me a hard look but handed me the phone.

When I answered, he said, "Faye, I need to tell you something. Linda and I broke up for a while, but we just got back together this evening. I don't want you to get the wrong idea about you and me. I really like you, but can we just be friends?"

That was fast. He'd just kissed me a few hours before. My heart sank, but I summoned my most casual voice. "Uh, okay. Sure."

We hung up, and I felt like the stupidest girl in the world. I went to my room and spent the rest of the evening hiding under the covers, sobbing my eyes out.

THE NEXT SATURDAY, which was the first day of Thanksgiving break, a car pulled into our driveway. Dad was out in the groves, so I ducked into my bedroom, closing the door behind me. I didn't care for the way some of the citrus workers looked at me.

My mom answered the door. "Why, Francie. So nice to see you. Please come in."

I burst out of my room, surprised to see my friend. She usually worked at her dad's real estate office on weekends.

"What have you got going today?" she asked.

"The usual chores. And I've started working for Mr. Barrett, too. Why?"

"I have a better idea," she said, eyes twinkling. "How would you like to go to Daytona Beach with me?"

Such magical words, *the beach*. Of course I wanted to go. I'd never seen the ocean, and I'd been dying to go ever since we moved to Valencia. Mom and Dad kept promising to take me, but they hadn't gotten around to it.

I nodded and then turned toward Mom. She laughed. "Yes, you can go. I'll tell Mr. Barrett that you can't work today. Just be back by dark." But then she stopped, her eyes big, hands lifting toward her mouth. "Just a minute. Who's driving? Your parents?"

Francie shook her head and held up car keys. "I am. I got my license last week, and my dad let me borrow his car."

I held my breath, waiting to see what my mom would say. It would be the first time I'd driven anywhere with a friend without a parent along. She thought for a minute, her shoulders hunched, and then said, "All right. If your parents think you're safe to drive, I'll accept that. But *do not speed*, you hear me?"

"Yes, ma'am."

There was a long silence. Finally, I asked Francie, "What should I bring?"

She laughed. "I forgot this is new for you. Just your bathing suit, flip-flops, and a towel. I packed food and Cokes."

I'm going to the beach, beach, beach!

An hour later, Francie drove right up onto the hard sand and parked. I hadn't realized that cars were allowed to drive on beaches. Francie looked amused when I squealed in delight. The experience was old hat to her, but it was one of the highlights of my life.

We got out and skipped to where the waves, curling up in little zigzags, met the hot sand. I'd thought it would be too cold to swim, since it was late November, but the day was warm. I stuck my toes in and discovered that the water was cool but not cold. The sand dissolved out from under my feet when I tried to stand still. I edged in a little farther, up to my thighs, and a wave knocked me down on my behind. I couldn't keep the smile off my face.

We bodysurfed and ran on the beach and got home just before dark, sunburned and salty and extremely happy. This was the way November was supposed to be, instead of snowy and cold. I loved my new life in Florida.

I had gone the whole day without speaking Kyle's name or thinking much about him. Who cared about Kyle, anyway?

Chapter 9
"Stand by Me"

In the three weeks since Benny had scared me with his car, I hadn't run on the road once, just the track. But that needed to change. In spite of being exhausted from a lack of sleep, on Monday, I got up as soon as the sun rose and went running by myself. I had to increase my mileage if I wanted to run the Boston Marathon, and I needed to get over my fear. Running in the daylight didn't scare me, just the dark. The road in front of our house wandered to Valencia Lake, four miles away, so I ran to the end of the lake, sat on a bench there for a few minutes, and turned around and jogged home.

I practiced noticing what was around me while I ran. Three medium-sized alligators lay on the sand beside the lake. They didn't even glance at me as I ran past. It seemed that alligators weren't as scary as people. Farther on, a great blue heron dove straight into the water and came up with a big fish. It flew toward the shore and landed awkwardly. I stopped to watch as it jiggled the foot-long fish around to be in line with its throat. Then it swallowed an inch at a time. The heron's throat became fish-shaped until finally even the tail disappeared inside. The bird flew off, and I smiled and ran on.

When there wasn't anything interesting to look at, I recalled the faces of people I'd known during my life. I especially liked to remember my favorite teachers. Some of them had been very kind to me, and I didn't want to forget them.

A couple of miles into the run, a picture of a woman's face formed in my mind. She had shoulder-length blond hair that was long and wavy, full lips, and a tiny mouth, almost like one of those expensive china dolls. Her face was familiar, but I couldn't place her. I didn't think she'd been one of my teachers. Possibly a babysitter. When I was little, I'd stay with babysitters while Mom worked, but I couldn't remember one who looked like that. I enjoyed trying to recall her face more clearly while I ran.

But rain was threatening, so I cut my run short. At our cottage, I could hear through the open window that Mom and Dad were in the kitchen, arguing. I stopped outside the front door to listen.

Dad yelled, "We can't stay here any longer. Why can't I get through to you?"

Mom said in her calmest tone, "I hear you fine. I just don't agree. We've only been here a few months, for heaven's sake. We agreed to stay until Faye graduates from high school, and that's what we're going to do."

A cold sweat covered me. Would Dad make us leave? He usually did, in spite of Mom's protests. I wondered what kind of trouble he'd gotten into. I crept closer to the kitchen window, and an azalea branch scratched my cheek. I let out a groan. Mom and Dad instantly stopped talking. I waited, hoping they would start again.

Instead, Mom said, "Faye, is that you?"

Sighing, I rubbed my cheek and went inside. I asked as innocently as possible, "What's going on? Is everything all right?"

Dad slammed a cup down on the drain board. "Just getting some water before I go back outside." He turned to Mom. "Think about it, all right?" Then he grabbed his work gloves off the table and headed out the door.

Mom said to his back, "I've said all I'm going to say on the matter." She looked at me. "Stop lurking. We're just having a little disagreement. Nothing to worry about." She rolled her shoulders. When Dad was gone, Mom turned to me. "Why are you up so early? Nightmares again?"

"I just wanted to run."

She looked at me as though she didn't fully believe me. "You haven't had nightmares in years. Why do you think they're back?"

"I don't know." They had started after Benny had scared me when I was out running, but I didn't dare tell that to Mom. She would take any excuse to make me stop.

She sighed. "All right. Have it your way." After a pause, she asked, "What do you want for breakfast?"

I hoped Mom had won that round of the never-ending argument with Dad and we could stay in Valencia for at least five more months. Staying for another year and a half was too much to expect. But after the marathon, when my scholarship to college was assured, I wouldn't mind moving so much.

THE THREE OF US ATE Thanksgiving dinner together after Mom and I took the Barretts' turkey and fixings over to them. I'd been thinking about the Boston Marathon, and I couldn't get over the feeling that something about it was familiar. I couldn't ask about it directly, because they probably wouldn't answer.

When we had all dug into our food, I said, "I've been trying to remember all the places we've lived on Thanksgiving." Mom and Dad had fun with it and thought of eight or nine different places. They laughed as they remembered all the different homes, some more run-down than others. Our cottage in Valencia was one of the best.

"The first Thanksgiving was in Massachusetts," I said. "Did we ever live there?"

Mom said, "No, honey. We were a few months in upstate New York, but that's about as close as we got."

"Something about it seems familiar."

"Upstate New York is pretty similar. Maybe we'll go there one day and you'll see. We could visit Plymouth Rock, too." She scanned the table. "Bud, would you pass Faye the sweet potatoes?"

Mom's eyebrow was twitching the way it did when she was lying. I had no idea why she would lie about where we'd lived, and I didn't want to push the subject when things were going so well. I got quiet, and Mom and Dad talked for a few minutes about the states they'd never visited. Pretty soon, they fell silent, too.

Mom lied to me even when she was having fun, even when there was no reason to lie. Dad probably did, too, but I couldn't tell with him. Sick to death of my family, I concentrated on eating as much as I could. Since I'd started running so many miles, I felt like a bottomless pit.

FRANCIE INVITED ME for a sleepover that Saturday night. I'd never been to a sleepover before, so I accepted. I was taking a risk that I'd wake up Francie's whole family with my thrashing and screaming. I'd have to warn her about my nightmares before we went to bed.

Her house was much larger than our little cottage and blissfully quiet. Her parents were at a party, and Kyle had gone back to college. Fortunately, I wouldn't need to face him. Francie and I heated up Thanksgiving leftovers and listened to records in the living room. Later, in the dark, I told her how Benny had scared me to death. I warned her that I might wake up screaming.

"That little creep. I've been in school with him since first grade, and he's always been a jerk. We've got to do something about this. He can't get away with what he did to you."

"Of course he can. He's a boy. He can do anything."

She turned on her bedside lamp and stared at me. "Surely you don't believe that."

I counted it out on my fingers. "All right, let's just look at athletics, for instance. Boys can play football, and girls get stuck being cheerleaders. Boys can win medals in track, whereas girls can't. There aren't any sports for girls in Valencia except for intramural softball. But boys have everything from archery to... well, everything. So tell me about the difference between boys and girls."

She thought about it for a while. "You may be right about athletics. But that's going to change. This is 1967, after all—women's liberation is a big deal. Don't change the subject. I'm not going to let Benny get away with harassing you."

"All right. What do you have in mind?"

She considered. "Maybe something to do with his car. Or else somebody ought to scare him when he's alone."

I laughed with anticipation. This was getting fun. "How about we let the air out of his tires, then?"

"Yeah, that works. Not too mean, but it should make the point. We can leave him a note so he'll be sure to get the message."

We giggled and made plans. Benny lived in town, about three miles from Francie's house. She wasn't allowed to borrow the family car without permission, so we would have to walk. Or run. At three in the morning, long after Francie's parents had come home and gone to bed, we stuffed pillows under the covers to make it look like we were still lying there. It was hard to muffle our nervous laughter as we tiptoed out.

The night was clear and cool. Stars shone down on us like blessings. Valencia closed up by ten on weeknights and eleven o'clock on weekends, so that night we were able to run down the middle of the street. I wasn't afraid at all, running at night with my friend beside me. Our feet hit the pavement in sync, and I felt so light I thought I could run all the way to the coast, or beyond.

Benny's huge rattletrap of a car was parked on the street in front of the house. The porch light was on, but the rest of the house was dark. I took the back tires and Francie the front. After I unscrewed the cap from the valve, I pushed in the point with a nail file. A loud whooshing made me jump. Stopping for a minute, I looked around, but nothing moved.

I was on the second tire when a dog across the street barked. Then another dog down the block answered. Francie and I looked at each other, trying to decide whether to run away or finish the job. I gestured that we should take off, but she shook her head and bent down to finish letting the air out of a tire.

The door to Benny's house burst open and a man yelled, "What's going on here?"

Francie signaled for me to run, but I stood rooted to the spot. All I could do was stare at the man in the doorway.

"What are you girls doing?" He was in a robe and flip-flops, walking quickly down the sidewalk. Francie and I were both standing on the side of the car closest to him. He grabbed my arm—not hard but firmly enough that I couldn't squirm out. "Who are you, and what are you doing to my son's car?"

Lights flickered on in the house. A woman stood in the doorway. "Mike, what's going on? You're waking up the whole neighborhood."

"Call the cops, Emmy. They're vandalizing Benny's car. And wake Benny up. I need him out here." While he held me, the man stared at Francie. "I know you. You're Richard Ivey's kid. Get over here."

The next few minutes were hours long. Neighbors came out to see the flat tires, chuckled a little, and went back inside. But Benny's father made us sit down on the sidewalk and wait for the cops.

His wife said, "Oh, Mike, didn't you do something like this when you were a kid? It's the middle of the night. Let them go. See how scared they are."

And we were. I was trembling so hard I wasn't sure I could stand up if I tried. Francie looked the same. But Benny's father refused to budge. "No, they need to learn a lesson."

Then Benny ambled out and stared at us. He'd put on shorts and a T-shirt but was barefoot. He just shook his head as if he had no idea who we were or why we would do such a thing.

Mr. Maxwell pulled our note out from under the windshield wiper and carried it to the porch. I glanced at Francie. She nodded toward her house. It was a good time to run, but I couldn't move. Mr. Maxwell read the letter and called Benny over.

"Son, I want you to listen to this." He read aloud: "This is for running an innocent girl runner off the road. Think about it, you jerk."

He peered at me. "Hey, you're the girl who ran in the track meet. I recognize you from TV." He turned to glare at his son. "Did you run one of these girls off the road?"

"No, sir."

He turned back to us. "Did this happen to one of you? Did my son run you off the road?"

My mouth was too dry to form words, so Francie answered for me. "Yes, sir, he drove his car so close to my friend that she had to run on the shoulder, and she fell into an anthill. She could have broken her ankle."

A police car drove up. Fortunately, it didn't use a siren or flashing lights. Two men, one in a uniform and the other in slacks and a dress shirt, got out. The uniformed one asked, "What's going on here?"

Nobody answered. I wondered what my parents would do when they received a phone call to come and bail me out of jail. I felt the beginning of one of my spells. My vision got cloudy, with neon lights dancing around and blocking out the porch light. My head felt as if somebody had hit me with a hammer. To keep myself from fainting, I put my head down between my knees and listened to the silence that dragged on.

Finally, Mr. Maxwell said in a strange tone, "Nothing, Officer. It was just a misunderstanding. I don't think we need you."

One of the officers said, "It looks like somebody let the air out of your tires."

"No, my son must have run over some nails." Mr. Maxwell shook his head and shrugged.

The man in street clothes turned to me. "Are you all right, miss?"

By this time, my vision was beginning to clear, and I didn't feel so strange. My head still ached, but I looked up and nodded.

"Well, then, why are you girls out in the middle of the night?"

"We were going for a run, sir." My voice squeaked. "It's cool out now, so it's a good time to run."

The corners of his mouth curled up. "Is that so? What are your names, and where do you live?"

I considered making up a name or address, but for once, my ability to lie deserted me. I couldn't think of anything but the truth, so I told him. I started to breathe hard and shook like an out-of-balance washing machine.

He looked over at Francie. "I'm going to let you two go now. But I want you to run right home. We'll follow you to make sure you get home safely. And from now on, do your running in the daylight. It's not safe for young girls out late at night." He handed each of us a card. "If you have any more trouble from this young man or anybody else, you give me a call. And don't take the law into your own hands." He grinned, showing that we hadn't fooled him. I nodded, afraid I might break into tears of relief.

The police radio squawked, and the officers looked back at their car.

Mr. Maxwell said, "How about if I drive them home? I don't mind, and I think my son has something to say to them."

The officers agreed and drove away. When they were gone, Mr. Maxwell said to Benny, "I'm ashamed of you, son. I really can't blame these girls for trying to teach you a lesson. Now, apologize for what you did."

Benny's face flushed. "It wasn't like they said. They're trying to make me look bad."

"Benjamin, what did I just say to you?"

Looking at me with a combination of hostility and embarrassment, Benny eventually said, "Sorry. I didn't mean to scare you."

"All right, then." Mr. Maxwell turned to his son. "In the morning, you can pump up these tires. Get back to bed. I'll take these girls home."

"We'll be happy to run, sir," Francie said hopefully. "It's not that far."

"No. I'll take you."

He drove us to Francie's house without saying another word. When we thanked him for not telling the cops what we did, he said, "I'm sorry for my son's actions. What he did was wrong." He hesitated. "But don't do anything like that again. If I see you out at night again, I'll call both of your parents. You hear me?"

"Yes, sir."

We tiptoed into the house, clutching the cards from the police officer. Francie's parents' bedroom door was still closed. The house lights were still off. I couldn't believe our luck. We'd gotten away with it.

Francie and I lay in her twin beds and laughed wildly before we spent hours talking ourselves down from the excitement. I fell asleep knowing there was one person in the world I could trust. And I woke up in the morning without having had a single nightmare.

Chapter 10
"Money (That's What I Want)"

On Sunday afternoon, Francie called. "Uncle Stan wants to hire a teenager to help him in his carving store during the Christmas season and maybe afterward. I told him you'd be good. What do you think? It would give you some more money for Boston."

My first thought was, *She has an uncle?* I'd never heard of him. To Francie, family was so ordinary that she didn't think to mention it unless something special came up. It was another reason I envied her life. And then I realized that I'd missed the rest of what she said. "What on earth is a carving store?"

She laughed. "Uncle Stan carves totem poles, bears, eagles, and a hundred other things out of cypress wood and sells them in a funky country store a couple of miles from our house. He's a little quirky, but he's really nice."

"What country store? I don't remember seeing a country store."

"You might have run right past it without noticing. It's back from the road a bit. Anyway, I'm not sure how much he sells, but he likes to carve, and he makes ends meet. Kyle worked there when he was in high school. Now Uncle Stan needs to hire another teenager to help out at the cash register. I already have a job, so I suggested you, and he's fine with it. But you'll need to come in for an interview. Will tomorrow work?"

I wasn't sure what to say. Working at a real job seemed like a giant step up from working for Mr. Barrett. "Uh, I'm not sixteen yet. Don't you have to be sixteen to have a real job?"

Francie laughed. "No, no, you've got the wrong idea. When you get done for the day, Uncle Stan opens the cash register and takes out a five- or ten-dollar bill and hands it to you. You won't be on the books at all. And he'd be happy to teach you how to carve, too, if you want. Just because I have absolutely no talent doesn't mean the same is true about you."

That got my attention. In elementary school, I had loved carving small animals out of soap. "Okay, yeah. I'd like to do that. I'll ask my mom."

"FRANCIE'S UNCLE MIGHT hire me to help out at his carving store," I said to Mom as we were cooking supper. "I can make lots more money working there than for Mr. Barrett."

She pursed her lips. "I don't know. I don't like how much you're away from the house already. There's plenty of work here for you."

"Please, Mom. If I have a job, I can pay for my lunches out of my salary. It'll save you money."

She pulled the meatloaf out of the oven and sliced it. I thought the deep crease between her eyes had more to do with her considering my request than her wondering whether the meatloaf was done, so I waited. After a moment, she said, "All right, I'll let you interview. And then we'll see." She even agreed to drive me to the interview.

On Monday afternoon, we found the store with no trouble. It was in an old log cabin that had belonged to Stan and Laney's grandparents. Francie was right—I had run past it several times without even noticing it. Stan was quite a bit older than his sister Laney, and his long white hair straggled down his back. But he had a great smile. He was on the phone when we arrived, so he gestured for us to look around.

The store was crammed with wooden creatures, ranging from a six-foot-tall bear with a fish dangling from its mouth to tiny birds that seemed to be on the verge of taking off and flying around the store. There were also dollhouses, complete with tiny beds and rocking chairs. Stan had created a world so fantastical that I wouldn't have been surprised to find homes for hobbits tucked inside the jumble. I laughed from pure joy. Mom just shook her head, probably imagining having to pack up all that stuff in order to move.

Stan only asked me a few questions in our interview: "Are you reliable? Are you available to work on Saturdays before Christmas and maybe after Christmas, too? Do you want to learn to carve? Can you start this Saturday?"

The answer to every question was yes. *Oh, yes.* Earning more money would get me out of the house and away from the constant chores. It would also help me pay for the Boston Marathon. The miracle I had wished for had arrived.

The only issue was how to get to and from work. Mom refused to drive me unless it was raining, saying she already had too much to do. It was a long way to walk, but if I ran, I'd be all stinky and sweaty when I got there, and there wasn't a shower in the store. Stan scrounged around and found a bicycle he was willing to fix up for me so I could get to work. But I started shaking when I thought about riding home by myself after dark. Bad things happened in the dark.

WHEN I WAS LEAVING for work on Saturday morning, Dad handed me a canister of mace that he'd bought in a sporting goods store. "Here, you might need this. Keep it with you all the time." It was small enough to fit in my pocket. He showed me how to line up the lever with an arrow and push down the button to make it spray. Dad wouldn't let me practice with it, because there were only five or six sprays in the canister, and he didn't want me to waste any of them.

The act of spraying it, he said, was the easy part. "If you're in danger, shoot first and ask questions later. Hold it as close as you can to a person's face when you press the button, and hopefully, the guy will be downwind." He grinned as he handed it to me. "It won't kill any-body, but it should keep them busy long enough for you to get away."

I wished I'd had it when Benny had tried to scare me to death. I could have reached right into his car window and sprayed it at him, and he wouldn't have been laughing when he drove away.

At the store, Stan taught me how to use the cash register, how to deal with difficult customers, and how to carve. He even allowed me to call him Uncle Stan, and I daydreamed about how nice it would be if he were my real uncle. I was in heaven.

Chapter 11
"Don't Let Me Down"

After our run the next Monday, Francie and I went into the clinic to help Laney restock her supplies. I was on my knees, shoving boxes of large bandages into the lower cabinet, when Coach Lopez came in, carrying a bundle of mail.

"Hi, girls. Sorry I wasn't able to work with you today. Other responsibilities. But you're doing really well. I wish the boys were as motivated as you are."

We laughed. It was true. Most of the boys goofed off when the coach wasn't around. But they weren't planning on running the Boston Marathon in five months.

He turned toward Laney, who was putting new sheets on the cots. "Actually, Laney, I want to talk to you about driver's ed. You got any time in the afternoons after school? Mrs. Samples has to drive her mother to Orlando for cancer treatments, and I'm looking for a replacement. It'd be on Tuesdays and Thursdays."

Laney nodded. "Sure, I'll do it. My teaching certificate's up-to-date." She looked at me. "Francie already has her license, but I bet you'd like to get your learner's permit, Faye. You should sign up for driver's ed."

My heartbeat quickened. "That would be great. I'll be sixteen in January."

"All right, then. We can talk about it later." She turned and smiled at Coach Lopez. "Do I start this week?"

"Yeah. I'll get the materials together. Thanks." His tone became lighter. "Uh, Faye, some letters came for you after the track meet." He thumbed through the pile of mail in his hand. "There's a boatload of requests for newspaper interviews." Noticing my expression, he hurried to continue. "I'll ignore them. But there are a few other letters, too. Let's see." He pulled out three envelopes. "This one is from somebody who wants you to model athletic footwear for their catalog. And this is from a man in Utah who wants to marry you, because you're so fast and could breed a bunch of boys to start a running dynasty." He laughed, and we joined in. "There's one more." He opened it. "Oh yeah, this one is from a man who thinks you're his long-lost daughter. That one's kind of sad." He paused to put the letters back in their envelopes. "Do you want these letters, Faye? Or should I throw them away?"

"Man, crackpots come out of the woodwork when a girl does something out of the ordinary," said Laney, shaking her head.

"Throw them away, I guess," I said, shrugging. "No, wait." Francie and I could read them later for a laugh. "I'll take the crackpot letters. A souvenir of my time in Valencia. But throw away the ones from the reporters." I shuddered. He handed me the letters, and I stuck them into my geometry book.

Laney was right. There were a lot of crackpots in the world. *A running dynasty.* What a crazy thought.

WHILE WE WERE STRETCHING on Tuesday afternoon, Coach Lopez gestured for us to join him in the infield. He looked like he was about to cry. After staring at us for a long time, he said, "I'm sorry, but I won't be able to coach you anymore."

As I tried to make sense of what he was saying, Francie asked, "Why on earth not?"

"The principal threatened my job if I continue. And I had a hard time getting this job, what with my family coming here from Cuba." Misery was obvious in every inch of his body. "I'm sorry."

Francie looked like a steam engine about to explode. "What could be wrong with coaching us? Is it getting in the way of your work with the boys?"

"That's what he said, but it's not true. He got called on the carpet by the superintendent when Faye ran in the meet, so he's not about to stick his neck out again." He spat into the grass. "I'm sorry, but I don't have any choice."

Francie and I stared at each other. She looked as horrified as I felt. I said, "We're sorry, too. You're a great coach."

We all stood there for a few seconds, not knowing how to end this terrible conversation. Finally, Coach shook his head, took a deep breath, and said, "I've set up a training schedule to prepare you to run the marathon in April. You're both in good shape, and I'm sure you can do it, even without me. Here it is." He held the pages, filled with squiggles, out to us. "Study this, and do what it says, and you'll be all right."

Francie took her copy, but I hesitated. "Coach, I want to run the Boston Marathon more than anything. But isn't it still against the rules for females to run in it?"

He fidgeted with the clipboard. "Strictly speaking, it is against the rules for females to register. But the rules need to be changed. The race committee will probably be looking hard at runners who register under names that might be female. The registration papers are stapled to the training schedule. I figure you could be Frank Ivey," he said, gesturing at Francie. He turned to me. "And you could run using your initials. What's your middle name?"

"Faye is my middle name. My first name is Dana. But nobody calls me that."

"Dana. That's perfect. That can be a man or a woman's name. You'll register as Dana Smith."

"But, Coach, what if my parents won't let me go?" I usually tried to ignore the little voice in my head that said I was wasting my time training so hard, but having our coach quit made that voice even stronger.

"Just take it one step at a time, and focus on running right now. Maybe they'll be open to it by April. All right?"

He was trying so hard to be positive that I tried, too. "All right. Sure." I took the papers and gave him a feeble grin.

His lips became a straight line. "I'll try to find you another coach, but I can't think of anybody right now. I guess if you follow the program I wrote out for you, you'll be all right."

AFTER THAT, ALTHOUGH we still ran every day, we couldn't keep up with Coach Lopez's schedule. Then Francie twisted her knee in PE and couldn't run for a couple of weeks. I ran without her, but it wasn't any fun, and my mileage dropped.

I could feel the Boston Marathon, and my track scholarship, slipping away, and I had no idea how to get them back. Going to college began to seem like a sweet fantasy made up by a girl in a novel. Definitely not me.

The future I dreaded was starting to close in. I would end up doing farm labor for the rest of my life. Or sitting in an office, typing boring letters. I felt like I was drowning, and all it would take to go under for the last time would be for me to stop fighting.

Finally, Francie started running again. On our last run before the Christmas break, I brought up the Boston Marathon. "We've got to find another coach."

"I know. I asked my dad if he would coach us, but he doesn't have time." Her dad had some big real estate project going on and was rarely home these days.

"There's got to be somebody." I thought about it while we ran a lap around the track. "Why don't you ask your dad if he can find us somebody else? And I'll talk to Reese, too."

"All right. I'll ask him again." She sounded as depressed as I felt.

CHRISTMAS EVE WAS BUSY at the carving store. Customers had bought out most of Stan's inventory. At six in the evening, he handed me two twenty-dollar bills. "You can go home now. I can handle it from here." He smiled. "Merry Christmas."

"Thanks, Stan. Merry Christmas to you, too." He was letting me off two hours early. I wasn't about to argue, though, because I was dead on my feet.

I had spent a month carving a pelican as a Christmas gift for my parents and had finished it the day before. About three feet tall, it stood on a post with its head tucked in, long beak against its chest and feathers ruffled, as if it were about to go to sleep. Truthfully, the feathers looked more like roof shingles, but it was the best I could do. I'd painted the bird in bright colors, figuring it would stand outside the door of our cottage and welcome guests. I hoped my parents would like it.

I called Mom to pick me up early. I would be able to go to church with my parents after all. Getting into the truck, I saw that Mom's eyes were red rimmed and her lips were pressed together. She looked really mad. As far as I knew, I hadn't done anything wrong.

"What's up?" I asked.

She said, "Get in. Your father is an idiot."

Okay. They'd been fighting again. Nothing new in that, although they usually gave it a break at Christmas.

As soon as I walked into the house, I smelled something strong that reminded me of... *pot*? Dad was sitting in the living room, playing his guitar. He sang whiny, emotional songs. A half-filled beer bottle sat on the coffee table.

I stood still for a second to take this in. Unless somebody else had been in the house, Dad had been smoking pot and drinking beer. I'd never known him to take a drink, although Mom had said he used to drink a lot when he played in a band. He'd stopped drinking after he had an accident of some sort. As for marijuana, I didn't think adults smoked that stuff, especially not my *dad*.

I stood just inside the door, gawking. Mom headed toward their bedroom, saying, "Faye, I left your supper on the stove. Eat it quickly, and get dressed for church." She turned around and glared at Dad. "Bud, are you going with us?"

"Huh?" He stopped in the middle of the song and looked around, his eyes red and glassy. "Oh. Yeah, I'll get ready." He leaned his guitar against the couch and drained the beer. "Hon, are there any brownies left?"

She stomped into the bedroom and slammed the door. I grabbed my plate and stuffed food in my mouth then rushed to get dressed. When Mom came out in a new red dress, I leaned in and asked, "What happened to Dad?"

"The sheriff came around, looking for a guy who used to work here. He was long gone, of course, but it upset your dad." She sniffed. "And then Mr. Barrett caught one of the pickers smoking pot, and he fired him. I'm not sure if he knows your dad was smoking it, too. I keep waiting for the knock at the door." Shaking her head, she said, "And here at Christmas, too. I don't know where we'll go." She seemed ready to burst into tears.

Dad came out of the bedroom, looking handsome in his grey suit. He'd splashed on English Leather and gargled with mouthwash, so the evidence of alcohol and pot was gone. He grinned at me and put his arm around Mom. "You look good enough to eat."

She pushed him away. Life was back to normal.

At church, I sat between my parents. Mom sang the Christmas carols in a beautiful alto that could harmonize with anything, and Dad had a great tenor. I carried the lead, and the three of us sounded wonderful together. The sweetness of it brought tears to my eyes.

I wondered how long the harmony would last.

Chapter 12
"Happy, Happy Birthday Baby"

My sixteenth birthday arrived on January 17. My birthday wasn't usually that big a deal, just a regular day, except that Mom would bake me a chocolate cake and my parents would sing "Happy Birthday" while I blew out the candles. I would get a few presents—clothes mostly—and that would be that.

But turning sixteen was special. In my daydreams, I would pass my driver's test in the morning and then take my parents' truck out for a spin after school. In the evening, I would have a party with a big cake and a huge stack of presents. And smiling parents like the ones on TV shows. A girl could hope, couldn't she?

My birthday turned out to be on one of the coldest days of the season. Even though it was usually relatively warm in Central Florida, winter brought a few really cold spells. The temperature had hovered around thirty degrees all night. If the citrus froze, it would be worthless, and Mr. Barrett might have to let us go. Dad had been up all night, working the smudge pots—buckets filled with fuel oil and set afire to keep the fruit from freezing. Unfortunately, the burning pots sent up thick black smoke that covered everything and stank like a skunk. He must have kept at least two dozen pots burning all night.

By breakfast time, the temperature had risen enough that Dad could blow out the smudge pots and come inside. He thought he'd saved the fruit, so he was weary but smiling. He ate a few bites and fell into bed.

Mom made me French toast for breakfast, and as usual, we had fresh-picked grapefruit. To demonstrate that I was an adult, I said, "I want to start drinking coffee."

She smiled. "Okay. How do you want it?"

"Uh, black." I was determined to be a *real* coffee drinker, and to my mind, real coffee drinkers drank it black.

She poured me a cup. I'd tasted coffee before, but my parents drank it with milk and sugar. This was bitter and awful. I made a face and set the cup down with a plunk. Mom shoved the milk and sugar closer, but I shook my head. I drank the entire cup, wincing every time I swallowed a sip.

When I was finished, I asked Mom, "So when can I get my driver's license?"

We'd had the conversation before, and it always ended the same way: "Wait until your birthday, and then we'll see." But today was my birthday, so she couldn't use that excuse anymore.

"You can go ahead and take the written part of your driver's test after you've finished driver's ed, but there's going to be a problem with getting the practice hours you need. Your dad and I are too busy right now to take you driving, and besides, we don't have the money to add you to our insurance. So I hate to tell you this, but it might be a while until you're able to get your license. I'm sorry."

How could she do such a terrible thing to me, and on my birthday, too? Without thinking, I yelled, "Why can't you take me driving? That's not *fair*."

Dad called from the bedroom, "What's going on out there? Can't a guy get some sleep? Keep it down."

Mom and I locked eyes. She said, "Remember when I took you driving last year, and you kept stalling out because you couldn't work the clutch? I swore then that I'd never do it again. It makes me too nervous, and I've got enough to worry about as it is."

"Then what about Dad? He could do it."

"You'll have to ask him. But he's very busy right now. He'll probably have more time after the citrus has been picked."

That wouldn't be until spring. My heart sank. I wasn't done with the subject of driving, and she was not getting off that easily. But I could hear the school bus chugging down the road. The rest of the conversation would have to wait until after school.

As I headed out the door, holding back tears of fury, Mom said, "I'll have your special dinner ready when you get home."

I stomped out, letting the door slam behind me. The daydream was already unraveling.

When I got to school, Reese was waiting at my locker. "Happy birthday," he said, blushing. He handed me a small white box with a bow on top. I hadn't seen much of him recently. Before Christmas, he'd regularly eaten lunch with Francie and me, but then he got the lead in the school play and started rehearsing during lunch. The play also kept him too busy to run track. I'd missed spending time with him.

I didn't recall mentioning my birthday to him. Francie must have told him. Surprised, I opened the box, and inside was a pretty necklace with a sparkly rhinestone. I managed to stammer out, "Thank you," before he leaned over and kissed me on the cheek. His face was as red as a fireplug as he bolted away from me and galloped toward his class.

I stood in the hall, clutching the necklace and wondering what had just happened. It was possible he was trying to tell me he wanted to be my boyfriend. But not likely. I didn't have much experience with boys, but I thought I would have noticed if he'd been flirting with me. While I stood there, wondering, the bell rang, and I had to run to class.

Afterward, I grabbed Francie and showed her the necklace. "What do you think? Is this a boyfriend-girlfriend kind of gift?"

"I don't *think* so. I know he's shy, but he's not twelve, after all. He'd probably hang around you, ask you out, things like that, if he was interested in you as a girlfriend."

I wasn't sure whether I was relieved or not. "That's what I thought, too. But nobody's ever bought me a necklace before."

She gave me a questioning look. "But do you like him? You haven't said."

"He's a good friend. I like him that way." Shaking my head, I added, "Not as a boyfriend."

"Oh, I forgot. You've got a crush on *Kyle*." She grinned at my guilty expression and seemed about to say something else when the bell rang. We headed to the next class.

I zoned out during geometry, thinking about past birthdays. Moving backward, I tried to remember where I'd been on every birthday. I did fine until around the age of nine or ten, when I lost track. Every year, we'd lived in a different place, and the schools tended to blend together. I was drifting along, trying to look interested in the boring lecture, when a memory—or a fantasy—popped up that almost made me cry out in surprise.

I was wearing a white dress with a big flower, possibly a rose, embroidered on the front. And white socks with ruffles. My black patent-leather shoes were so bright I could see my face when I bent over to look. And I had a big birthday cake with a few candles on top. I wasn't sure, but there might have been four of them. There was a big pile of presents, like the stack in my daydream. I sat on a high stool, licking frosting off my chin. *No, wait*—someone else was wiping it off with a warm, wet cloth.

That was where things got weird. I was pretty sure Mom wasn't the one wiping off the frosting. I wasn't positive, but it seemed to be the woman whose face had come to mind when I was running. I had no idea who she was. And I knew for sure there were no pictures in the family photo album of any party like that.

Was it somebody else's party? If so, whose? Maybe this was one of those times when my brain made up something that wasn't true. That happened so often when I was having one of my spells that sometimes I got confused about what was real and what was pure imagination. My head started feeling weird, so I swallowed a pill from my container.

The bell rang, and I walked out with Francie.

"What was going on with you in class?" she asked. "You were a million miles away."

"Francie, do you remember stuff from when you were really young, like four?"

"Sure. I got a bicycle that year. It was too big for me, and I fell and ground gravel into my forehead, and we had to go to the hospital to get it taken out. See, I still have the scars." She raised her bangs so I could make out the tiny white dots. "Why?"

"Oh, I just remembered a birthday party, and I think I might have been four or five, but I'd forgotten all about it up till now." I shook my head and smiled.

"Neat," she said, hurrying toward her next class. "By the way, happy birthday."

AFTER SCHOOL, COACH Lopez introduced us to Coach Jess Williams, who had been the track coach at the black high school that was shut down the previous year because of desegregation. When he'd lost his job, he'd gone to work selling real estate at a different company from Mr. Ivey's. Coach Williams was middle-aged with light-brown skin, crinkly eyes, and a big smile. I liked him immediately.

Coach Lopez beamed. "This man is the best. I thought he'd moved away, which was why I didn't call him right away." He nodded toward us. "This is Francie, Richard Ivey's daughter. You know him, right?" Coach Williams nodded, and he and Francie shook hands. Coach Lopez continued, "And this is Faye Smith. You might have heard about her."

"Oh, yes, I've heard about her. I saw her on television, too." He smiled at me. "I'm happy to know you, Faye."

We shook hands. After we told him we wanted to train for the Boston Marathon, he chuckled. "I'd be happy to coach you. It'll be a pleasure to coach somebody who has the courage to dream big. I like that."

I didn't know how to say what I needed to say next, so I blurted out, "I'm real sorry, but I can't pay you very much."

At that, he laughed. "Who said anything about paying me? I wasn't expecting to get paid. No, I miss coaching. And it'll get me to start running again myself. I've slacked off recently." He patted a tiny tummy.

Francie and I were ready to begin right then, but he shook his head. "We'll start tomorrow after school. You'll need to increase your mileage, and I'll work you hard. That okay with y'all?"

Oh yes. It was okay. Better than okay.

We were ready to leave, but Coach Williams continued to stand there, looking as if he wanted to say something but didn't know how to begin. Finally, he said, "I know Francie's dad, but I should probably meet your parents, Faye. You know, get their permission to coach you."

I stammered out, "I don't think that's a good idea."

Nobody said anything. Coach Williams looked down at his feet, a sad expression on his face. Coach Lopez opened his mouth, but no sounds came out. And Francie just stood there, gaping at me. *Oh God.* They must have thought I didn't want him to meet my parents because they were racists. Maybe that was true, but mainly, I didn't want to rub my parents' noses in my plan to run the Boston

Marathon. They'd never asked why I was training so hard, and I hadn't volunteered the information.

"Uh, they're really busy right now," I said. "You can meet them later. They won't mind if you train me, Coach Williams. They didn't meet Coach Lopez, either."

The silence drew out. Then Coach Lopez said, "That's right. They didn't."

Coach Williams shrugged. "All right, then. See you tomorrow. But call me Jess. Or just Coach."

INSTEAD OF LETTING me off at the road, Laney drove up our driveway and stopped in front of the house.

"You didn't need to do that," I said. "I'm used to walking."

"I know. I need to talk to your mom for a minute. You don't mind, do you?"

"I guess not." This had never happened before, so I didn't know what to think. Something was up, for sure. Laney got out of the car, and so did Francie.

I opened the front door. "Surprise!" The shout made me jump. Inside were Mom, Dad, and Mr. Barrett, all grinning like fools. A bunch of balloons hung from the ceiling. I laughed so hard that if I were a dog, my whole body would have wagged.

Francie had gone back out to the car and brought in a present wrapped in white paper. She'd kept the secret all day at school without even a hint or a sideways glance. "Did you really think I'd let your birthday go by without giving you a gift?"

"But I didn't get you one for your birthday. I'm sorry."

"Hey, you didn't even know me in July. You can make up for it next year." She laughed, and I relaxed.

It was a special treat to see Mr. Barrett. His wife was failing, so he rarely came out of the house anymore. I liked the old man and his perpetual stories, but things had been tense between him and my dad since the incident with the marijuana. From what I could tell, Dad had been working harder lately, and he must have been behaving himself if Mr. Barrett was willing to leave his wife to come to our house.

Mom had prepared shrimp cocktail, french fries, garlic toast, and a salad. And of course, chocolate cake with sixteen fabulous candles. It was a rare feast at our house.

Three presents were stacked on the coffee table, all wrapped and beautiful. They almost looked like my daydream. After we ate, I wiped tears from my eyes and looked at my mom.

"Go ahead, open them," she said, smiling.

I tore into the presents, starting with my parents'. Inside a huge box was a pair of white go-go boots that I'd eyed in a store one day. I hadn't realized Mom had noticed. They'd look fantastic with a miniskirt—if Mom allowed me to wear one—and fishnet stockings.

I ran to hug both parents. "Thank you. I love them." I could hardly wait to wear them somewhere special.

Mr. Barrett said, "Honey, I need to get back to Betty. Why don't you open mine next?" He'd clearly wrapped it himself, using the Sunday comics. Inside was a nice pair of leather gardening gloves that fit perfectly. I'd worn out my old ones, and I needed them.

"Thank you so much," I said, wishing he were my grandpa. I hugged him.

A blush rose from his neck up to his leathery face. "I've gotta go now. Thank you for the dinner, Sue. Happy birthday again, Faye."

Last was Francie and Laney's gift. Francie was so excited she was nearly bouncing up and down on the couch. "Okay, okay," I said, happiness flowing out of me. I opened the box, and inside was a new pair of sneakers in my size. They were different from my other shoes—sleek and blue with padded heels and a silver racing stripe down the side. They looked as if they were made especially for running.

"Oh my gosh. These are amazing. I've never seen anything so beautiful." I held them up for my parents to see. The sharp look on my mom's face told me I had made a mistake. In addition to encouraging me to run, which she didn't like, those shoes must have cost more than the go-go boots. My mom was probably embarrassed. I hurried to correct my error. "They'll be great for running, and the go-go boots will be great for dancing. I can't believe I got two pairs of fantastic shoes tonight. Thank you both." I hugged Francie and Laney, holding back tears. Everything was so wonderful that I wanted to pinch myself to be sure I wasn't dreaming.

That Francie had remembered how hard it was for me to run in my crappy Goodwill shoes made my heart feel full. She hadn't said a word when I slapped on four or five Band-Aids before every run. A girl couldn't ask for a better friend. And Laney was great, too. I sometimes wished she were my mom, although I'd never have said that out loud.

I slipped on the shoes, and they fit perfectly. "Where did you get such beautiful shoes?" I asked Francie.

"Mom ordered them all the way from Germany. There's nothing like them in this country. I got a pair, too, but I've been waiting to use them until we could do it together."

I could hardly wait to go running the next day. A new coach and a new pair of running shoes. *Wow!* This birthday almost lived up to my fantasy birthday.

Francie and Laney got up to leave, so Mom and I followed them out to the car. When we were outside, Mom said, "Francie, please get in the car. I need to talk to your mom." Francie glanced at me and did as she was asked. I melted back toward the house, giving the two women a little privacy, but I could hear everything they said.

Mom glared at Laney. "I appreciate all you've done for my daughter—bringing her home from school, giving her presents, teaching her to drive. Everything. You've been a good friend to all of us. But I think you're forgetting something. I'm Faye's mother, not you. You're overstepping, and you need to stop."

Laney jerked as though she'd been slapped. She took in a deep breath and held it for a long time before letting it out. "I'm so sorry, Sue. I didn't know you felt that way. Faye's my daughter's best friend. I was just trying to help. I never meant to upset you." She paused, biting her lower lip. "What would you like me to do?"

"Just stop trying to be her mother. That's all. Those shoes were too expensive."

Laney brushed her eyes. I thought that she might break down, but she stood up straight and said in a shaky voice, "Uh, okay. Would you like me to return them, then?"

Mom glanced back at me. I shook my head, eyes wide. She turned back to Laney. Her voice softened a little. "It's too late for that. Just don't buy her any more expensive presents, please. It's not appropriate."

"All right." Laney hesitated. I got the impression that she was trying to think of something to say that would make everything all right. Then she reached out to Mom and touched her shoulder. "I think the world of Faye, and I know that you all don't have a lot of money. I thought the shoes would be helpful."

Mom pulled away from the comforting hand. "Well, they're not. But thank you for coming. I don't want to lose your friendship."

Very stiffly, Laney said, "I apologize for overstepping my bounds." She turned to me and said in a soft voice, "Good night, Faye. See you tomorrow."

After they left, I helped clean up from the party and tried to act as if nothing had happened. But when I went into my room, I took my new running shoes with me. I wouldn't have put it past Mom to make the shoes disappear overnight if I left them out.

Chapter 13
"I Want to Hold Your Hand"

After my birthday, Reese began waiting for me to get off the bus in the mornings so he could walk me to my locker. On Thursday, he said, "Why don't I carry your books?"

Did he think I was an invalid? My books weren't that heavy. "Uh, no, thanks. I'm fine."

He backed off, looking a little hurt.

I had no idea why he would ask such a strange thing, so I checked *Seventeen* magazine, which told me that boys liked to carry their girlfriends' books. *Oh.*

When he asked again the next day, I said, "Sure," and handed over the books. He stood a little straighter as he added my books to his own. After that, he started eating lunch with Francie and me every day, and he talked more to me than to Francie. I waited to see what would happen next.

On Monday afternoon, just before I ran out onto the track, he stammered a question. "Will you go to a movie with me on Saturday night?" *Well, well.* He might be the shyest boy this side of the Mississippi, but he'd finally built up enough courage to ask me out on a date.

Of course I said yes. Unfortunately, I didn't get all pitter-pattery around Reese the way I did with Kyle, but I was willing to give him a chance. After all, it was my first official date. Reese was the nicest guy I knew, and I hadn't heard from Kyle in a couple of months. Maybe I could convince my heart to change who it got pitter-pattery over.

Also, I'd never actually been to a movie theater, and I was dying to go. My dad sometimes took us to drive-ins, but my parents thought sit-down theaters were too expensive. There weren't any movie theaters in Valencia, anyway, so we'd have to drive to Orlando, an hour away.

My parents said I could go as long as Reese came to the door to pick me up and they could talk to him. He was fine with that. I had a smile on my face all week as I anticipated the evening. On Saturday night, after I was dressed, I examined myself in the mirror. My auburn hair was parted in the middle and hung in ringlets down my back. I often ironed my hair to straighten it, but the humidity made it curl within a couple of hours, so that night, I just let it be. Pancake make-up covered most of my freckles. Bright-blue eye shadow reflected the color of my eyes. Orange lipstick matched the minidress I had bought that afternoon at Goodwill. And finally, black fishnet stockings contrasted with my white go-go boots. I felt like a color wheel. I added Reese's necklace and a wide-brimmed black hat, and I was done.

When I went into the living room, Mom gave me the stink-eye about my short dress, but Dad whistled. Mom was halfway through a speech about how trashy I looked when Reese knocked on the door, right on time.

He was dressed in a white button-down shirt and dress slacks. His hair curled nicely below his collar, probably pushing the school limit for hair length. I wasn't sure how he'd grown it so long without my noticing, but he looked a little like George Harrison—not particularly handsome, but not bad, either. His acne had mostly cleared up, too.

Dad was sitting on the couch, fingering his guitar, a beer on the table in front of him—maybe his sixth that afternoon. He stood up and shook Reese's hand then invited him to sit down. Then he picked up his guitar and started playing some stupid song, as if he'd forgotten we were even in the room.

But Mom grilled Reese. What kind of car was he driving? Had he ever had a ticket or a wreck? Was he aware that I had to be home by eleven?

Reese didn't get ruffled by Mom's questions and answered as though he faced a similar inquisition every day. At school, he was quiet and shy, so this was a side of him I hadn't seen, except when he'd stood up to my mom at Laney's party.

I was starting to get anxious that we'd miss the beginning of the movie or that things with Mom would go downhill, so I walked to the door and gestured to Reese. *Come on. Let's go.* He stood up and turned to go.

Dad set down his guitar and stood. He was taller and heavier than slender Reese. He turned his attention to me. "Punkin, I'm sorry, but you can't..."

I grabbed Reese's arm and pulled him out the door before Dad finished his sentence. "Bye," I called behind me in as cheerful a tone as I could manage. "See you at eleven." Not that Dad would be around. He'd be out somewhere, so he wouldn't have the slightest idea what time I got home. But Mom would notice, and I'd get grounded if I was late.

I HAD NEVER SEEN ANYTHING as beautiful as that movie theater, with its carved walls and ceilings, heavy plush draperies, cushy seats, and giant screen.

Reese asked, "Do you want something? Popcorn and Coke?"

"Sure." I opened my purse to pull out some money, but Reese wouldn't let me.

"I'll get it."

Mom had told me it was the boy's responsibility to pay for the date, and apparently, Reese's mom had told him the same thing. It didn't make any sense, since he probably had no more money than I did.

The movie was about a young guy who graduated from college and returned home for the summer, only to have an affair with an older woman who was a friend of his parents. *Eww.* Even though I was grossed out by the plot, I loved watching a movie on the big screen like a regular person. During the movie, Reese eased his arm behind me on the back of my seat, but he didn't touch me.

Back in Valencia, he pulled the car into an orange grove and stopped the engine. Between the rows of trees, it was quiet and private. I could see stars above and smell the sweet scent of orange blossoms. Reese leaned over and put his arm around my shoulders, pulling me toward him. My heartbeat was so loud I was sure he could hear it, but he didn't say anything. Our lips met. His were kind of dry, and I tried to lick mine to make our mouths fit together better. But he must have misunderstood my intention, because the next thing I knew, his tongue was halfway down my throat, and I nearly gagged.

I pulled away. "Reese." I wasn't sure what message I wanted to give, but I knew I needed to slow this thing down.

He said in a strangled voice, "Sure. Let's go." I breathed a sigh of relief when he started the car. He walked me to my door and gave me a quick hug.

"I had a great time tonight. Thank you." Mom had taught me to say that at the end of a date, and he seemed to appreciate it, because he gave me another, longer hug without trying to kiss me.

"Me, too. See you at school."

I went inside, and that was that. My first date. Not as great as I'd anticipated, but not too bad, either. I didn't want him to feel rejected because I'd broken off our kiss, but I didn't know how to bring up the subject. If he asked me out again, I'd try to do better.

Chapter 14
"You've Got Your Troubles"

Reese was busy rehearsing for the school play, so I didn't see much of him for a couple of weeks after our date. I didn't know if he was ignoring me or what, but there wasn't anything I could do about it, so I put my energy into running.

February was perfect running weather in Central Florida—highs in the sixties, azaleas shimmering with pink or white blossoms, fragrant purple clusters of wisteria, and low humidity. Francie and I ran down country roads in the mornings before school, often accompanied by Jess, who came along to protect us from drivers trying to run us off the road. Some drivers weren't willing to cross the solid line even a foot to give us room to run. Many of the worst offenders were women. They glared at us as we trotted onto the shoulder to avoid getting run over, as if we were insulting them by daring to run out in the open. They weren't like Benny, who really was trying to scare me, but they scared me anyway. I was always the first to move onto the shoulder.

Speaking of Benny, he hadn't bothered me again. I occasionally saw him in the halls, walking with his cheerleader girlfriend, but he looked away when I passed. Even though he wasn't a problem anymore, I stayed close to Jess when we were running, in case some other nutcase bothered us. It felt a little awkward at first, running with a black man, but after a few days, I forgot about his race and got comfortable calling him by his first name.

Jess liked to run. "Like Jesse Owens, the man I was named for, the fastest man alive. Not the fastest *black* man—the fastest man. Nobody's ever beat his record. And he's from Alabama, the next state over. Jesse Owens won four gold medals for track at the 1936 Olympics and wasn't treated right by the US government. President Roosevelt didn't even send him a congratulatory telegram."

After knowing Jess for only a month, I'd heard the story numerous times, and I tried not to roll my eyes when he started on it again. Instead, I attempted to sidetrack him. "Hey, Jess, tell us about the Boston Marathon."

The corners of his mouth curled up, and he winked at me. He was willing to switch to a different monologue. "Ah, the biggest event in distance running in the country, except for the Olympics. There are other races, but Boston is the only marathon. Both times when I finished it, I thought I was in heaven. Heaven, I say. You girls are gonna feel the same way when you cross the finish line. The crowds cheer you on, and you get to finally stop running." He cackled and slapped his knee.

He'd told us this one several times, too, but I never tired of hearing it or imagining crossing that finish line.

"When y'all run that race, you'll be part of history. Yes, indeed. Women were included in the earliest Olympic running events. One woman fell down after running the eight hundred meters in the 1926 Olympics. That was only about half a mile, but the judges ruled that women's bodies were too frail to compete in running. That's not true, as you well know. But women weren't allowed to run the eight hundred meters again until the 1960 Olympics. Soon, women will be allowed to run marathons with the men, and you'll be part of that."

Francie and I glanced at each other and smiled. The man had so much wind that he could chatter even after running ten miles in the cool winter mornings. Although at least thirty years older than we were, he could run us into the ground. I hoped I would be able to justify his faith in me.

That particular morning was misty, with steam rising from the ponds and lakes we passed. The heavy mist obscured the dawn and made me wonder if I was on a different planet. The mist would burn off soon, and the day would warm up, but before dawn, the cool air was refreshing.

I tried to keep up but kept having to stop to rest. My breath came out raspy, and I slumped to the ground, putting my head between my legs.

Jess bent over and asked, "Are you sick or what?"

I kept my head down and shook it as I struggled to stay awake.

Francie squatted beside me and asked in a whisper, "Hey, are you on your period?"

I whispered back, "No. I haven't had my period in a couple of months. Am I going to die?"

"If you are, so am I. My mom said that hard exercise like this can disrupt a woman's cycle. Maybe that's it." I heard concern in her voice. "So what's wrong, Faye? Did you eat breakfast this morning?"

I nodded.

"If not that, then what?"

"I'm still not sleeping very well," I said, trying not to cry as I looked at their concerned faces. "I wake up nearly every night with these terrible nightmares. They started a few months ago when a guy from school ran me off the road one night." Francie nodded, and I told Jess about the dream of being in a dark place and screaming and nobody would come and help me. "It seems to be getting worse." I glared at Jess. "But don't try to stop me from running. If I don't run the Boston Marathon, I'm nothing."

Francie and Jess stayed quiet. We watched the mist recede and the sun, bright and welcoming, rise above the orange groves.

Jess asked, "Are you afraid of something, Faye? Or did something terrible happen to you when you were younger?"

"I don't know. Not that I know of."

"Teenage girls can be really sensitive to things going on around them." He sounded tentative. "Is everything all right at home?"

No, everything was not all right. My dad constantly harped about wanting to move to someplace where the work wasn't so hard, but my mom refused. They fought about it all the time. Francie knew about the fights, but there was no way I was going to tell Jess.

"Yeah, it's all right."

He said, "I know a woman who's a counselor in town. Her name is Terry Johnson. She works with other teenagers, and she might be able to help you."

A counselor? Was I that bad off? It didn't matter. "My parents wouldn't pay for that."

He hesitated. "But if she would do it for free, would you go?"

"I don't know... I guess so."

"Great. I sold a house to her a few months ago. I'll see what I can do."

We sat quietly for a while. Then I asked, "Are you afraid of anything, Jess?"

He answered right away. "I'm afraid of getting lynched for running with white women. Every time I leave the house, my wife kisses me and says, 'Now you be sure and come back to me.'"

We sat still, stunned. I couldn't tell for sure if he was serious.

"My God, if you're afraid of that, why do you take the risk and run with us?" Francie sounded as concerned and confused as I was.

"Because I don't want to give in to my fears. If people don't take the chance, how will things ever change? Y'all two need me, and I can help you. But I'm still afraid. This is the South, after all."

I raised my head and stared at him. "I didn't realize you were afraid, too. You seem so strong and... confident."

"I think everybody's afraid of something, Faye. Getting older helps you do a better job of living with it, I guess. And you learn that what you're afraid of rarely happens. Even lynchings don't happen as often as they used to. I'm willing to take my chances to do something good in the world." He paused. "You ready to get started again? We're a long way from school, and you're almost late for first period. I don't want the principal coming down on me because I got you back late. He already doesn't like me much." Grinning, he said, "We need to stretch out before we start. Can't risk you getting injured only two months before the marathon."

On the way back, the other two ran slowly, adapting to my pace. My legs wouldn't go fast, no matter how much I willed them to. I didn't like being the turtle instead of the hare. But it was going to change, I vowed. I'd do whatever I needed to run that race.

THE PHONE RANG AT NINE o'clock on a Thursday evening. Mom had already gone to bed, so Dad answered. After a few seconds, he called to me. "Faye, it's *Tommy*. Don't talk long. It's already late, and it's a school night."

Tommy? Why would he call me? Tommy was this shy, brilliant guy in my biology class. The only conversation we'd ever had was when we had to share a microscope to look at slides.

"Hello?" I tried to sound cool, but I wasn't sure how successful I was.

"Hey, Faye. Don't say my name, but it's Kyle."

"Oh." I paused for a minute, trying to figure this out. The last time I'd spoken to him was at Christmas, when we went over to his family's house for dessert. He'd been with Linda that day and had barely paid any attention to me. "Hi, Tommy."

I pulled the phone and its long cord into my room and closed the door. I'd learned that I needed to lie on the bed and pull the covers over my head if I wanted to have a private conversation. When I was reasonably sure my parents couldn't hear me, I whispered, "Why are you calling me? And why did you say you're Tommy?"

He inhaled and blew out for a long time. I could practically picture him holding the joint. It gave me time to calm my heartbeat and breathing. In spite of how he'd jerked me around before, I couldn't help but hope that this time would be different. But was I being disloyal to Reese, even though I'd only been out with him once? I hoped not, but I wasn't sure.

"I miss talking to you. And you told me your mom thinks I'm too old for you. So I figured they'd only let us talk if they think I'm somebody else." I could hear his pride at putting something over on my parents.

"Uh, I miss talking to you, too. But what about Linda?" I couldn't help asking the question, even if it made him mad.

"Oh, we broke up."

"Again?" Those two were like a revolving door.

"This time it's for real. Besides, we're at different colleges."

"And I'm three hours away in Valencia."

"Yeah, but you're nicer."

Well. That was as far as I wanted to push that. I didn't want him telling Francie that her best friend was a bitch. Actually, I hoped he wouldn't say anything to Francie at all about me or this conversation. I knew I wouldn't. She would say I was jerking Reese around, and maybe she'd be right.

There was silence on the phone for a long time, but it felt friendly. "So what's new?" I asked, still unclear why he'd called me.

"There are even more antiwar marches now than there were a few months ago. It keeps getting worse. Last night, I was driving down the street while a march was going on. I had the right to drive down that street, but a bunch of them surrounded my car and started screaming at me. They even rocked the car a little. It was all I could do to not get into it with them. The police finally came and made them let me through."

"Jeez. That must have been scary."

"A little, I guess. But mainly, it pissed me off. We're all sitting in our safe college classes, and boys who aren't so lucky are getting drafted and dying in Vietnam. I want to quit school and join up, but my parents won't let me."

That's what he wants to talk about? Again? Am I only worthwhile to him as a listening post? In a little more than a year, I might be at the University of Florida with Kyle, and if the war continued, I would definitely be one of the protestors. I took a deep breath. "I'm honored that you think I'm mature enough to have an intelligent conversation with you. You know I don't agree with you, right?"

"Yeah. I remember. I thought you might have changed your mind."

"I didn't. But that doesn't matter. What matters is that you need to stay in school. It's dangerous over there. You might get killed. Besides, your parents would be devastated if you quit."

After a while, in a reluctant tone, he said, "I'll stay in school for now. But you're not right about the war."

We argued back and forth for a while, in a friendly way, until Dad yelled, "Dana Faye, get off the phone. It's a school night."

I said to Kyle, "I've got to go."

"Could I call you again? Maybe next week, same time, same station?"

"I guess so." Then, making my voice louder, I said, "Good talking to you, Tommy. See you at school tomorrow."

When I placed the phone back in its cradle, Dad strummed a loud chord and gave me a goofy grin. "Who's Tommy, anyway?"

"Just a guy in my biology class. He's helping me with my homework."

My dad winked. "Sure he is. You be careful, punkin. You're barely sixteen. Those teenage boys only want one thing."

"Oh, Dad." I stomped back into my bedroom. There was no use getting into it with him, because he probably wouldn't remember what he'd said in the morning. Besides, for all I knew, he was right.

Chapter 15
"Come Together"

On Friday night, I was in my room, looking at a sketch I'd drawn early that morning when I woke up at four and couldn't go back to sleep. It was of the woman who regularly popped into my mind when I was running. Maybe she was someone I ought to remember.

Mom was watching TV by herself, so I wandered into the living room. She'd made some popcorn and propped up her feet. Dad had gotten a second job playing country music with a band, and things at home were more relaxed when he was gone. During the next commercial, I showed Mom the sketchbook. "This woman's face keeps coming to me, and I don't recognize her. Do you know who she is?"

She flipped through the book. Then she looked at me, eyes wide. "I had no idea you'd gotten so good. These are fantastic. I don't recognize her, either. Maybe you made her up."

"I don't think so. That's why I'm asking you. Could she have been a babysitter or something? It seems like I remember her from a long time ago."

Mom stared at the picture again, squinting. Then she turned back to me. "She might have been one of your babysitters when we lived in Ohio. You took quite a shine to her. Mimi, I think her name was. But why are you drawing her so much?"

"I'm not sure. She just keeps coming to me. I even dream about her sometimes, but it's kind of hazy, like she's underwater or something. There's a house that goes along with her." I opened my sketchbook to the drawing—a two-story house with a porch on the front and dormer windows. Kind of like Francie's house.

When Mom saw this picture, she laughed. "I don't remember her living in such a fancy house, but it might have been hers. I do know it's not any place we've ever lived. Wishful thinking on your part, I'd say."

"How old was I when we lived in Ohio?"

She considered. "Four or five, I think. It was before you started school—I remember that. I'm surprised you can remember something from so long ago." She turned back to the television. "James West is really in trouble this time, and I want to see how he gets out of it." She patted the seat beside her. "Why don't you sit down and watch the end of the program with me?"

"No, thanks." Maybe Dad would remember her. I'd ask him when I got a chance.

A WEEK AFTER I NEARLY fainted while running, Jess handed me a business card. "You have an appointment with Mrs. Terry Johnson after school tomorrow. It's at the same time that you usually run and lasts for an hour, so you'll still be able to get a ride home from Mrs. Ivey."

I stared at the card, panic pushing itself up through my stomach and into my chest. "But I don't know what to do."

Jess laughed in a kindly way. "She'll tell you what to do. Mainly you just talk about what's bothering you. But you'll need to get your parents to sign a form saying it's okay for Mrs. Johnson to see you. Will that be a problem?"

There was no way I would ever ask my parents for permission to see a counselor. Besides the money problem, my dad hated all of that "talking trash." I'd heard him make fun of it when the subject came up, saying it was just a way to con people out of their hard-earned money.

Jess was waiting for my answer. "Uh, I don't think we have the money to pay for this."

He nodded. "I didn't think so. She said she would see you a few times for free. Will your parents object? Should I call them?"

"No. No, you don't need to." I thought fast, trying to figure a way out of this situation. The nightmares weren't getting better, in spite of my best efforts to stop them. I hadn't been able to increase my distance in weeks, and Jess and Francie had had to go on the last two long runs without me.

I could forge my parents' signatures, as I did for most everything else. "All right," I said, trying to be brave. "I'm sure they'll sign this tonight."

Francie ran up to us. "What's going on?"

I slipped the appointment card into my pocket while Jess said, "Not a thing. Get going. I want you to run five miles today with ten-minute splits." We all knew he was going easy on us because I was sickly. But the pace worked for me, and Francie didn't complain. We took off running while he yelled suggestions about our form.

DURING LUNCH THE NEXT day, I told Francie about the counseling appointment. She nodded. "I know Terry. She's a friend of my mom's and a really nice lady. She gave a lecture on dealing with depression to our health class last year. I bet she can help you."

"Do you think I'm depressed?" I hadn't thought about that. I didn't feel depressed, but maybe I was.

"Who knows? But she helps a lot of kids with problems, no matter what they are."

I had to ask. "Francie, do you think I'm crazy?"

She tilted her head to the side and made a huffing sound. "No, of course not. Why would you ask that? You're the sanest person I know."

"Well, something is wrong if I have to see a counselor. The nightmares are terrible and getting worse."

She was quiet for a minute. "What does your mom say about them?"

I snorted. "She thinks they're caused by running. According to her, every problem I ever have is either caused by running or by epilepsy. She says they'll go away if I cut down my miles." I hadn't told Francie about the lady whose face came up when I ran or the hours I'd spent drawing her picture. She really *would* think I was crazy if I told her about that.

Francie chewed a bite of bread, looking thoughtful. "Have you tried not running for a while and seeing what happens?"

I shook my head. "No way. This is my only chance of getting to college and having a different life. You know that."

She sighed. "Yeah, I know. Would you like me to come with you, then? Would that help?"

"Oh, yeah, that'd be great." I felt like I was drowning and had just been thrown a life preserver. "Thank you, Francie."

THE TWO OF US SAT IN Mrs. Johnson's waiting room that afternoon. I wasn't sure I could talk to an adult I didn't know, and I was shaking so hard I had to dig my feet into the floor to keep from sliding off the couch.

"Will you go in with me?" I asked.

"Uh-uh. This is your special time to speak with her alone. I'll wait for you right out here."

"I want you to stay with me."

"I know, but she won't let me. You can tell me later what happens."

I knew I was acting like a baby, but I couldn't help it. I stared at a painting of the ocean, wondering what I'd gotten myself into. The inner door opened, and a sophomore I recognized came out with a pleasant-looking black woman right behind her. The girl gave us a little wave and blushed before hurrying out.

"Hi, Faye, nice to meet you," said the woman, shaking my hand. "I'm Terry. You were brave to come today." She gestured toward her inner office, and I walked in, shoulders slumped, not daring to glance back at Francie. Inside was a small couch with a few chairs grouped around it. Terry said I could sit anywhere. I chose one end of the couch and crossed my legs and arms.

Terry sat in a chair and looked over the forms I'd forged with my mom's name. She set them aside then focused her gaze on me. "Maybe we could start by your telling me why your coach thought you should come and see me."

"Because I nearly fainted while I was running."

"And why was that?"

I knew I should tell her about the nightmares, but I just sat there like a lump. I felt increasingly desperate as the silence stretched out. As much as I wanted to, I couldn't speak frankly to a stranger. I shrugged.

She changed the subject. "Do you like school?"

"I guess so."

"Do you have a boyfriend?"

"No. Not really." I wanted to stop talking about stupid topics and tell her what was bothering me, but the words wouldn't come.

She waited for me to say something else. Was my boyfriend Kyle or Reese? Kyle called me occasionally, and we had good conversations, but that was it. I'd gone out with Reese a couple more times recently. Even though I liked him, I wasn't wild about him the way I was about Kyle. I didn't know what to say, so I kept quiet.

Terry rubbed her face, thinking. Then she brightened. "You haven't been in Valencia long, have you?"

That one, I could answer. "Six months now. It's one of the longest times we've stayed anywhere." I smiled, and that seemed to break the logjam inside me. We talked for a while about moving. She had moved a lot as a kid, too, and we had that misery in common.

Finally, she asked about sleeping. I took a deep breath, and miraculously, the words came easily. "I have nightmares nearly every night. Usually it's that I'm alone in the dark, and the smell of pee is so strong that it turns my stomach. And I'm scared. So scared." I shuddered. "Then I wake up screaming and can't go back to sleep."

"That must be terrible," she said in a tone that told me she believed me and understood. "Have you ever experienced anything like this in real life?"

I started to shake my head, and then something hit me. I remembered that, until I started school, I was so afraid of the dark that I had to sleep with the overhead light on. If Mom tried to turn it off, I would scream until she turned it back on again. Things got better after school started. Funny that I'd forgotten that.

"Faye, are you all right?"

I realized I'd zoned out. "Uh, I guess so."

"What just happened?"

"I, uh, I get these spells sometimes. I've got epilepsy. It's like I'm on the verge of seeing something, but a black curtain comes down and hides it. Then I have trouble coming back. I've had it all my life."

Terry sat back in her chair. "Do you get these spells all the time? Or does something trigger them?"

I considered that. "No. Not necessarily. But I just remembered that I used to hate sleeping in the dark. I guess I got over it for a while."

"Do you sleep in the dark now?"

"Yeah. My parents don't like to keep lights on when they don't have to. It wastes electricity and costs money."

She pressed her lips together and was quiet for a moment. "When you think about being in the dark, what else comes up in your mind? Take your time."

I let my mind wander. After a while, in a flash, I remembered seeing my mom's face outside a window. She was smiling, but she looked like a monster. I tensed, and the curtain came down again. When I tried to tell this to Terry, I couldn't speak. My mouth moved, but no words came out.

"All right, stop now. Breathe, and think about something you like to do."

I thought about running in the fog in the early morning with the doves cooing, frogs croaking, and the cool mist hitting my face. I began to feel slightly better. The memory got clearer over the next few minutes, but I could still feel how scared I'd been when I saw Mom through the window. I didn't understand why I was so scared of Mom, though. She didn't look like a monster, even when she'd just woken up in the morning.

All I could figure was that this wasn't a real memory but something my weird brain had concocted for some reason of its own. I froze up again and had a hard time breathing.

After a while, Terry said, "I'd like you to imagine running in the mist when it's dark. And know that you are safe. Completely safe. You feel wonderful, running in the dark and being safe."

It seemed like a strange thing to do, but I gave it a try. As I combined the two thoughts, my throat opened, and after a while, I could breathe more easily.

Terry smiled. "Good job. You're going to be fine." She told me to go home and, before I went to sleep, think about running in the mist instead of how afraid I was that I'd have the nightmare.

Over the next few weeks, working with Terry, the nightmares slowed down. They didn't stop altogether, but I started getting more rest. At her suggestion, I also bought a night-light, and that helped.

I began to feel stronger than I had in months, and I was running fast again. After four visits, I said goodbye to Terry. She told me I could come back anytime if I needed her. I hoped I wouldn't need her.

AFTER WE FINISHED OUR workout one Tuesday in early March, Francie brought up the subject of the marathon. "Mom says it's time to work out the details of our trip. She's planning on going with us as a chaperone. We should buy our airplane tickets soon. How are you doing for money?"

"Uh, I'm not sure." Stan paid me well at the carving store, but I spent quite a bit, too. I'd started buying school lunches every day because I needed more food than just cheese crackers. And I'd bought a few new clothes and some makeup. "I think I'm probably close to two hundred fifty dollars." Unfortunately, I'd been too busy to count my money for a while. I resolved to do it right away.

But the money was a minor problem compared to the major one, which was that I hadn't yet asked my parents for permission to go to Boston. They'd told me I couldn't do it the first time I'd asked them, but that was months earlier, when the whole thing was just a distant dream. I needed to ask them for real. I didn't even want to think about what I'd do if they said no. Whatever happened, I couldn't put it off much longer.

"Can't I just run away and leave them a note?"

"Nope," Francie said. "My mom wants to talk to your mom about it. She's waiting for you to tell her when would be a good time to call."

There was no getting around it, then. "Okay. I'll ask them on Sunday." They were usually in their best moods on the one day of the week that they had off from work.

"Mom says we can wait to buy the tickets up to about two weeks before the marathon," said Francie. "Don't you dare chicken out on me."

Sunday, then. I had five days to figure out a plan for getting my parents' permission.

THAT NIGHT, I OPENED my jewelry box, where I kept my money, and turned it upside down. A fistful of bills fluttered downward and onto the bedspread. Two small drawers at the bottom held coins, and I dumped them onto the bed, too. This was a ritual I loved. When I'd first started earning money, I counted it every Sunday night, placing the bills into separate piles and betting myself which pile would be the highest. The one-dollar pile had always won, but it was fun to anticipate a day when the ten-dollar pile would tower the highest, or maybe the twenty-dollar pile.

Over the past couple of months, I'd been so busy that I'd taken to stuffing my paper money into the jewelry box in random order and keeping most of the coins in my pocketbook. When I wanted money, I'd reach in and pull out whatever amount I needed and then stuff the rest back in.

That night, I realized there were so many bills inside the jewelry box that the lid barely closed. *Uh-oh.* I would need to take the singles to the bank and exchange them for tens or twenties and possibly find a different hiding place. I didn't want Mom to know I had this much money until I asked permission to go to Boston.

I performed my regular ritual of placing the bills into piles. As usual, the one-dollar pile was the highest. There were forty-eight ones, seventeen fives, nine tens, and three twenties. The total came to $283, plus more than five dollars in coins. I inhaled sharply, and my eyes filled with tears as it slowly dawned on me that I really had been able to earn enough money for the race just by working at the carving store and occasionally for Mr. Barrett. Saving more than two hundred fifty dollars had seemed impossible the previous fall. If I cut back on my spending, I should be good, even if the airplane ticket and other expenses were higher than Francie had estimated.

I placed the dollar bills in my pocketbook so I could take them to the bank and exchange them for tens. I would definitely ask my parents on Sunday afternoon. They had to know why I was training so hard, and they hadn't told me I couldn't do it in quite a while. So they knew about the marathon, and I knew they knew. All we needed to do was talk about it.

I imagined how the conversation would go. The first thing they would say was that they didn't have the money. And then I would pull out my wad of cash and show it to them. They would be amazed that I could save so much money, and then they would agree that I deserved to go to Boston, especially when it meant getting a scholarship to college. Even though they were worried about me being so far from home, I figured they would be reassured when I told them Laney would be there as a chaperone. I wouldn't allow myself to consider any other possibility than that they would give me permission. I was sure I could convince them.

But that wasn't until Sunday. I had other things to think about right then. Before I asked my parents about the marathon, I needed to focus on passing my driver's test. After waiting so long, the time had finally arrived.

Chapter 16
"Helter Skelter"

I passed the written test to get my learner's permit, and on Friday afternoon, I was in the driver's seat of the school's driver's ed car with Laney as my passenger. The class included a few hours of driving with an instructor, so we were on a newly paved road with several long, slow curves on the outskirts of town. I drove carefully, adjusting through a long left turn. That particular turn even had one of the few hills in Central Florida. Midway through the turn, I saw a car crest the small rise, coming toward us. It was halfway in our lane. I could see the driver looking over her shoulder at something in the back seat. Kids, probably.

Sweat dripped down my neck, and I frantically tried to remember what the manual had said I should do in this situation. *Why, oh why doesn't that woman look forward?*

"Slow down, Faye," Laney said. "Get close to your side. Use your horn."

I obeyed, gripping the wheel with both hands. The horn seemed especially loud to my ears, but the woman didn't look up. Was she deaf, or what? The car kept coming toward us in our lane. In a tight voice, I asked, "What now?"

"Swerve to the shoulder. Now."

I swerved to the shoulder, but then I overcorrected and swerved back into the road, nearly crashing into the other car. "Go right, *right*!" screamed Laney, holding on to the dashboard and jamming her foot on the brake on her side of the car. I jerked the wheel back

119

again, and we careened off the road. The car bumped through a stand of weeds, then under the spreading limbs of a large oak tree covered with Spanish moss, and hit the tree trunk with a deep *thunk*. I was thrown against something hard. Everything went black.

THE NEXT THING I KNEW, it was dark, and something wet was running down my face. I tried to reach up to feel what it was, but somebody—I couldn't see who—had hold of my arms and was shaking me. Then I realized it was a strange grown-up lady, and she was sitting beside me, yelling, "Faye. Faye." She seemed really upset, as if she'd been crying. I wondered, in a woozy sort of way, if it was me she was yelling at and why she was calling me Faye. That wasn't my name. She had to have me mixed up with someone else.

Another grown-up lady was outside the car, banging on the window, a wild look in her eyes. I didn't know her, either. I rolled down the window. In a small voice, I asked her, "Where am I? What happened?"

"I'm sorry. I guess I accidentally ran you off the road. You're under a tree. Can you move? What hurts?"

I shook my head, trying to figure out what was happening. "Everything hurts. Where's my mama?"

The outside lady looked confused, but the one sitting next to me spoke. "Sweetie, I'm Laney. Remember?"

"No. Where's my mama and daddy?"

"They're back at your house. Now feel around your body and tell me what hurts."

"*Ow*, my foot hurts bad. It's stuck. I can't get it out." I was about to start screaming, but the lady tried to calm me.

"It's okay, Faye. Maybe your foot was caught when we crashed. You stay here. I'll go for help if I can get this door open."

"Faye? Who's Faye?" I felt like Alice falling down the rabbit hole. My daddy liked to read me that book before I went to sleep at night. I was very, very small.

"You are, of course. You must have hit your head in the accident. Just stay still. We'll get help."

My mouth could barely form words, and I spoke slowly and carefully. "My name's not Faye. It's... Pilot. No, that's not right... I forget. But it's not Faye. Why are you calling me Faye?"

"I think you hit your head, sweetie. Just sit still. I'm going to see if I can get out of the car while this lady goes for the ambulance. Understand?"

I mumbled something. The outside lady helped the inside lady out of the car. And then the outside lady left. The inside lady, the one called Laney, walked around, wobbling a little.

I sat still, trying to remember my name. *Pilot* wasn't quite right, but I knew it was something like that. Why couldn't I remember my own name? Why had that lady called me *Faye*?

The next thing I knew, some men dragged me out of the car and into an ambulance. At the hospital, a doctor checked me out and told me I'd bruised my foot when it got caught under the accelerator, and I had a big lump on my head. I would have to stay at the hospital overnight so he could keep an eye on me.

Everybody asked what happened, but I couldn't remember. I felt like I was on a boat, rocking, rocking. When I closed my eyes, I was sure I was going to fall out of the boat and into the water, so I held on tight to the railing.

Laney came in and told me that a lady had accidentally run us off the road.

I didn't remember that. I stuck out my lower lip. "Where are my daddy and mama? I want them. Now."

Laney said they were on their way.

My bed was rolled into a different room. Another doctor came in. "I'm Dr. Whittaker," he said before holding up two fingers. "How many fingers do you see?"

I giggled. "Two."

Then he asked, "Can you tell me what year it is?"

I didn't know what he was talking about. I shook my head, but only a little, because every movement hurt.

"Do you know where you are?"

"A hospital?"

"Do you know which one?"

"No." I stuck my thumb in my mouth and wouldn't answer any more questions.

He said, "That's all right. You did fine. Now, I want to take a test to study your brain waves. All you have to do is lie still and breathe."

I lay still and breathed. After the test was over, he said everything looked fine, but I probably had a concussion. I didn't know what that was, and I was too scared to ask. Nothing made sense. I closed my eyes and tried to remember my name.

After a while, two people I didn't know came into my room and hugged me. I pulled away from them. "Who are you?" They weren't familiar at all, and I was close to screaming again.

The man stepped back, but the woman bent over me and asked, "Don't you know us, Faye?"

"I'm not Faye, I'm... Pilot." That was close enough to my name, even though I knew it wasn't quite right. In my Alice in Wonderland voice, I asked again, "Where are my mama and daddy?"

The people turned to Dr. Whittaker, who leaned over me. "These are your parents. Don't you know them?"

I shook my head, but not too hard because I had a huge headache. Tears streamed down my cheeks. The doctor asked the people to leave, and I calmed down a little when they went out of the room. He started filling out a sheet of paper and asked without looking at me, "How old are you... Pilot?"

I shook my head. "I'm not sure."

He held my hand for a minute before he said carefully, "Pilot, you're a little confused right now. But I promise you'll get better soon."

I asked, near tears, "Are my mama and daddy okay? I shook them and shook them, and they wouldn't wake up."

"Yes. I want you to rest now, and you can see them when you wake up." He gave me a shot. It hurt, and I almost cried, but then I got really, really tired.

WHEN I WOKE UP, A WOMAN was sleeping in an awkward position in a chair beside my bed. My head felt a little better, but I was sore all over. After a few seconds, I recognized her. *Laney.*

When I moved, she woke up and smiled. "There you are. You slept for three hours. How do you feel?"

"Like I got hit by a truck." I smiled because I had gotten hit by a truck-sized tree.

She smiled back. "What should I call you?"

"My name, of course. Faye." I had a vague memory of telling somebody my name was something different. Something like *Pilot.* But that couldn't be right. I shook my head. It hurt but not as much as before.

Laney said, "Your parents are here. Bud and Sue. Do you want to see them?"

I hesitated. I felt as if something had gotten jarred loose in my brain, but it didn't yet have a home. Before I could answer, the doctor came in. He did another exam, asking me how many fingers he was holding up. I got that right.

Then he asked, "What year is it?"

This time, I was sure. "It's 1968."

"And how old are you?"

"Sixteen." Such dumb questions.

He asked in an even voice, "Do you remember when I asked you some of the same questions before you went to sleep?"

"I think so. Sort of."

"Do you remember what you told me then?"

I shook my head.

"You said that the people waiting outside weren't your parents. Do you remember that?"

"Maybe." Even though I couldn't pull the memory up clearly, I knew there had been some truth in what I was saying. I just couldn't figure out what it was.

He patted my hand and stood up. "I'm glad to see you're doing better. We'll do some more tests, and I'll let you know what we find. Meanwhile, would you like to see your parents?"

"Yes."

The doctor left after giving Laney a pointed look. She stayed in her chair. My parents came in. Mom's eyes were red and puffy as though she'd been crying, and she gave me a big hug. Dad leaned over and kissed my cheek then sat down in a chair and opened the newspaper. Mom's voice sounded strained. "We were so worried about you. And then when you didn't recognize us, I didn't know what to think."

I tuned her out and tried to figure out what had happened. The memory was hazy, but I almost remembered something that kept skittering just out of reach.

After a few minutes, I couldn't hold my eyes open. "I need to take a nap now."

"Sure, sweetie," Mom said. "Your dad has to get home, but I'll stay the night with you."

Laney said goodbye, promising to be back in the morning and that she'd let Francie know I was okay. Both she and Reese had called a bunch of times, worrying about me, but they weren't allowed to talk to me yet. I was so tired that I barely heard what she said.

IN THE MORNING, DR. Whittaker discharged me, but he said he wanted to see me in his office on Monday to go over the test results and check on how I was doing. As Mom and I gathered my things, a police officer walked into the hospital room. It was Detective Hunt, one of the men who'd caught Francie and me at Benny's house.

When she looked at his badge, Mom jumped as if she'd been shot. I jumped, too, terrified that he was going to give away that we'd already met. Fortunately, he didn't seem to remember me. He asked some questions about what happened and then said, "The wreck wasn't your fault. The other driver got a ticket for reckless driving. Her insurance will pay your medical bills." As he walked out, he said, "Drive carefully."

"Let's go," Mom said, her hands shaking like palm fronds in a heavy breeze. She didn't even wait for the nurse to take me out in a wheelchair, just led me to the elevator and through the front door. The thought of getting back into a vehicle, especially so soon after the wreck, made me want to scream and cry—or run back into the hospital and hide under the bed. Of course, I couldn't do that, and my legs were too wobbly to walk home. I forced myself to get in on the passenger's side, and I braced my feet against the floor in case we wrecked. Mom drove carefully, but the pavement rushed past much too quickly, and I felt sick to my stomach.

To distract myself, I asked Mom, "Were we ever in a car wreck when I was little?"

She glanced at me. "I'm surprised you remember that. It was a long time ago. Your dad slid on some ice and ran into a tree."

"But were the two of you knocked out?"

"I'm not sure. Briefly maybe. You weren't hurt, though. The radiator was messed up, and we had to get the car towed to a garage. Do you remember that?"

"I... I'm not sure." Something didn't feel right about what she was saying. Her voice sounded strained, and I thought her eyebrow was twitching. But I didn't trust my perceptions. "Was the accident in this truck?"

"No, I think it was in our old Plymouth car. You must have been four or five when we had that wreck. The Plymouth never ran right afterward. We kept it for another year or two before we gave up on it and got the truck. Do you remember it?"

"Not really." I paused. "Mom, did I ever have a nickname? Something like Pilot?"

She laughed. "Why would we ever call you Pilot? No, your dad calls you Punkin a lot. Could you have gotten mixed up?" Glancing at me, she said gently, "The doctor told us you were confused and thought your name was Pilot." She reached over and squeezed my hand. "I'm so sorry you had to go through that. But you're going to be fine."

Fine looked like a long way away from where I was. But I appreciated that she was trying to make me feel better.

THE NEXT DAY, FRANCIE came to visit. I asked her to walk with me around the orange groves. I was limping a little but not much.

She asked, "How's your foot?"

"It's okay. It doesn't hurt so much today."

"Do you think you'll still be able to run?"

I balanced on the good foot and circled my bad ankle around. "Yeah. But it might be a day or two."

"What about the marathon?"

"My head hurts a lot, but the rest of me will be okay in a few days, I think. It shouldn't be a problem to make up the time I lose." I glanced back at the house to make sure Mom wasn't around. "I need to talk to you about something else." I hesitated then rushed in. "I think my parents aren't my real parents. And..." I winced, knowing she would think this next part was crazy. "I think my real name is Pilot, or something like that." She didn't respond right away, so I said, "What's more, I think I remember different parents." She still didn't speak, so I was forced to ask, "What do you think, Francie? Could that be true?"

"You hit your head, right?" Her voice was kind. When I nodded, she said, "People get mixed up after a concussion. My cousin Brant got a concussion when he was playing football, and he couldn't walk straight for a week. He couldn't even remember what year it was. Maybe that's what happened to you."

"The doctor said the same thing. I'm not sure what to believe. I'm starting to think that something is seriously wrong here."

"Did you ask your mom about all this?"

"I asked her about another wreck, and she made up a story that wasn't true."

"How do you know it wasn't true?"

"Because a muscle above her eye twitches when she's lying. And her voice sounds funny, like she's talking through a balloon or something."

Francie sighed. "This is all pretty weird. Let's say your memory is right. What, exactly, do you remember about those other parents?"

"Ever since I've been running, I've had pieces of memories come up during and after I run. It's almost like a snapshot is set in front of my eyes and then snatched away. Has that ever happened to you?"

She shook her head. "Nope. Not at all. I think about how hungry I am and what I want to have for supper or which boy I think is cute. That sort of thing."

So something was definitely strange about me. I'd thought so. Were these really memories, or just *spells*, as my Mom insisted when I asked about them?

I described the woman I had been drawing. "I think she was the mom I expected to see at the hospital. When the other one came in, I was really scared because I figured something bad had happened to my real mom. And this fake mom was taking her place. Sort of like a horror movie or something."

"What about your other dad?"

"I can't picture him. But I'm pretty sure he's not Bud."

"Huh." We walked up and down the rows of orange trees. "I keep wondering what Sherlock Holmes would do in this situation. But nothing comes to mind." She sighed. "Do you remember anything else about these people, your real parents?"

"Not much. But remember on my birthday when I told you about a birthday party when I was little? I was four, I think. The other mom wiped cake off my face. It definitely wasn't Sue."

Francie rubbed her chin and looked thoughtful. "Didn't you tell me that sometimes strange thoughts come into your mind, and you get these fake memories?"

So Francie didn't believe me. Maybe she was right. I groaned, and my head started hurting again. I didn't feel like arguing with her. "Yeah. Maybe I'm really crazy." Sometimes I did feel as if I were going crazy. Other times, I thought I was sane and my parents were the crazy ones.

We threw dried oranges at a bunch of vultures that were perched in a tree. They flew away, flapping their giant wings, and white poop dripped down the tree. We laughed and started back toward the house. Francie said kindly, as if speaking to a three-year-old, "You aren't crazy. But if Bud and Sue aren't your real parents, how do you think you came to be with them?"

I'd thought about this constantly ever since the accident, so the words burst out of me. "I think I'm adopted. There's a million possibilities of how it could have happened. Maybe I was so bad that my real parents couldn't handle me. Or they were so poor that they had to give me away. Or they were spies from another country, and they had to escape in a hurry. I think I remember that my real mama had a foreign accent. Maybe they died, and these people adopted me. Or there was another car wreck, a different one from the one Mom talked about. I can't remember how it happened, but it's the only thing that makes sense. For some reason, nobody will tell me what really happened. It's driving me crazy."

Francie looked away. "I can't imagine you ever being so bad that your parents would give you away. So that one's out. But they could have been poor. Remember reading about poor houses in English class? Lots of people used to be so poor they had to put their children in orphanages. Do you remember anything like that?"

I shook my head, wondering where this was going.

"Lots of people are in car wrecks, so that might be it." She sounded thoughtful. "But if your real parents died, I would think you'd have been adopted by some family members, not strangers. So if your parents haven't said anything about it, I doubt that was it." She paused. "But... spies. I like that one. Maybe your parents were Russian, and they were friends with the Smiths. They managed to give you to them before they left the country. And that's why you move around so much—so the FBI won't find you. Ooh." She poked me in the ribs. "Do you remember any Russian words?"

"No." I knew she was teasing me, but I didn't tell her that we moved around so much because my dad was running from the law for other reasons.

She said, joking, "Make sure you keep running. Maybe some Russian words will come back to you."

She was trying to cheer me up. I teetered on the verge of being irritated that she didn't believe me, and I tried to think of how to respond. "I want to show you something." I took Francie inside, and we went into my bedroom, where I pulled out our family photo album. "Look. There are pictures of me as a baby, and then none until I'm in school."

She thumbed through the pages. There were only three baby pictures of me. In one, I was wrapped in a blanket and being held by my mom, in another, I was splashing in a kiddie pool, and in the third, I was wearing a pretty dress. The photos were in black and white, and they had faded over the years.

"Aw, you were so cute," she said.

"Yeah, but they could have been any baby. And that's all there are until I was in first grade. See." I pointed out the huge gap between my baby pictures and the ones that were clearly of me. I had added all my school pictures to the album, along with the others that Mom had snapped of some of the places where we'd lived. "Why aren't there any pictures in between?"

"I don't know. It's a little strange, I admit, but there's probably an explanation. And a gap of a few years in pictures is hardly enough for you to think you were adopted. You should ask your mom about it."

"I *have* asked her. She doesn't answer."

"Well, ask her again."

"Okay." This was going nowhere. I closed the album and placed it back on the shelf.

Francie said, "You're looking sleepy. Why don't you take a nap? I've got to go anyway. By the way, Reese is planning on coming over in a little while."

She was right about me needing a nap. My head felt like a toy that needed winding. After I slept for a while, I'd be happy to see Reese. I hadn't told him about the problems with my parents, but I enjoyed hanging out with him. It was nice to do normal teenager things, like playing board games or talking about sports. Or kissing when my parents were out of the room.

As I was falling asleep, I realized that I hadn't asked my parents if I could go to Boston. There was no way I could bring it up right then, with everything else going on. I'd deal with that when I felt better, assuming that Laney was even willing to take me since I'd wrecked the driver's ed car.

Chapter 17
"How Can I Be Sure"

Mom and I found the doctor's office in a small building near the hospital. Dr. Whittaker's assistant took us to an examining room and left us there. After a half hour, the doctor came in, carrying a pile of papers.

"How are you feeling, Faye?"

"Fine, I guess. Still a little tired, though."

He checked my eyes and ears, listened to my heart, and asked me to follow his finger as he moved it in front of my eyes. He nodded and wrote something down. "That's normal. You should start feeling better soon." He shuffled through his papers. "Your tests are all normal. Did you ever figure out why you thought your name was Pilot?" There was a twinkle in his eyes.

Mom spoke fast without looking at me. "She was out of her mind, sir. Nothing she said made any sense for a while. The knock on her head did it, I think."

"Faye, what do you think? Do you even remember the things you said in the hospital?"

The doctor had been nice to me, so I decided to take a chance. I took a deep breath. "Yes, I remember them now. I was kind of confused for a while. But I do think I remember having a different name and different parents when I was little." It was no longer a secret. I could feel a giant chasm opening before my feet.

He shifted his gaze to my mom. "Mrs. Smith, is her memory correct?"

Her tone was forceful and frustrated. "No, sir. I've told her over and over that she's imagining things. She's always had an active imagination. She gets these spells when she seems far away and thinks she's remembering things that never happened. Her dad calls her Punkin, and I guess it could sound a little like Pilot. And I've always worked, so she stayed with a lot of babysitters when she was little. She must have gotten them mixed up."

He looked at me. "Tell me more about these spells, Faye."

It took me a while to put together an answer as I tried to find the right words. "Well, several things happen. Sometimes I get these squiggly lines in front of my eyes, and I can't see anything for a few minutes. Other times, I feel like somebody's holding a picture in front of my face, or it seems like a curtain is about to be lifted and I'll see something important. But it never happens, and then I get sick to my stomach. That lasts for just a few seconds, I think. And I have this terrible nightmare. I'm in a dark place all alone, and I'm scared out of my mind. I wake up screaming." I paused to think. "That's it, I guess."

He had taken notes while I was talking. "Going back to the squiggly lines in front of your eyes. Do you ever get a headache after you see the lines?"

I nodded, surprised that he understood me so well. "Sometimes. But not always."

"And what about the other times? Do you get a headache, or do you ever black out when you get these strange sensations?"

"I've never blacked out, but I do get a weird feeling in my head, and sometimes I forget where I am for a few seconds. I might get a headache then, too. But more often, I get sick to my stomach."

He nodded and then turned to Mom. "Have you taken her to a doctor for these problems?"

"When she was little, I took her to a doctor, and he said she might be having small seizures. He said if they got worse, we would have to see a neurologist, but we never had the money. He prescribed some medicine for when she had one of her spells. I guess it's worked, because she hasn't gotten worse." Her face was red. Beads of sweat were forming on her forehead, and her eyebrow twitched.

He shuffled through his papers for a few seconds then looked up. "I don't think she's been having seizures. Her tests look good. What was the medicine?"

"Phenobarbital. I keep getting the prescription refilled."

"I don't think she needs to take it anymore. But you'll need to taper her off of it. Here's how you do it." When he finished talking to my mom, he turned to me. "Faye, I think you are having migraines. They start with a visual aura, like you describe, and then they may or may not lead to a headache. The headache, when it comes, can be intense or mild. Does that describe your experience?"

Migraines. I'd heard of them, but I didn't know much. I nodded.

"If they get worse, I can give you some medicine. But it sounds like you're managing pretty well. I'll give you a pamphlet about it before you leave." He paused. "As far as the 'spells,' as you describe them, I'm not sure what to make of them. I wonder if you're having flashbacks." When he saw my look of confusion, he continued. "Flashbacks are something from your past that you might not remember, but it happened, and at times, pieces of it come back into your mind." He looked at Mom. "Did anything like what she describes happen?"

Mom laughed. "Different parents? No. Definitely not. I have her birth certificate at home if you want to see it. Like I said, she could be remembering babysitters. But we did have a car wreck when she was about four, and that might be part of it." She shrugged. "What can we do about these spells?"

He frowned and looked away. "The only thing I can think of would be counseling. I don't think any medicine is going to help. Would you consider counseling? I could refer you to someone."

My face went hot. I probably blushed up to my hairline, thinking about Terry. Fortunately, nobody was looking at me.

They were quiet for a while until my mom said, "Sir, I appreciate the thought, but we don't have the money for counseling. We're simple working people. Faye's doing better now. If she didn't insist on running so much, everything would be fine. But I can't talk any sense into her."

He turned to me, concern in his eyes. "Does running make your symptoms worse?"

"No, sir. Not at all." I knew it wasn't completely true, and probably so did Mom, but neither of us said anything.

He nodded. "Running's good exercise, and I know more women are starting to run. You can go back to it whenever you're ready. Don't push it until you've got your energy back, though." He stared hard at my mom. "I don't think she has epilepsy now, and she probably never did. She might have had a seizure at one point because of a high fever. But taper her off the pills, all right?"

Mom nodded, her face red.

He said we should come back and see him if things got worse and assured us that, other than the spells, I seemed to be a normal teenager. He patted me on the shoulder and left the room.

When Mom was driving home, she said, "I know you lied to that doctor, missy."

I didn't respond, but I thought, *And so did you.*

THE NEXT DAY, I STOPPED by Laney's clinic before meeting Francie for our regular run. Laney sat at her desk, trying to write with her left hand. Her right arm was in a sling, and she had a big bruise on her cheek. But when she saw me, she smiled and stood up to give me the best hug she could manage.

I held on for as long as I dared and tried to hold back the tears. A few leaked out anyway, but I kept them to myself.

"Hi, sweetie," Laney said. "Are you all right?"

"Yes, ma'am. I'm much better. How about you?"

"Oh, I bruised my shoulder, but I'm mending. No major harm done."

"What about the car?" I asked, wondering if I would be charged for the damage. After all, I had been driving.

She laughed. "The car is the least of our problems. It's dinged up, but it can be fixed. It's in the shop now. Don't worry about it. That's what insurance is for."

It was time to take responsibility. I cleared my throat and forced myself to look directly at her. "I'm sorry about the wreck. I know I overreacted."

"No, Faye, you're a new driver. It was my responsibility to keep you safe. I guess I didn't react quickly enough." She sucked in her breath. "Maybe I'm not such a great driver's ed instructor. I've never been in a difficult situation before."

We stared at each other. I didn't know which of us was telling the truth. Possibly we both were. The whole thing had happened so quickly that I couldn't say for sure.

"Well, I'm sorry," I said, awkward in my new role as equal to an adult.

"Yeah. Me, too." We hugged again. When I didn't make a move to leave, she asked, "Was there something else you wanted to talk to me about?"

This was going to be hard, but I needed to do it. I took a breath and opened my pocketbook. "I want to show you something." I told her about the doctor's visit and then handed her a bottle of the pills I'd been taking for as long as I could remember. "Do you have access to a chemistry lab or something?"

"I can send things to a lab in Orlando if I need to. Why?"

"I just wondered if you would have these pills analyzed. They're supposed to be phenobarbital, but I just want to make sure." I felt like a dog that had done something wrong and was cringing, waiting to be yelled at for its behavior. Somebody—either Laney or my mom—was bound to yell at me for doubting those pills.

She took the bottle and removed the lid, shaking out a few pills. Giving me a funny look, she said, "Let's check it out." On a shelf was a nurses' book of pills, with pictures. She opened it to the photo of phenobarbital. The pills in my bottle were round and white and pressed, similar to but not exactly like those in the picture.

We stared at each other. "Honey," she said, "I don't know what this is, but I don't think it's phenobarbital. Is this what you've been taking all along?"

I didn't need to cringe after all. I nodded, unable to speak.

She drummed her fingers on the table. "I've got to say, this pill looks a lot like aspirin."

"Really? Will you have them analyzed?"

"Of course I will. But it might take several days to get the results." Taking an aspirin bottle from the cabinet, she shook one into her left palm. The pills I'd been taking were in her right hand. We examined the two types of pills. The aspirin had something stamped on it, and the mystery pill didn't, but otherwise, they were exactly alike.

She sounded a little shaky. "These are Bayer aspirin. I imagine the generics wouldn't have the *B* stamped on them." Looking down at the two pills, she said, "We'll know soon." She placed two of my pills in an envelope then picked up the prescription bottle. "It plainly says here that it's phenobarbital. But look, the date is from 1956. Didn't you notice that?"

"Mom just said we're using an old bottle. The pharmacist gives us a discount if we use our own bottle, and she gets it in a big bottle that she fills the little bottles from."

Laney shook her head. "Faye, that doesn't happen. My husband takes a lot of pills for the pain in his leg, and no matter how many pills he takes, the pharmacist always gives them to him in a new bottle. Every time."

"Oh." This information was as shocking as driving into a tree. I couldn't have known about the prescription bottles. Things were unraveling in my family faster than I could believe.

Her next words echoed my own question. "What is happening in your family?"

I didn't know. Mom and Dad had had a big fight after we came home from the doctor's office. They walked out into the orange grove so I couldn't hear, but I could see their arms waving. Dad seemed madder than Mom. When they came back inside, their faces were bright red, and Dad went outside to work until it was dark. He almost never missed supper, but he did that night. Mom and I ate without him, and we watched the news without saying a word.

I didn't want to tell Laney any of this. I needed to think about the rest of my suspicions before I confided in her. I shrugged. "I'm not sure. But it has something to do with these pills. Can we talk about it again after you get the lab report?" I said goodbye and hurried out to meet Francie.

LANEY WAS RIGHT. THE report she received later that week said I'd been taking aspirin. She showed it to me. "I've been a nurse for twenty years. In that time, I've seen parents do some weird things. At least this didn't hurt you. You might ask your mom why she deceived you, but she probably figured just thinking you were getting medicine would help you. And maybe she was right." She continued, looking thoughtful. "Your parents love you very much, Faye. I think you need to show them the lab report and ask them why they were giving you aspirin."

I agreed to do it, but I didn't say when. As I was leaving, she asked, "Have you asked your parents about going to Boston yet?"

Oh gosh. I didn't know if I should lie or tell the truth. If I lied, she might feel compelled to call my parents and talk to them about it. "Yes, ma'am. They're thinking about it."

There, that was only partially a lie. It would keep her from calling the house, and I would get to ask them on my own timetable—which would have to be soon. I needed to find out what was going on in my family, Boston Marathon or no Boston Marathon.

Chapter 18
"Don't Worry, Baby"

For several days, I spent every spare hour checking out Russian spies. If the Smiths had adopted me when I was four or five, that would have been in the mid-1950s. After sorting through piles of microfilm in a dark room at the public library, I found that, even though several spies had been expelled during that time, none of them had children. After that, it seemed ridiculous that I'd even thought my real parents might be spies, so I gave up that line of research. But I wasn't sure what came next.

Francie and I talked about my strange memories every day while we ran our laps, but she thought I'd gotten things mixed up and there had to be a perfectly reasonable explanation for them. She also reasoned that my mom must have really thought I had epilepsy but didn't have the money to buy the real medicine, so she substituted aspirin. Such a trusting soul, Francie.

After another conversation that went nowhere, she asked, "Why don't you look at your birth certificate and see what it says?"

I felt as if I'd been mowed down by a truck. Of course that was what I needed to do. I stopped in the middle of a turn and stared at her, appreciating her brilliance. Francie stopped, too, but then started running again.

"Do you know where your birth certificate is?" she called over her shoulder.

In her settled life, she probably knew exactly where her birth certificate was and could put her hands on it in a second. Sometimes she struggled to comprehend my stories about the rootlessness of my life before we moved to Valencia.

I started running again and strained to catch up to her. Francie had gotten really fast. "Yeah, but..." I didn't know how to continue. Frankly, I wasn't sure I'd ever seen my own birth certificate. But I knew where to find it. Mom kept our important papers in a fire-proof metal box somewhere in her bedroom. She had always carried my transcripts and birth certificate when she registered me at a new school. She would probably get suspicious if I asked to look at it. So if I wanted to know the truth, the next time I was alone in the house, I would have to find that metal box.

Mom and Dad's room was always off-limits to me. I hadn't been in there in years. Once, when I was little, I'd gone into their bedroom and taken Mom's jewelry box off her dresser and placed it on the floor, where I happily played with her few necklaces, bracelets, and earrings. She had some pop beads I particularly loved. Even though Mom had told me before that their room was off-limits, I must have forgotten, because when a shadow darkened the bedroom door, I looked up, eager to show Mom how I'd decorated my stuffed bunny with her jewelry. I wasn't prepared for the dark cloud that was her face, and it scared me so much I burst into tears.

She jerked my arm to pull me to my feet, and it hurt. I cried loud-er. She slapped my hands until they were red, and she yelled at me to get out of her bedroom. I must have told her I was sorry a hundred times before she forgave me. Later, after she'd hugged me and apolo-gized for slapping me, she gave me the jewelry box. It was the same one where I kept my money. But I'd learned my lesson. I never en-tered her room again without permission, and just thinking about it made me nervous.

Mom was almost always in the house or near it. She cooked the Barretts' meals in our kitchen and then ran them over and placed them in the old people's refrigerator. She was only gone for about five minutes on those trips, not nearly long enough for me to search.

Ever since Christmas, though, she'd regularly gone to church on Sundays, and she'd be away for a couple of hours. I'd have to do it then, assuming I could get Dad out of the house.

I didn't think that would be hard.

"I'll get it. Don't worry," I assured Francie.

THE NEXT SUNDAY, DAD and I were eating breakfast when Mom came into the kitchen. As she gathered up her purse and Bible, she asked in a hopeful tone, "Would you two like to go to church with me?" Every week, she asked the same thing, and we always turned her down.

This time was no different. Dad barely looked up from the paper. "Not this time, hon."

I said, "Uh, I'm going for a run with Francie in a little while. Sorry, Mom. Maybe next week."

Mom grunted but left without another word. I took a deep breath and closed my eyes, trying to let go of the guilt I always felt when I disappointed her. Maybe I really would go the next week. But that day, I had something else to do, and it wasn't just going for a run with Francie.

After she left, Dad sat for a few minutes, reading the Sunday paper while I stretched in the living room. It was time for Dad to go outside. I crossed my fingers and waited.

Five minutes before I was supposed to meet Francie, Dad cleared his throat. "I've got some work to do in the back grove. Catch you later." And he was out the door. I knew he wasn't going to work, because he didn't take his suede work gloves. I suspected he had something stashed out there—either drugs of some kind or whisky.

The previous month, Mom had put her foot down about keeping liquor in the house. When he'd brought a bottle inside, she'd given him a hard look. "You remember what happened the last time you kept liquor in the house?"

I watched him walk down the driveway and turn left into the grove and then waited for a full minute before approaching their bedroom door. Hopefully, this wouldn't take long.

I let the bedroom door swing open and peered inside. The room was neat, with the bed perfectly made and nothing but a few knick-knacks on top of Mom's dresser and Dad's chest of drawers. I tiptoed in and opened the closet door. Inside, light reflected off the metal box sitting on the top shelf. I took it down and tried to open it. Locked. I had to find the key. It wasn't on top of the dresser. I opened drawers and felt beneath underwear. No key. I felt in all their shoes and in the pockets of Mom's dresses and Dad's suit coat. Nothing.

I started blowing out short breaths like a woman in labor. Trying to control my panic made me so clumsy that I knocked over Dad's bottle of English Leather. Fortunately, it bounced off the rug and didn't spill or break. I picked it up and glanced around.

A clock ticked loudly on their nightstand, and I knew Dad might be back any second. Steadying my hands, I opened Mom's new jewelry box. And there it was, lying among loose buttons and safety pins.

Eureka! I stuck the key in the lock, and the lid snapped open. Sweet relief rushed through me.

Inside was a stack of papers with my birth certificate on top. I unfolded it and took a look. Dana Faye Smith, born January 17, 1952, in Atlanta, Georgia. Walter and Sue Smith were listed as parents. I breathed a sigh of relief and set the paper aside.

Because Dad was still out in the grove, I took the opportunity to glance through the other papers—my parents' wedding certificate, Dad's high school diploma, loan applications, and a letter to someone in Boston. *Hmm. Boston.* That was interesting. I would check it out if I had time.

At the bottom of the box was a black envelope. Opening it, I took out a row of faded black-and-white photos from one of those drug store machines. It was of Mom and me when I was a baby, and I was laughing like crazy. Cute. Why wasn't this in the family album?

After staring at it for nearly a minute and not seeing anything unusual, I turned it over. On the back, in Mom's handwriting, I read, "Dana Faye Smith, born January 17, 1952, died September 24, 1953."

I didn't breathe for a few seconds as I stared at the back of that page. I couldn't make sense of what she'd written. If this baby was Dana Faye Smith, deceased, then who was I?

I'd have to think about that later, because I'd used up all my time. Quickly, I put the papers back, careful to keep them in the same order in case Mom had a secret filing system. I set the birth certificate aside. I would show it to Francie before putting it back, but I hesitated about taking the photos. Even though they had been at the bottom of the box, the envelope was limp and smudged as though it had been handled many times. I could justify taking my own birth certificate, but I wasn't quite ready to admit I'd seen those photos. They were dynamite. I stood there in shock, wondering what I could possibly do next. Eventually, I placed them back in the envelope and returned it to the bottom of the box.

Just as I was setting the box back in the closet, somebody knocked on the front door, and I nearly jumped into the next county.

Someone asked, "Faye, you in there? Are you ready?"

Francie. Of course. I took a deep breath and tried to calm myself down. I left my parents' room just as I'd found it, and hoped they wouldn't suspect I'd been inside. After slipping the birth certificate inside my geometry textbook and stashing it on my bookshelf, I ran for the front door.

Arranging my face into my best estimate of normal, I opened the door and met my friend. "Sorry it took me so long. Just goofing off. I'm a little nervous about running so far."

She laughed. "I know what you mean. Never in a million years would I think I might run fifteen miles." Frowning, she said, "Are you stretched out? You look a little funny."

"I'm fine. Let's go." I jogged down the driveway.

All during our run, Francie kept asking me what was wrong, but I insisted I was fine. That couldn't have been further from the truth. At first, I felt as if I might break in half or curl up into a ball on the ground and scream in agony about the contents of the black envelope. But the act of putting one foot in front of the other cleared my mind enough that I could think semirationally. I needed to tell Francie what I'd found, but once the words were spoken, I could never take them back. It was all too raw to talk about right then, even to my best friend.

Eventually, around mile fourteen, the pieces came together. I realized that everything I'd told Francie was right. The baby in the pictures wasn't really me. It was Dana Faye Smith, who had died. For whatever reason, I had become her. But I used to be someone else. Pilot?

No matter how much I'd talked about being adopted, deep down, I hadn't really thought I was. I'd assumed there would be some other explanation and that I'd laugh when I found out what it was. The whole *spy* thing had been more or less a joke, a fun way to handle my suspicions.

But there didn't seem to be another explanation or any way to get around what I finally understood to be the truth. My parents weren't my real parents. And I wasn't really Dana Faye Smith.

Holy shit. Part of me wanted to forget I'd ever seen those pictures and go on with the life I knew, at least until after the marathon, and maybe even until I graduated from high school. Then, when I was safely away at college, I'd ask Mom about them.

Another part of me wanted to cry and scream and beat my head on the ground because my parents had lied to me my whole life about something as fundamental as who I really was.

Still another part wanted to ask Mom a whole lot of questions and not back down until she answered them.

By the end of the run, even though I was exhausted, I was over the worst of my freak-out. The part of me that wanted to talk to Mom had won, and I was trying to figure out how to do it so she wouldn't know I'd seen the photos. I'd started to remember all the nice things she'd ever done for me, and I needed to give her a chance to tell me about the adoption before I talked to anyone else. Depending on what she said, I'd decide whether to tell Francie what I'd discovered.

Chapter 19
"Help!"

Two evenings later, I helped Mom make supper while Dad was out in the fields. She stood at the counter, chopping onions, while I snapped green beans at the kitchen table. This was my opportunity, but I wasn't sure how to begin.

Mom asked in a bored voice, "How's school going?"

I didn't think she cared, as long as I passed. She had always signed my report cards without commenting about my grades. But they were usually bad. Thanks to Francie's tutoring and my determination to get into college, this time was different. "Let's see. I'm getting a C in geometry and an A in English. An A in phys ed. Uh, a B in biology, and I think a C in Spanish. Oh, and a B in choir."

"Why a B in choir?" She was just making conversation. This would be my best report card ever, and we both knew it.

"Uh, there was a choir competition in Orlando, but I couldn't go."

"You didn't tell me about this." She turned and glared at me, holding the knife upright as if preparing to throw it at something. "I imagine running got in the way. Am I right?"

"I guess so." I looked down and concentrated on snapping the beans.

She sighed. "What am I going to do with you? I wanted you to sign up for typing and shorthand, but you insisted on taking college-bound classes. I'm glad you're doing so well, but you need to be more realistic."

"But Mom, I don't want to be a secretary any more than I want to be a farm worker. I want to live in a city and be a gym teacher. And for that, I need to go to college." I couldn't keep the eagerness out of my voice. I wanted so much for her to understand and to support me—so much that I ignored the knife and her disapproving expression.

"We've talked about this, Dana Faye."

"Yes, ma'am, I know, but the school counselor says that even if I don't get a scholarship, I can probably get loans, and I can work, too."

Deep down, I thought she would be pleased if I went to college, since she hadn't gotten to go, and that she was being mean because she didn't want me to be disappointed when it didn't happen. I didn't want to even consider that she thought I'd flunk out because I was too stupid to succeed.

But she didn't answer, just continued to chop onions for the chicken salad for Mr. and Mrs. Barrett's supper, *bonk, bonk, bonk* on the cutting board.

I took a deep breath and grabbed my chance. "Hey, Mom, I was wondering about something."

"What?" She seemed lost in her own thoughts.

I had pondered for hours about how I should proceed. I couldn't ask directly about the photos of the baby who died, because then she'd know I'd been in her private papers. I had to start in a roundabout way. "Why aren't there more pictures of me when I was little? There's a big gap between the pictures of me as a baby and when I was about five."

She whirled around, knife still in her hand. "I've told you before that those pictures got lost in a flood. What is it you want from me?" Her eyes were red from chopping onions, and her mouth was set in a straight line.

The truth was what I wanted, and this wasn't it. I held my ground. "Why aren't there any pictures of me during that time?"

She sighed, shaking her head. "Oh dear Lord, let me think." She paused. "All right, you want the truth? The truth is, your dad pawned the camera so we could pay rent. It took me a few years to save up enough money to buy another one. Now are you satisfied?"

The sadness in her voice softened me. I had never heard this explanation before. Could it possibly be true? I needed to give it more thought. "Oh. Sorry, Mom. I didn't know."

"Well, now you do. It was a tough time for us. So leave it alone, will you?"

But then I remembered the photos and hardened myself again. *Yeah, I bet it was a tough time for you. The real Dana Faye died, and somehow I came into the picture.* Suddenly, it dawned on me to wonder how the baby had died—and if I was in danger. I'd been planning to ask more questions, but I got distracted by that train of thought.

Mom set down the knife. "I'm going to take a little rest. Finish making the chicken salad, would you?" She was crying, and probably not just because of chopping onions. She walked into her bedroom and shut the door.

All I could think was, *Crap. What if she discovers I took my birth certificate?*

She emerged a half hour later, eyes still red and puffy. She looked wearier than I'd seen her in a long time.

I went to my room, confused about what to do next. It was clear that my mom was never going to give me a truthful answer about the little girl with my name, no matter how gently I worked up to the subject. And Dad wouldn't be any better. He'd probably just get mad and say I needed to mind my own business. No, I was going to have to do something about the situation myself.

First, I needed to tell Francie what I'd found. But I knew she didn't really believe my theory about being adopted. I would need proof to convince her or anyone else. That meant taking the photos and showing them to her. Together, we'd decide what to do.

While Mom was out of the house, taking the Barretts' supper to them, I rushed into her bedroom and unlocked the metal box. Flipping through the papers, I discovered that the black envelope was gone. An electric shock shot from the crown of my head to the tips of my toes. Mom must have known I'd found them, so she'd hidden the photos somewhere else. That was the only explanation I could think of, and it also explained her red eyes. But I'd been cheated out of my evidence, and I was ready to pound that metal box into smithereens.

Through the window, I saw Mom coming down the steps of the big house, and I quickly put everything back. At the last instant, I took the Boston letter that I hadn't taken the time to look at before. I would check it later. When she came inside, I was in my room with the door closed, pacing and waiting for her to confront me about the photos. I waited an hour, but nothing happened. Feeling like I was about to shake to pieces, I went out for a second run after supper.

After my parents were asleep, I locked my door and looked at the Boston letter. It was just a folded piece of paper with an address label on the front. The address wasn't familiar. Inside was a note from the city about the Boston Marathon, listing the streets that would be closed during the race. Why would my parents have this when they said we'd never lived in Massachusetts? It was a minor mystery, though, compared to the major one about my birth. I stashed the letter in the envelope with my birth certificate.

I locked my door that night and planned to keep it locked from then on. Mom didn't say anything to me about the pictures, even though I waited, braced, for the confrontation. I didn't know who these people were, but I realized I might be in danger. Just like the first Dana Faye Smith.

MY FIRST OPPORTUNITY to tell Francie everything came during lunch the next day. Reese often ate with us, but on that day, he was busy, so we were alone. We carried our trays to a table outside, far away from the other kids. I was trying to figure out where to start when she asked, "How are things with you and Reese?"

"Reese? Oh, we're fine." Our kissing had improved, but my insides still didn't flip-flop when our lips met. I tried to sound enthusiastic, but my heart wasn't in it.

Kyle had called me a couple more times and then stopped. I was glad I hadn't mentioned his phone calls to Francie. She would have kicked me in the butt for falling for her brother over and over, when she had already told me he wasn't worth it.

She noticed my attitude and jumped on me about it. "Why are you jerking Reese around if you don't like him? He's too nice for that."

A pang of remorse pierced my heart. "I know, but I can't help it. I really like him, but he's more like a good friend."

"Instead, you're hung up on Kyle, who doesn't know you exist."

Hmm. She understood more than I thought. And she was right. I was just a lowly high school junior, while Kyle was surrounded by glamorous college girls—and probably the luscious Linda.

"I wish somebody would follow me around like a lovestruck puppy like Reese does you." Francie's tone was wistful.

"Listen, that isn't important right now. I need to talk to you about something else. This is life or death."

"Okay. What is it?" She had something on her mind, because she was acting kind of dreamy.

"What's wrong with you?"

She said, "I just got asked to the prom. By Jeremy. Do you know him? He's a senior, and he's in my chemistry class. He's kind of shy."

Why was she acting wistful about Reese when she'd just gotten her own date? "That's great, Francie. I've been so busy I forgot all about the prom. Did you say yes?"

She looked at me with wonder in her eyes. "Are you kidding? Of course I said yes. Hasn't Reese asked you yet?"

I shook my head. "No, and it doesn't matter now. Listen, remember when I told you about being adopted?"

She nodded, clearly bracing herself to argue with me again.

"I found my birth certificate. But in the same stack of papers, I also found some pictures of a baby, and on the back, my mom had written the baby's birth date and *death* date." I drew this out so she'd understand how crucial it was. "That baby died when she was eighteen months old. But she had the same name and the same birth date as mine." I stared at her, waiting for her to apologize for doubting me.

She shook her head, looking dubious. "Let me see the pictures. Do you have them with you? Where were they?"

"Uh, they were in my mom's metal box where she keeps important papers. Here's my birth certificate." I opened my geometry book and pulled out the envelope.

Francie unfolded the paper and read it several times. "Is this what you've always been told about your birth? The date and place and all that?"

"Well, yes. But it's probably not mine."

She set down the birth certificate. "Okay. Now, where are the pictures?"

"Gone," I said miserably. "I went back to get them last night, and they were gone."

She scratched her head then took a bite of her sandwich. Sounding irritated, she said, "All right. Tell me about them."

"They were on one of those rows of pictures from drug store machines. Black-and-white. You know what I'm talking about?" When she nodded, I continued. "The baby and my mom were laughing in all four pictures. I recognized her. She was the baby in our family photo album, not me. She didn't even look much like me."

Francie inhaled deeply and set down her sandwich. Finally, I had her full attention. "Does this have something to do with your parents being Russian spies?"

I winced and shook my head. "Uh, I was wrong about that."

She looked away, considering. "Do you think she was maybe your sister, and she died, and your parents gave you her name or something? Man, that's weird."

"I don't know. Maybe that happened. But it seems like the birth dates would have been different. Unless we were twins. Or they adopted me."

"Yeah, maybe. Whatever happened, you've got to find those pictures." She hesitated. "Why didn't you take them when you got the birth certificate?"

"I... I don't know. I guess I was just so stunned that I was afraid Mom would find out and kill me or something."

Francie grew pale. "Wow. That's scary. But it's not true. Your mom wouldn't hurt you. You know that, right?"

I nodded, not completely sure.

"But we really need to find those pictures before we can do anything else. It's the only proof that you aren't who they say you are."

We. She'd said "we." That word was music to my ears.

I sighed. Of course she was right. I, or *we*... somebody needed to find the pictures. But I didn't know how to begin.

Francie took a few more bites of her sandwich. "I don't think your mom would have thrown them away, since she's already kept them for so long and they're obviously important to her. But she must have hidden them somewhere else. We're going to have to find them. When should we do it? And how do we get your parents out of the house so we can search?"

"So you believe me now?"

She nodded. "Yeah. You wouldn't have made up those pictures. I don't understand what's going on, but for sure, something is."

A deep sense of satisfaction settled in my body. As horrible as this whole thing was, at least somebody believed me. I probably could have run the marathon right then and not even gotten out of breath.

Francie interrupted my thoughts. "Look, I know this is really big stuff, and I'll help you all I can. But... do you want to go to the school play on Saturday night? My dad is letting me take his car. Maybe we can combine the search and the play somehow."

Yes, oh yes. I'd been so involved in my own drama that I hadn't paid much attention to Reese and the school play. I'd figured I'd go to the dress rehearsal one afternoon instead of the actual play. I had no way to get to school since Reese was in the cast and Dad always took the truck on Saturday nights. I wasn't going to run all the way to the school at night by myself. Thank goodness for Francie.

We made our plans. Getting my parents out of the house when I wanted them out was going to take all of my talent for scheming.

WHILE MOM AND I WERE washing dishes that night, I said offhandedly, "Dad really likes playing music. I've never heard him play in a band. Have you?"

"Yeah. I told you that. When you were little, I used to leave you with a babysitter for a few hours and go listen to him play. But now I'm always too tired." She added in a hard voice, "He's quite good. But he plays in bars, and they serve liquor there. I can't stand drunks."

Uh-oh. Bad direction. Mom was a nutcase about drinking. If it had been a hundred years earlier, she would have been one of those women marching for temperance, barging into saloons and breaking bottles of booze.

"Oh, well," I said as though that topic was finished. When we were done with the dishes, I asked, "Hey, Mom, can I go to the school play with Francie on Saturday night? And then can she come over and spend the night?" This was the first time I'd ever asked to have somebody sleep over. It was a big deal, and I was sure she knew it.

Mom hesitated. "It's fine for you to go to the play with Francie. She's a good kid. But I don't know if I can sleep with two teenage girls giggling all night. I work too hard to miss a night's sleep."

"We won't giggle all night. Well, we might giggle for a while, but we'll go to sleep before it's too late." I hesitated and then added, as though it had just occurred to me, "Hey, maybe you should go out with Dad and hear him play. I bet he'd like that. And people will probably be doing more dancing than drinking." I was on thin ice, considering that I'd never been to the bar where he played—or any bar, for that matter. But I kept my tone upbeat and confident. "Anyway, we'll be asleep when you get back."

I could see the mental battle play out on her face. She probably knew how happy Dad would be if she went to hear his band play. Music was all he talked about those days, other than moving. And she didn't want to move. Finally, she said, "I guess that will work. But you have to be home by midnight. I'll get your dad to run me home between sets, so I'll be here when you get home."

"Oh, all right." I rolled my eyes and stomped around, pretending it was a huge compromise for me to be home that early, but really, I planned on being home way before midnight.

Chapter 20
"Kind of a Drag"

Finally, Saturday night arrived. We'd read *Romeo and Juliet* in English class, but I'd never seen the play. Francie and I had front-row seats in the school auditorium. As soon as the play started, I was transported back to long-ago Verona. After a while, I could even follow the gist of the dialogue.

Reese surprised me. I hadn't seen him rehearse, so I'd had no idea that he would be a confident and even sexy Romeo. When he said, "See, how she leans her cheek upon her hand! O that I were a glove upon that hand, that I might touch that cheek!" I leaned my cheek on my hand and wondered how I would respond if he said something beautiful like that to me. Maybe that was the problem—I wanted Romeo instead of Reese.

Since I was in the first row, I could see how he kissed the girl playing Juliet—as if he enjoyed it. I wondered who he liked kissing better, the actress or me. I hoped it was me. Francie nudged me and covered her grin with her hand.

When Romeo and Juliet declared their undying love and got married secretly, I had to keep telling myself, *It's just a play, it's just a play*. At the end, when Romeo died and Juliet died lying on top of him, I was in tears, along with Francie and at least half of the audience. And then they were up and bowing, and Reese, not Romeo, blew me a kiss. I vowed to be more attentive to him.

Afterward, Francie and I waited around to talk to the cast members. When he'd changed into street clothes, Reese invited us to the

156

cast party at the home of one of the actors. I glanced at Francie. We needed to get back to the cottage and search before Mom and Dad got home. But Dad's band played until two in the morning, and I seriously doubted he would be up for driving Mom home between sets. My guess was that my parents wouldn't get home until two thirty at least. We should have plenty of time. We both wanted to go to the party. So we went to the party.

Everybody danced, and the host parents served us food and soft drinks. The actors joked around and played with their lines. At one point, Reese knelt and proclaimed in his actor's voice, "It is the east, and Faye is the sun." I felt exotic and desirable and gave him a long, sexy kiss. The other kids hooted. I loved it.

AT THE END OF THE EVENING, Reese said, "Will you go to the prom with me? I'm sorry I waited so long to ask you. I was so involved with the play that time just crept up on me."

"Of course I'll go with you. I'd love to." I gave him a big kiss to show that I was excited about being asked. But I knew I was acting, just like a character in a play. The prom would be fun, but it was hard to think about anything other than finding the photos and deciding what to do with them. And of course, running the Boston Marathon, which would be a week after the prom.

Before I went home, Reese said, "You don't seem like yourself. Is something bothering you? Is it... someone else?"

Oh gosh. I wasn't ready to tell him about the photos and my doubts about my family. I'd tell him later if I found out anything important. It was funny that he thought there was someone else. My crush on Kyle seemed long ago in a simpler, less complicated lifetime.

"No. I'm fine. Just worried about the marathon." I kissed him slowly and deeply. "I'll try to do better." We laughed, and he grinned.

He'd probably forgotten all about the kiss he'd given that other girl in the play.

Francie and I were home by eleven thirty. I knew Mom would call the house exactly at midnight and I'd better be there to answer the phone, so we started our search in my parents' bedroom. I thought I would have a heart attack being in there again. In fact, my heart beat so hard and loud that I wouldn't have been surprised to find that my parents heard it all the way in town.

First, we searched through the dresser drawers. The photos by themselves were small, but if they were still in the black envelope, they'd be bulkier. Just in case Mom had taken them out of the envelope, we searched for something the size of the photographs—two inches wide by three or four inches long. I searched through their drawers and directed Francie to the closet to go through their shoes and jackets.

Nothing. We lifted the mattress off the box springs and found only a couple of Playboy magazines, which we didn't touch. *Ick.* We lifted the rug. Nothing. We went through the metal box again, but the photos still weren't there.

They clearly weren't in my parents' bedroom. When we were finished, I stood at the door and checked to make sure we'd put everything back to normal. And then we moved on. We searched the kitchen, the living room, and the bathroom. And that was pretty much everywhere there was to search.

I was right—Mom called at midnight. She sounded like she was having a good time. After a little chitchat, she said, "Now, I expect you girls to be sound asleep by the time we get home."

"Fine, Mom. We will be."

At one in the morning, I started to get tired. We only had an hour or so until we really did have to get to bed. We'd saved the trash for last. Holding our noses, we went through the inside trash and then the outside trash. We even sifted through the ashes of the trash that

Dad had burned the previous week. The photos wouldn't be there, of course, because I'd found them after that, but we were being thorough.

We stared at each other in frustration. Francie asked, "Could she have hidden them in your room?" Unlikely, but we searched it anyway. We found all my little treasures: the less-than-glowing report cards from all my different schools, my bedraggled stuffed bunny, the Cracker Jack ring a boy had given me in the fourth grade, and the family photo album. But there was no row of black-and-white photos of Mom and a strange baby.

We had to get to sleep. Francie had brought her sleeping bag, and she slipped into it on the floor beside my twin bed. I got into bed and turned off the light. We talked quietly, brainstorming about where the photos could be. The last possibility was in the truck. My parents would probably sleep late the next morning, so we'd search it then.

That didn't make sense, though. Mom probably wouldn't hide anything in the truck, where I might find it. If I happened upon the photos, how would she explain the damning writing on the back? No, they wouldn't be there. The photos might be in her pocketbook but probably weren't. They would be too easy for me to find if I went looking for lunch money.

I didn't want to consider that we had failed or that the pictures might be gone. I didn't see how I could cope with my life if we didn't find them.

Finally, we saw the lights of the truck and stopped talking. When Mom peeked into my room, we breathed evenly as though we'd been asleep for hours. That was the last thing I knew until morning.

WHEN I WOKE UP, IT was daylight. Francie was still asleep, and the house was quiet. I decided to do the final search on my own, because it would be easier to make up an excuse if I got caught.

I searched the truck, Mom's sweater pockets, and her pocket-book. Nothing. I was about to go back to the bedroom and have my-self a quiet cry when I noticed Dad's guitar case leaning up against the coffee table in the living room. It was the last place to check. Not that I thought for a minute that Dad had taken the photos. No, Mom's handwriting was on the back of them, and she was in that picture. Dad might not even know the photos existed.

Moving as quietly as I could, I picked up the guitar case and slipped outside, where I laid it on the picnic table. I clicked open the latches and raised the lid. Faded red velvet lined the inside of the case, and the battered guitar lay on top.

I lifted the guitar and shook it, but only a pick fell out. Holding the guitar in one hand, I felt around the case for anything unusual. I found nothing other than a set of strings, two picks, and a pair of needle-nose pliers for cutting strings.

As I laid the guitar back inside the case, I noticed a slight tear in the fabric lining. Sticking my fingers inside it, I felt a piece of paper. Could it be? I slid the paper out, trying not to enlarge the tear. And there were the photos, right in front of me, without the black enve-lope. I had already started to think that I had imagined them. But this was my proof.

A pain settled into my stomach so hard and deep that I bent over and almost cried out. This was the end of one life, the life of the fake Dana Faye Smith. It might be the beginning of another life, but I didn't know who I was. In terms of my real parents, what kind of weirdos would name their kid Pilot?

The pain passed, and I stood up, slipped into the house, and set the guitar back where Dad had left it. I tiptoed into my room and closed the door behind me. Francie was still snoozing. I slid into bed and examined the photos. Mom was much younger, of course, and she looked happier than I ever remembered seeing her. The baby was happy, too. The real Dana Faye was nearly bald, with wispy hair at the top of her round head. But she was laughing hard, as though some-body had just blown on her tummy.

Did somebody sit with me when I was a baby and laugh like that? Or blow on my tummy? I couldn't help myself—I started to cry. My sobbing woke Francie. She whispered, "What's wrong?"

I handed her the photos. She glanced at them then turned them over to read the handwriting on the back. "Holy crap," she whispered. "Just like you said." She handed the photos back. "I'm so sorry, Faye. What do we do now?"

"I don't know."

"I've been thinking about it, and I'll tell you what I've come up with. We've got to go to the cops with the pictures. Or at least tell my mom. She'll know what to do."

I thought about that. If I could force myself to confide in Laney, she'd probably help, as she had with the aspirin. And she'd likely take my side against my parents if it came to that. But she'd probably make me go to the cops.

"I need to think this whole thing through before I do anything like that. If they really are my parents, they're going to be so mad at me for going through their stuff that they might kill me. At the very least, they'll make us move away immediately. Dad wants to do that anyway. But I want to finish out the school year here." I paused, thinking furiously. I could hardly speak the next words, even though I'd been thinking them for weeks. "And if they aren't really my par-ents, I might have to go to an orphanage or something until the po-lice find out who I really am."

Saying the words out loud made the whole situation sound even worse. I started to cry again. Francie cried with me. After a few minutes, she blew her nose. "All right, let's change the subject." She sounded as sad as I'd ever heard her, but she didn't hesitate. "I hate to bring this up after everything that's happened, but the marathon's in less than four weeks. Have you even asked your parents if you can go?"

I couldn't lie to her again. "No. I'm sorry. First there was the wreck, and then the pictures. It's hard to think about Boston when I don't even know who I am."

I held my breath and waited for her response. In a calm and even voice, she said, "Do you want to quit, then?"

Quit. That word reverberated throughout my entire being. Did I want to spend the rest of my life thinking of myself as the girl who *could* have run the Boston Marathon if only things in her life weren't so terrible? Or as the girl who *could* have gotten a scholarship to college if she'd just persevered? No. No. *No.*

I sat straight up in bed. "Of course I don't want to quit. Don't worry. I'll ask them today. Even if they aren't really my parents, they're *acting* like my parents. So I guess I'll need their permission."

After Francie left, I steeled myself to ask the big question, but I couldn't bear the thought of what I would do if my parents said no. So I put it off again. I had one more week until Laney was going to call them to finalize the arrangements, so I would wait till the last minute and hope for the best. Miracles had happened before, and maybe another one would come my way in the next week.

Chapter 21
"Bad Moon Rising"

After much thought, I decided to try and act like everything was normal, at least until after the marathon. I thought I could pretend that my life wasn't falling apart for a few more weeks. It wouldn't be easy, but I reminded myself that my most important goals were to run the Boston Marathon and get a scholarship. Whoever I had been as a child was less important than who I was as a teenager and who I was going to be as an adult—a gym teacher, if everything worked as I wanted.

But to pull it off, I would need to stay away from home even more and hang out in my room as much as possible when I was home. I had nearly stopped worrying that Mom would ask me about the photos, but it didn't make sense that she hadn't. I hoped I could keep my expressions neutral so she wouldn't notice that I was completely freaked out around her. I didn't know if these people were murderers, but I could never again relax around my so-called parents.

Francie told me about a new resale shop in town, and we went together the next afternoon. She didn't need to shop at resale stores, but most of her savings would be used for the marathon, so she decided to check out the store with me. The place was much nicer than Goodwill, and it was upstairs, off an alley, so I was unlikely to run into cheerleaders or other rich girls from school. We walked in, a little nervous because neither of us had ever worn a formal gown before. We were skinnier than most of the other girls, though, so there were a few nice dresses left, and there were no other customers.

The owner, Robin, welcomed us wearing a miniskirt and red cowboy boots. Rock and roll blasted from speakers high on the walls. There was a three-way mirror on a pedestal. We took over the two dressing rooms, and Robin brought us dresses to try. With each one, we wandered out to the pedestal and did a complete turn, to either enthusiastic claps from Robin or dead silence that told us we should move on.

I settled on a long yellow sleeveless dress. It was fairly ordinary but looked great with my auburn hair. Over-the-elbow gloves in the same color came with it. Price: twenty-five dollars. Sold. I just hoped the previous owner wouldn't be at the prom. Francie found an orange organza dress that flared when she whirled and looked fantastic on her. Add shoes and bags and wraps, and we were set.

With all our moving, I hadn't expected that I would ever have the opportunity to go to something as grand as a prom. I was always the outsider, after all. Even when Reese asked me to be his date, I hadn't thought it would happen. But after I bought my dress, I hugged myself and grinned for all I was worth.

FRANCIE HAD OTHER PLANS on the following Thursday afternoon, so Jess and I decided to do a ten-mile run out in the country. It was hot and steamy in the early evening when we set out.

Jess was in a festive mood because he'd sold two houses that week and stood to make hefty commissions. "I'm thinking about putting a down payment on a little house for my son and daughter-in-law. They're staying with us while they look for jobs."

"That's nice," I replied, barely able to talk with the fast pace that Jess had set.

"And then maybe I'll look for a new house on a lake for my wife and me. I'll buy me a boat, too. I'd purely love to go fishing in the evenings after I get off work."

"Great." Out of the corner of my eye, I noticed some white men milling around on the edge of a trailer park that we had to pass to get back into town.

Jess must have seen it, too. In a level tone, he said, "Stay close to me, and don't make eye contact." We changed sides so Jess would be closer to the sidewalk where the men had congregated and were talking in low voices. I couldn't quite catch what they were saying, but they were clearly upset. I kept my eyes straight in front of me and hoped we'd get through this area and into downtown without any trouble.

I held my breath and tried to act nonchalant as we strode through the groups, picking up our pace. We were almost to the far end of the trailer park when one man stepped out from his group of three, right into our path. We started to veer away, and then two more men blocked our way. Jess and I exchanged a look and stopped but kept shuffling our feet in case we had to sprint off in a hurry. As we stood there, chill bumps raced up my spine and down my arms all the way to my fingers. I forced myself to breathe through my nose so I wouldn't pass out. I had thought Jess was exaggerating when he'd talked about being afraid of running with white women. I couldn't believe this was happening in daylight, half a mile from the center of town.

One man seemed to be the leader. He was large—tall and heavy as if he might have been a football player years before but had since gone to fat. He said to Jess in a conversational tone, "Hey, boy, whatcha doing out with a white girl?"

Jess adopted a shuck-and-jive attitude that I hadn't witnessed before. Instead of his usual upright posture, he slumped over, making himself as nonthreatening as possible. There was a pleading note to his voice. "Well, sir, we've just been on a run. This here's a high school student, and I'm her coach." He nodded. "If you don't mind, her parents are waiting for her in town. We'll be on our way."

"Not so fast," said another beefy white man. He set his beer can down on the road and stood up straight, unraveling until he was about six inches taller than Jess. He cracked his knuckles. "You got no business out with a white girl, least of all on this day."

I asked, "What's happened?"

They snickered, looking at Jess. The leader answered, "Your boy's been shot by a white man—that's what's happened. And the nigras are all riled up. There's about to be a riot. The cops made us leave downtown, but we're getting ready to go back."

I smelled alcohol on their breath. Jess and I glanced at each other. The confusion I saw in his expression must have matched mine.

"What do you mean, my boy? My son James?" Jess asked, fear in his voice.

That made them laugh. The first one said, "Well, I don't know about that one way or the other. But your *boy*, Martin Luther King, has done been shot and killed." He spat out the name as though he'd tasted rat poison.

Oh no. Dr. King is dead? An image of him standing at the podium, proclaiming, "I have a dream..." made me tear up. I inhaled and blew out through my mouth. I'd find out what had happened later and let the tears come. Right then, my concern was getting out of there alive.

Jess said, "Well, sir, thank you for the information. We'll jest get along home now." He moved to slide between the men, with me following behind him. But one of them reached out and grabbed his arm.

"Not so fast. One of your kinfolk threw a rock in my window." He gestured toward the broken-down trailer closest to the road. Sure enough, there was a big hole in the picture window. "I'll need you to pay for it. I think about two hundred dollars will do it."

"Sir, I don't carry money when I'm running. Just let me get home and get my wallet, and I'll come back and pay for the window. I'm sorry about that." Jess was trying to pull his arm free. He gave me a glance that said, *Run*, but I shook my head. No way was I going to leave him.

The man snickered again. "Like we're going to let you go, boy. No, somebody's got to pay for my window, if not in money then in blood." The three exchanged a look.

The third man—he had a blond crew cut and the hardened look of ex-military—pulled me off to one side. I tried to jerk away, to rush to Jess, but the man grabbed my shoulders. I shook him off. He said to me in a low voice, "You stay out of it. Your boy won't get hurt too bad if he don't have to worry about defending you." I was trembling so hard that I might not have been able to run away if I'd gotten free, so I stopped struggling.

The really tall man stood in front of Jess and lifted his beefy fists into a defensive posture. He spat out brown tobacco juice to the side. "Okay, boy, here's the deal. I'm going to beat you in a fair fight. You get the first punch." He smiled to reveal a mouth with several missing teeth.

The other man let go of Jess and moved off to the side. "Hit him, boy. Now's your chance."

Jess stood there, tense, barely breathing, arms at his side, and did nothing—just kept looking at the ground.

The first man, the one with a huge gut and a wheeze, pulled back his fist and punched Jess in the mouth, hard. Blood spurted from a split lower lip. Jess shook his head and wiped his mouth. And continued looking at the ground.

What was wrong with him? He was strong, and he could have taken that drunk redneck with one blow. I wanted to yell, "Hit him, Jess. He's just a fat bully." But I held back my words. Something was going on that I didn't understand.

The fat man taunted him and took several more jabs, bloodying Jess's cheek and mouth, and doubled him over with a punch to his stomach. Jess let it happen.

I couldn't stand watching my friend get beaten up by these horrible drunks. Glancing around, I noticed a few women huddled in a knot in front of one of the trailers, watching but doing nothing. No help there. The man who had been guarding me evidently figured I wouldn't do anything, so he was watching the beating. He didn't see me pull the canister of mace from my pocket.

With shaking hands, I turned the lever so the spray nozzle was in line with the arrow that indicated the canister was ready to shoot. I aimed it at the man closest to me and pushed down on the button. A fine spray emerged from the hole and landed on his face. I pushed it down again. He gasped and then screamed, his hands reaching up to cover his face.

That got their attention. Holding my breath so the spray wouldn't come back at me, I moved closer to the others... and took four quick sprays, two in each man's face. They screamed and cursed, but they let go of Jess and ran for the water faucets outside their trailers. I grabbed my friend's arm, and we stumbled away as fast as our shaky legs would allow.

Jess was huffing, trying to catch his breath, but he managed to put one foot in front of the other. Within a minute, we were beyond the trailer park, although I kept glancing back to make sure nobody was coming after us. The road was clear.

Jess said, panting, "Let me sit down over there by that tree for a minute. I can't make it back to town just yet."

We maneuvered behind a big azalea bush and collapsed on the ground, leaning against a palm tree. We were out of sight of the road and safe for the time being, at least until those men got cleaned up and decided to search for us. I twisted the lever back into the safe position and put the canister in my pocket. And then I looked closely at

Jess. Blood trickled down his cheek and from his lip, and one eye was swollen. I wanted to give him a hug, but I wasn't sure where I could touch that wouldn't hurt.

He leaned to the side and vomited into the bush then pulled a handkerchief from his pocket and dabbed at his cut lip. In a shaky voice, he said, "Thank you, Faye. I don't know for sure, but those men might have killed me if you hadn't blasted them. Was that mace?"

My ragged laugh threatened to get hysterical but tapered off to a sob. "Yeah. It sure worked. I was afraid it would get you, too. But I guess it didn't."

"Nah. You were a good shot."

We leaned against the tree and listened as cicadas took up their night song. Finally, I asked in a small voice, "You really think they might have killed you?"

He thought about it. "I don't know. I surely don't know. But I was afraid of it. I was most afraid of it."

"Why didn't you fight back? You're strong. Those were just fat bullies. They'd probably have backed off if you hit one of them good."

"Oh, child." He sighed. "You haven't been in the South long enough to know better. If I'd hit him, either they'd've killed me right then, or they'd come after me later. Maybe burn down my house or hurt my family. It's happened before. It might have caused a race war even worse than what's likely happening in town right now." He paused. "No, I could never hit back. I wanted to, though. I surely did."

Wow. He was the bravest man I'd ever met. I couldn't speak through the lump in my throat, so I patted him on his knee and wished for a better world.

After a few minutes, we walked back to town, his arm around my shoulders for stability. Within a few blocks, a police car pulled up to us, lights flashing. A white officer leaned out. "Are you all right, miss? Is this man bothering you?"

"No." I flashed him a look of pure hatred. He had the nerve to ask that?

He cleared his throat and seemed to notice that Jess was hurt. "You need a hospital, sir?"

Jess shook his head. "I'll be fine. I live not too far away. But I'd be obliged if you'd take my friend home."

"Sure. Get in, little lady."

I didn't want to leave Jess, but he pushed me into the car. "I'll be safer without you. Now, you go home and stay inside tonight. We'll talk tomorrow." He slammed the door and limped off.

On the drive to my house, I asked, "What's going on?"

"Dr. King was shot and killed in Memphis this afternoon." His tone was grim. "Blacks all over the country are threatening to riot."

I put my hand over my mouth and held back tears.

He continued. "Not too much has happened yet in Valencia other than a few broken windows. The mayor established a curfew, and we're sending everybody home. So far, it seems to be working."

I doubled over, trying to keep from sobbing out loud. Jess had been beaten up because of me. And he could have been killed. If he hadn't been out running with a white girl, he might have gotten away without being hurt. He wouldn't even have been out running if not for me. Before he'd started coaching us, he was an out-of-shape realtor, but he was safe. All along, he'd known something like this could happen, but he'd run with us anyway. I wanted to go back and spray those men again, spray them over and over until my mace ran out.

The officer asked, "What happened to you and that man?"

Most likely, Jess would not want me to tell him. I sat up, as tall as I could, and took a deep breath. "Uh, we were out running, and he fell down."

The officer watched me in the rearview mirror, but he didn't say anything.

Back at home, Mom and Dad were watching the news of the shooting on television. I couldn't stand hearing about more racial violence right then, so I went into my room, trying to figure out how I could make it up to Jess.

Chapter 22
"Wipe Out"

Money. Before we'd gotten stopped by the rednecks, Jess had talked about wanting to buy a boat. Even after buying my prom dress, I still had around $250 in my jewelry box. I thought I might be able to manage with only $200 for the marathon expenses. Fifty dollars wasn't much to give Jess, but it would at least help him pay for the window if those bad men hunted him down. And if they left him alone, maybe that money would help him buy a boat. It was the least I could do.

I walked to my dresser and opened my jewelry box. Inside, on the red velvet, was the necklace from Reese, but my wad of money was gone. I pulled out the drawers, but they were too small to contain that much money. All I saw were a few Indian head nickels I'd saved when I found them at the carving store.

I picked up the jewelry box, turned it upside down, and shook it. Nothing fell out.

I peered behind the dresser then pulled it out from the wall, but nothing was back there except some dust bunnies and an old pencil. Suddenly furious, I rammed the dresser back, bashing it into the wall.

Mom was instantly at my door. "Faye, what's wrong?"

"My money. It's missing." I frantically opened dresser drawers and dumped out the contents, hoping I'd dropped the money in a drawer the last time I'd counted it. When was that? Last Saturday, I thought, after Uncle Stan had paid me.

"What money? Calm down." Mom came into the room and grabbed me by the shoulders. "Now, sit down and tell me what you're looking for."

I sat on the bed and tried to think. "The money I saved from my job. For the marathon. It's missing."

She squinched up her eyes the way she did when she was really mad. "For the marathon? The *Boston* Marathon? You aren't going there."

The reality hit me like a punch in the gut. Unless I found that money, it wouldn't matter whether or not Mom gave me permission to go, because I truly wasn't going to Boston. I could never earn enough for my expenses in two weeks, even if I worked full-time. And for sure my parents wouldn't give it to me. If the cash wasn't where I'd left it, I had no idea where to look.

I looked at Mom and whispered, between sobs, "For months now, I've saved nearly every penny I earned from working. It was in my jewelry box. But now it's gone."

She stooped and picked up the jewelry box from the floor. Looked inside. Shook it. Felt around inside the lining. Then sat back down beside me, the box on her lap. "Yes, you're right. There's nothing in there. How much was it?"

"Around two hundred and fifty dollars. I think."

She gasped. "What? You had that much money? I had no idea you had so much."

"Yeah. But where is it? I can't find it."

"I don't know what to say. Did you move it somewhere else, maybe? Your pocketbook? Or your pants pocket?"

She went to the closet and looked inside then put a hand in the pants pockets and felt around. "Look in your pocketbook."

I knew it wasn't there, but I opened the clasp and peered inside. In one of the zippered pockets, I found the wad of forty-eight dollar bills I had meant to take to the bank to exchange for tens, but that was all. I slammed the bag down on the dresser and collapsed on the bed.

I'd thought everything bad that could happen to me had already happened. But I was wrong. I should never have let go of the ironclad rule or dared to hope that my life could be better. If I hadn't hoped, at least I wouldn't have been so disappointed when the rug got pulled out from under my world. I sat on the bed and stared at the wall, as hopeless as a person could be.

Mom finished feeling around in my pockets and shook her head. Then she sat back down on the bed, frowning. "As far as I know, nobody's been in the house all week." She buried her head in her hands and seemed to crumple. "Nobody except your father."

In an instant, her face hardened. Stomping to the door of my room, she yelled out, "Bud, have you seen Faye's money? It's missing." The television news continued its monotonous chant, and Dad didn't answer. She called again, louder. "Bud, would you come in here a minute?"

"What is it?" He sounded groggy, as if he'd been asleep in front of the TV. In a minute, he shuffled into my room, yawning. "What's up?"

Mom gave him a steely look. "Faye's money is missing. Do you know anything about it?"

"What money?" He shook his head, looking confused.

"A whole lot of money, that's what money. You were in the house alone yesterday when I went to town. What did you do with it?"

He stared at her. "What did I do with it? I don't have the slightest idea what you're talking about." He shrugged. "I'm going to bed."

Mom opened her mouth to speak but then closed it and watched him walk away. The expression in her eyes was one of absolute defeat. I probably looked exactly the same.

My mind went back to Harlan, Kentucky, when my dad had been accused of stealing money. Mom had insisted he didn't do it, but I didn't know what to think. It killed me to think that my own father would steal my savings, but it seemed like the only answer.

Liars. They might both be lying to me. I started to feel like Alice in Wonderland again, falling down the rabbit hole. I had no idea who to believe or where to turn. Nothing in my world made sense.

Mom stood up. "I'll deal with this. You get to bed. It's late. But even if we find that money, you aren't going to the Boston Marathon. And that's final." She stalked out of the room and slammed my bedroom door.

I locked the door, as usual, and pulled out my old stuffed bunny, the one that I'd cuddled as a child when my world seemed dark and full of confusion. Wrapping my arms around it, I curled up on the bed and cried for the lost money, the lost marathon, and most of all, for the lost child who was me.

Chapter 23
"I'm a Believer"

The tears finally ended, and my mind kicked into gear. I couldn't stop thinking about the Boston Marathon, and I had to face the truth. Even if I got my money back, Mom wasn't going to give me permission to go. I'd recognized that look on her face. No amount of begging would change her mind. It was a definite no. But I *had* to go to Boston. I would not give up. If I couldn't find my money, I would have to figure out another way.

Maybe I could borrow the money from Francie. No, that wouldn't work. Laney probably wouldn't let me go with her and Francie without Mom's permission.

My mind went around and around like a car motor that wouldn't turn off. After hours of thinking, I decided that either I would have to give up and find another way to go to college, or I would have to run away to Boston.

Maybe I could find my real parents, and if they were still alive, they would want me. And they would send me to college. Or the school counselor could help me apply for grants and loans. Or the University of Florida coach would give me a scholarship, anyway, if Jess recommended me.

Long shots, all of them. Still, I wasn't going to give up on getting out of my crummy life. Maybe my money would turn up. Maybe whoever had stolen it would feel guilty and leave it somewhere that I could find it.

176

Nah. That money was gone. I should have hidden it better. I hoped whoever had it would burn in the fiery pits of hell.

And I should have asked my mom in a different way—the way I had planned—instead of just blurting it out. She might have said yes then. Why wouldn't she let me go? I thought I would drown in my anger.

Giving up seemed to be the only solution. But if I gave up, I would be letting Francie down. She was my best friend, and we had pledged to do the marathon together. She might not have the courage to run by herself. Maybe Jess would run with her. He hadn't planned on going to Boston, but he might change his mind. It broke my heart that I didn't have any money to give him.

My other option was to run away. I didn't know how much it would cost to take a bus to Boston on my own. I still had forty-eight dollars left. If that wasn't enough, maybe I could borrow the money from somebody else. Maybe Reese. Or Mr. Barrett. If all else failed, I could hitchhike. Hippie girls did that all the time, I'd heard. But I didn't know if I was brave enough.

If I ran away, what would happen after the marathon? I didn't think my parents would forgive me for defying them. But at that point, I didn't care. The future I had envisioned was in ruins.

I DRAGGED MYSELF TO school in the morning, where the big news was the assassination of Martin Luther King Jr. The tension was thick and ugly. Many of the black kids were absent, and the ones who attended glared at us white kids. Most of our teachers didn't even try to cover the assignments but talked about Dr. King's legacy. This was the South, and not everyone agreed that the legacy was a positive one. I didn't get involved in the discussion, but after the previous night, my loyalties weren't the least bit divided.

At lunch, I wasn't ready yet to talk about the assault on Jess. Instead, I told Francie about the theft of my money. I held my breath when I told her, afraid that she would stop being my friend when she found out.

She was so mad that she banged the table with her palm and knocked over my apple juice. As we cleaned up the mess, she saw the expression on my face. "I'm not mad at you, Faye, but at whoever stole your money."

"I'm sorry, Francie," I said, trying not to cry. "I'll do my best to go to Boston like we've planned."

"I know you will. We can talk about that later. First, we need to figure out what's going on at your house. Something's really wrong. We have to tell my mom right now."

She was right. It was time to tell an adult about my family's secrets. We marched to Laney's clinic. When we got there, Laney told us to wait. There had been a fight that morning between two boys, one black and one white, and she had had to send both of them to the hospital. She had paperwork to complete. We sat on the bench outside the door and waited.

When she ushered us inside, I blurted out my suspicions about being adopted—about the memories that had been coming back to me, about the pictures and, finally, about the missing money. I could see her horror and sympathy in the way she sucked on her upper lip as I talked. Her eyes filled with tears when I told her about the baby pictures that weren't me.

After I had finished, she said, "I'm so sorry, Faye. Yes, I agree that something has to be done. I'll take you to the police station after school." She took a deep breath and shook her head. "But whatever is wrong in your family has been wrong for years, and it can wait until the end of the day. I've got other things to do now. So it's back to class for the two of you."

The bell rang, and Francie squeezed my hand before we separated to go to our afternoon classes. All that afternoon, I couldn't concentrate on anything except what I would say to the police and how my mom was going to kill me for telling the family secrets.

AFTER SCHOOL, LANEY drove Francie and me to the police station to see Detective Hunt, who was an old friend of hers from high school. He sat at his desk with a pile of papers spread around him. His eyes were bleary. "Hey, Laney, what brings you here? Been run off the road again?" He smiled his old-friend smile. "Have a seat, you all. You're saving me from having to figure out how to pay for additional officers on the street." He glanced at Francie and me. "How're plans for the marathon going?"

I looked down at the floor and waited for Francie to answer. She didn't say anything, and neither did I.

After a few minutes he asked, "You're still hoping to run that?"

Francie answered for both of us. "Hoping. Not sure."

He let that one lie. "How're you getting along, Faye?"

I wasn't sure where to begin, so Laney stepped in. "That's why we're here, actually. She's okay," she said in response to his look of concern. "But she insists that she remembers different parents from these. She thinks the Smiths adopted her." She cleared her throat and looked at me. I gestured for her to go on. "There's more. There aren't any photos in the family album of her between when she was a toddler and the first grade. She thinks she was adopted during that time and that the baby in the early pictures wasn't her. In spite of the fact that nearly every teenager thinks she's adopted, I do agree there's something awfully strange about her family." She paused, tilting her head as if waiting for him to comment before she continued.

He leaned back in his chair and gazed upward, staring at the ceiling for longer than seemed necessary. I glanced up but saw only white tiles. We waited.

Finally, he looked at me. "This true? You think you're adopted?"

I nodded, suddenly too shy to speak.

"And your parents have never mentioned it to you?"

"No. Does it make sense that I would have been adopted when I was four or five? Not a baby?"

"Sure. Parents die, or they go to prison, or they can't take care of the kids. But it's likely you'd remember something about that."

I leaned forward as my mind whirled. "I think I do remember something. It was a car wreck. I was in the back seat, and there was a big crash, and my parents wouldn't wake up."

"Then who was the other child in the pictures? The baby, the one who wasn't you?"

I hesitated then pulled out the photos. "These say that she was Dana Faye Smith." I handed them to him.

He looked hard at the photos of the baby and then up at me. "I don't know if this baby is you or not. I agree she doesn't much favor you, and since the picture's in black and white, I can't tell if she has red hair. But babies change as they grow older. This might be you."

I said quietly, "Turn it over."

He did, and his eyes popped out when he read the words. He whistled then looked at me, his eyes glistening. "Do you recognize the handwriting?"

"Yeah, it's my mom's. Sue's," I amended, realizing I was probably going to have to stop calling her my mom. My chin started to wobble, but I didn't look away.

"Do you know anything about this baby's death? Think, Faye, if you can remember anybody saying anything about it. Anything at all."

"No. Never once has either of my parents mentioned another child."

"Could it be a niece or some other relative?"

"Not that I know of. I've never met any of my parents' relatives."

He licked his lips and turned over the photos, studying them. "Look, Faye, I know this seems suspicious. It's definitely strange." He thought for a moment. "Did you ever have a brother or a sister?"

I shook my head. "No. When I asked about it, my parents told me that something happened when I was born, and Mom couldn't have any more children."

He grabbed his yellow pad. "Let me take some notes. Tell me again why you think you're adopted."

I took a deep breath. "Ever since I've been running, memories have been coming back to me. I remember my real mother. Here's her picture." I opened my sketchbook to the page where I'd drawn pictures of both women. "See, she's not at all like Sue, my current mom."

He studied the two drawings. "Neither one of them has red hair. Sometimes hair color skips a generation. But if Sue had blond hair and was twenty years younger, she might resemble this woman." He covered the mouths and chins. "They have similar eyes and foreheads."

I'd never noticed that. "I see what you mean. Maybe I just drew them alike. But I'm positive they're two different people. I remember another car wreck and a different name. My name was Pilot, or something like it, I think."

He covered his mouth with his hand as if trying to withhold a smirk. "Pilot? Nobody names their child Pilot."

"I know. But it was something like that." My eyes filled up, and I blinked back tears. He was saying what everybody else had said: that everything could be explained.

He steepled his fingers in front of his face and stared at the ceiling some more. Then he looked straight at me. "Faye, I believe you."

"You do?" I wondered if I'd heard correctly. I thought we were going through the motions by going to the police. I hadn't expected him to believe me.

"I don't know whether or not you were adopted, but when I met your mother at the hospital, I could sense how nervous I made her. Something is wrong there. Since you're so sure you had another family, I'm willing to start with that. Now, what's the first thing you remember?"

"With these parents?"

"Yes."

"Well, I remember my mom trying to force me to eat oatmeal, and I gagged on it. She was really mad at me."

"How old were you then, do you think?"

"I... I'm not sure. Four or five, I guess."

"Were you in school at the time?"

"No. I think I spent most of my time with babysitters or playing with my stuffed bunny."

"Have you asked your parents about these photos?'

"Not exactly. I did ask my mom why there weren't any pictures of me from when I was a toddler to when I was in school, and she said my dad pawned the camera and they didn't have one during those years."

He asked tentatively, "Have you considered that she might be right?"

I sighed. "Yeah, I've considered it. But it's not true. She also told me I had epilepsy, and I don't. The doctor says he doesn't think I ever had it."

Laney jumped in. "Sue has been giving her pills in a phenobarbital container since 1956. I had them checked out in a lab, and they're aspirin."

He started then shook his head. "Aspirin? Why would she do that?"

Laney said, "We don't know. Apparently, she wanted Faye to think she had epilepsy. None of it makes sense."

He turned to me. "Have you asked your parents about this?"

My face heated up. "No. Not about the pills. But I asked Mom about a car accident, and she says we had one. But it was different from what I remember."

He drummed his fingers on the table and then spent a few minutes writing on his yellow pad. Finally, he looked up at me. "The main question that occurs to me is why you're so afraid to ask your parents about these things. They are definitely suspicious, I admit, but there might be a reasonable explanation. Are you afraid for your safety if you ask them?"

I took my time collecting my thoughts before I answered. "My dad hasn't hit me since I was eight or nine. But I got those pictures from his guitar case, and if he found out I took them, he might beat me. He would ground me for life at the very least." I hesitated. "My mom is a different story. I don't really believe anything she says. Every time I ask her about some of these things, she starts to cry or gets really mad. I'm not afraid she'll hurt me, but I don't think I'll get a straight answer out of her. Ever. That's why I haven't asked her directly."

"Do you want somebody else to ask them for you? Laney maybe? Or me?"

This was quickly spinning out of control. I stopped to think about why we had come to the police station to begin with. "No, not yet. Maybe later. But would you be able to investigate these things before I talk to them?"

He considered for some time, drumming his fingers on the desk. "I'll have to do some research and talk to some people to figure out whether telling somebody they're sick when they're not is a crime. And the same with giving them aspirin instead of prescription medicine. It's definitely strange, but I don't know if it's illegal. I'll get back to you on that. It doesn't seem like you're in physical danger for the time being. But about being adopted... what about your birth certificate? What does it say?"

I pulled it out of my geometry book and handed it to him. "I was looking for this when I found the pictures."

He examined the birth certificate, holding it up to the light to see if there were any erasures or Wite-Out marks anywhere. "It looks fine. Let me just call and find out." He asked the receptionist to connect him to the records department of Grady Memorial Hospital in Atlanta, Georgia. He chatted with Laney about mutual friends while we waited. I thought about running in the morning, with the sun rising over the lake, and I began to calm down.

Eventually, the phone rang, and he answered it and talked for a few minutes. He put his hand over the phone and told us that a records clerk at the hospital was looking up my birth certificate in the files.

Then Detective Hunt spoke in the phone again. "Yes, that's it." After he hung up the phone, he nodded at me. "I guess you followed that. They're the same document."

"But..."

"I know, just because there's a birth certificate doesn't mean that the person who was born was you." After a long pause, he continued. "All right, here's what we'll do. Something doesn't add up with your family. There seems to be some secret you haven't been told about. It could be that you were adopted, or it might be something entirely different. Adoption records are sealed by the courts, so I don't have access to them. If you were adopted, your new name and your new parents would be listed on the birth certificate, not the old ones. So you'll have to get that information from your parents. But I can look into child custody violations, things like that."

I struggled to keep up with him. "Child custody violations?"

He chuckled. "You'd be surprised how many times a mother runs off and her sister or the grandmother takes the child, and the child doesn't know a thing about it." His eyes bored down on me. "Now, I don't want you to worry unnecessarily. There's a ninety-five percent chance that whatever happened to you can be explained. Maybe your parents couldn't afford the real phenobarbital, so they gave you aspirin instead and hoped for the best. I don't have the slightest idea what happened. But I'll look into whatever I can find."

He drummed his fingers on the table. "Every law enforcement agency in the country has a lot going on right now, what with the King murder, but I'll call you when I have something. It might be a week or two before I can get to it, so don't worry if you don't hear from me for a while. Feel free to call me anytime you want, especially if you start feeling unsafe. But, Faye, remember that it would be best for you to just ask your parents about all this."

He waited for me to answer, but I didn't say anything. Finally, he said, "Will this plan work for you? Are you going to be all right at home for a while?"

I nodded. Waiting for even a week to hear from him seemed impossible, but somehow, I'd get through it. There was no other choice. Besides, I had to figure out how to get to Boston with only forty-eight dollars to my name.

Just as we were leaving, he said, "Why don't we get your fingerprints? That way, I'll have something to compare if I do find anything. Just wait in the reception area for a few minutes while I set it up." He hesitated. "Don't worry, Faye. We'll figure this out."

Chapter 24
"Rain"

After my fingerprints were taken, I told Laney that Francie and I would walk back to school. We had things to discuss. No matter what was happening in my personal life, I still had to answer to Francie about the marathon. I knew she was going to be really mad once she had time to think about it.

We walked for a few blocks in silence. Then she said, "You asked your mom, and she said no. Tell me the rest of it."

"It wasn't quite that simple." I told her what had happened with Jess. Was it possible that it had only been the evening before? "When I got home, I looked for my money so I could give some of it to Jess. But the money had disappeared from the jewelry box where I kept it. My mom came in, and we looked and looked, but we couldn't find it." I fought back tears. "She asked what it was for, and I told her, and she said I wasn't going to go to the marathon, money or no money."

"Wow." Francie sounded stunned. "So that's it? It's over? Just like that?"

"No way. I really want to go. But she won't change her mind no matter how much I beg. I know her. So I'll have to run away to do it. And I'll need to get the money from somewhere else if I don't find mine. I don't want to let you down."

We walked in silence toward the waterfront, where there was a park. When Francie finally spoke, her voice sounded small and strained. "Listen, I don't think the marathon's important enough for you to run away to do it. And you don't need to feel responsible for me. I really, really want us to do Boston together, but I can do it without you. Maybe Jess will run with me."

"It's not just you. It's the difference between going to college and not."

"But running away is dangerous. You could get hurt or even killed. Too many crazy people are out there, looking for young girls to murder. There are other ways to get to college. We've talked about this. You're good. If you don't run the Boston Marathon, it doesn't mean you'll have to be a farm worker for the rest of your life."

We stopped, and I turned to look at her. I was so weary that I thought I might fall down where I stood. "It's my decision, don't you think?" I hesitated. "Would you loan me the money so I could take a plane or a bus to Boston?"

She leaned toward me. "I'm not ready to drop the subject of you running away," she said, her voice loud and intense. "Even if you live through it, you will get in big trouble with your parents. And I'll get in trouble for knowing about it and not telling anybody." She sighed and shook her head. "Besides that, I don't have the money to loan you, and there's no way my mom would take you with us without your mom's permission. So she wouldn't loan you the money, either."

My body and soul went numb. I had never felt so alone or so dejected. We started walking again. My feet couldn't feel the ground beneath me.

Francie said in a conciliatory tone, "Listen, why don't we think about this for a while before we make any decisions? Meanwhile, I'll see if Jess can come with me."

We got to the park and sat down on one of the benches. We watched a pontoon boat full of old people shove off from the dock and putt-putt away.

Francie asked, "Who do *you* think took your money?"

"I don't know, but Mom thinks it was Dad. A long time ago, he was accused of stealing some money, but it was never proved. And he's been acting weird recently, smoking pot and drinking and staying out all hours, playing music."

"Wow."

I knew she had to think that my family members were major losers. Including me. I thought the same thing.

"Why didn't you keep your money in a savings account at the bank instead of in your jewelry box?" She spoke loudly and sounded like she was talking to an immigrant who didn't know how things worked in this country.

"I don't know." It had never once occurred to me to open a bank account. Dealing with banks wasn't something people in my family did, as a general rule. We hid our money and pulled it out as needed, because we paid cash for everything. And we moved so often that it wasn't worth opening bank accounts everywhere. Apparently, that wasn't how "normal" people lived. But I didn't want to tell that to Francie.

It seemed I was going to lose my best friend after all. "I'll walk home. See you later." I started the four-mile trek to my house, feeling like warmed-over dog turd.

I'd only gone a few steps when Francie caught up with me and grabbed my shoulder. "I'm sorry I yelled at you. None of this is your fault. Nobody sane would think that their own father would steal their money. I don't know how you got to be so normal, coming from your family. Of course, maybe the answer is that you didn't come from that family. Anyway, I don't know whether I'll go to the marathon without you or not. I'll have to talk to my parents."

I shook off her hand and kept walking.

"Faye, please don't give up hope."

Speaking through the tears, I said, "Tell Jess I'm sorry, would you? I hope he understands. I'm sorry about everything."

Francie turned back toward the school, and I picked up one foot and then the other, heading for home.

ALL WEEKEND, MOM CRASHED dishes around, and Dad stomped in and out of the house without saying a word. They were both as mad as I'd ever seen them, although they didn't yell at each other in my presence. I went to work on Saturday, as usual, but I didn't have the energy to go on Sunday's long run with Francie, so I stayed in my room and listened to the slowest, most depressing music I could find.

Detective Hunt had promised not to contact my parents about my being adopted, but I wondered if he had broken his word and that was why my parents were so angry. Their argument probably had to do with my missing money, but I wasn't sure. Neither of them said anything to me, so I tried to stop worrying.

On Monday morning, I got up early and, as usual, went running with Francie and Jess. I couldn't imagine not continuing with my routine, no matter how pointless it seemed. If I didn't run, I would go crazy. I met my friends on the road outside Francie's house, and the three of us went for a seven-mile run before school. Just like normal. Except that nothing was normal anymore.

Jess had a black eye, his bruises had turned green, and there were stitches in his cheek. But he seemed to be in good spirits. He gave me a hug when he saw me and murmured, "I heard what happened. I'm so sorry, Faye."

I straightened up to my full height of five foot seven. "No, I'm sorry, Jess. If it hadn't been for me, you wouldn't have gotten beat up."

He looked at me as if I had gone insane. "Girl, that wasn't about you. The same thing most likely would have happened if I'd been alone, only it would've been much worse. Besides, you saved the day. No, don't trouble yourself about that." He sighed and looked away. "I was just in the wrong place at the wrong time. It won't always be that way. Dr. King's dream of equality is still alive, even if he isn't."

I didn't know how to respond, so I just stared at him. Francie punched me on the arm. "Even if you can't go to the marathon, I'm glad you're running with us now. It wouldn't be the same without you."

"Yeah. Me, too." I bit back tears and started jogging. The others followed me. Dark clouds hid the sunrise, and palm trees swished in a gusty wind. The rain hadn't started yet, but it wouldn't be long. I didn't care. The three of us had agreed to run in all kinds of weather, as long as there wasn't lightning. And those clouds weren't likely to hold lightning.

That particular morning, we ran down the streets of Valencia, which were mostly dark and deserted at six in the morning. I was running tight—arms close to my chest, shoulders raised.

Francie asked, "You all right?"

"I guess so."

Our feet hit the asphalt in unison. The rain held off. By our third mile, I'd loosened up. Although rain still threatened, the sky had brightened. We kept a steady pace, one that we could talk through. Francie and I were running astride, with Jess behind us a little way.

Francie said, "Hey, there's a band from Tampa playing at the community center this weekend. Jeremy and I are going. Do you want to double date?"

Her warm tone told me she wasn't going to dump me, even after our argument. I grinned and accepted her gift of friendship. "Sure. I'll talk to Reese about it."

We ran for a while in silence. Then she said, "I've got news. Kyle quit college, and he's going into the marines. He's home for a couple weeks before he reports to boot camp. My parents are having hissy fits, especially Mom."

"Wow." I tried to remember the last time I'd heard from Kyle. A month before, at least. I had a hard time thinking about anything beyond my own crisis, but it was clear I wasn't the only person in the universe who was struggling. "Well, tell him good luck for me." I hesitated. "Is he back with Linda?"

"Of *course*." She sounded disgusted. "He'll probably go to Vietnam, so I hope she doesn't break up with him again, at least until he comes back."

We ran for a while without talking. Then she asked in a gentle tone, "How are you really?"

I bit my lip. "The money hasn't turned up. I don't think it will. My parents are fighting worse than ever. I don't know if it's about the money or something else, and I don't dare ask. Oh, and the nightmares are back. It's the same dream, about being in the dark. I'm sleeping with the light on now, though. When I wake up in the night, I think about running, and I stop shaking. So it's not as bad as it used to be." We maneuvered around a giant pothole.

Francie said, "I'm really sorry. But maybe Detective Hunt will come up with some information that will change everything. Don't lose hope."

"All right."

The clouds burst open, and raindrops soaked us before we could even think of putting up our hoods. I'd always loved running in a warm rain. It washed my problems clean. In spite of everything that was wrong in my life, I sprinted ahead, arms held out at shoulder height and head arched back so raindrops could mingle with teardrops.

Chapter 25
"Like a Rolling Stone"

After supper that evening, Dad pushed his chair back, and he and Mom exchanged a look. *Uh-oh.* Something bad was about to happen. I recognized the signs.

Dad cleared his throat and gave me a hard stare. "I know your mama promised that we'd stay in Valencia until you graduated, but things haven't worked out here. I got a new job in Greenville, North Carolina, working on a tobacco farm, and they need me there as soon as possible. We're leaving in the morning, so pack up your things tonight and help your mama pack up the kitchen."

He stood and walked out, slamming the door behind him. Mom just looked down at her plate, a neutral expression on her face.

"Why?" I yelled. "Why would you do this to me?" I wasn't sure if she saw the hatred beaming from my eyes, but she couldn't miss the fury that had burst out of my mouth.

"Because your father needs to move on, and he's already been here longer than we've ever stayed anywhere else." She sounded resigned to the move. She reached over to pat my hand, which was clenched on the table. "Listen, honey, I've argued and argued with him, and I got nowhere. He told Mr. Barrett today and got paid off. So it's final. You'll make friends in North Carolina just like you did here. Maybe you can even come back and visit Francie during the summer."

"Nooo." I shook with anger. "I want to stay here. I bet Francie would let me live with her. At least until school's out. Please, Mom? It's just a couple of months."

"No. Definitely not. You're our daughter, and you'll stay with us. Besides, one of the day workers might have stolen your money. I don't like that scummy bunch. We need to get out of here."

My stomach sank. "But why do we have to leave all of a sudden? You may as well tell me what happened."

Mom sighed and kept her back to me. "I wasn't there, so I only know your dad's side of the story. Apparently, on Friday night, Richard and Laney Ivey dropped in at the bar where your dad's band was playing. They were drinking, but I don't know how much. And so was your dad. Anyway, during the break, Bud tried to flirt with Laney, and Richard hit him in the stomach. The two men got into a fight, although as far as I know, nobody was hurt. But Bud got fired from the band because of it. He loved playing in that band, and now he's too upset to stay here anymore. He needs to make a fresh start somewhere else."

Whoa. Dad and Laney. I remembered how the two of them had flirted when we first moved to Valencia. And then it had stopped, as far as I could tell. I hadn't noticed any sparks between them when they were in the same room. But given Dad's personality, I could see how he might try to flirt with her again—especially if he was drinking—and how it might have led to a fight. God, he was such a jerk. I wished I could divorce him, because I knew that Mom never would.

"This isn't fair. Don't I even get a vote? I want to stay here." I probably sounded like a toddler having a temper tantrum. If I'd thought it would do any good, I would have gotten down on the floor and sobbed and thrashed about. But she probably would have just stepped over me and gone about her business.

"No. You're the child, and we're the grownups in this family. After you're eighteen, you can choose what you want to do with your life. But for now, you'll do what we decide. And that's all I'm going to say on the matter." She stood up. "We've had our talk. Now we need to start packing. Start with your room, and then you can help me with the kitchen. We'll leave first thing in the morning, right after we withdraw you from school."

She moved into the kitchen and began washing dishes. I sat at the table, too stunned to move or even to argue anymore.

After a while, my mind began working. I thought about Reese and the prom I wouldn't get to attend. And Francie, my best friend, who would be running the Boston Marathon without me. And... and everything else about my life that was being torn to shreds. And Detective Hunt, who wouldn't know where to find me when he figured out who my real parents were.

I stood up and ran to the telephone. No dial tone. I tried dialing Francie's number anyway, but nothing happened.

Mom said, "The phone got disconnected this afternoon. Don't bother."

My voice was low and mean. "I have to talk to Francie. I can't just disappear."

She sighed. "All right. If you must. But if you're gone more than an hour, I'm coming after you with a switch. You're not too old for that." She turned around and glared at me. "I doubt that they've told Francie anything about what happened. And it isn't really why we're moving. It was just the last straw for your father."

I tore out of the house and ran the half mile to Francie's house. Knocking at the back door, I saw through the window that the Ivey family was sitting around their kitchen table, having an emotional conversation of their own. Laney was crying, and Richard was arguing with Kyle. Francie looked as if she were trying to shrink into the linoleum floor. When she heard my knock, she glanced my way then hurried to the door.

She stepped outside and closed the door behind her. Taking in my tear-stained cheeks and clenched fists, she said, "Faye, what's wrong?"

"We're moving in the morning. I came to tell you goodbye."

Francie's eyes widened, and her head jerked back as if she'd been slapped. "Whoa. Let's sit down. You're *what*?"

We sat on the stoop, and I told her the story. When I was finished, she shook her head. "My parents haven't said anything to me about it. What they're upset about is Kyle quitting school and going into the marines, not your dad flirting with Mom." She paused, thinking. "Your dad would move you away just like that? Like it's nothing to move to... where is it? North Carolina? What's wrong with him?"

"Yeah. That's the question. What pisses me off is that Mom goes along with anything he wants. Even though he probably stole my money, she still lets him get away with murder. And she doesn't seem to mind that he flirts with other women." I was fast losing control. Allowing myself to fall apart would do nothing more than waste my precious time with my best friend. I took a deep breath and said in a ragged voice, "I don't understand him, and I sure don't understand her. Why can't she think for herself? She and I could stay here, just the two of us. I'm sure Mr. Barrett would work something out."

Francie grabbed my hand and held on to it. "Did you ask her about that?"

"No, I didn't think about it. But I can't change her mind now. She won't back down. I'm screwed, and that's all there is to it."

In spite of my determination to stay in control, I started to cry. Huge sobs threatened to tear me apart. Francie put her arm around me and pulled me toward her. "I don't know what to say. I'm so sorry, Faye. But it's not the end of the world. We'll definitely write. And call. Maybe you can come and visit this summer." She paused. "I need to tell Mom about this and see what she says. But I can't talk to her right now. She and Dad are having a blowout argument with Kyle."

We sat together and watched the evening fall. Their dog, Lady, came and leaned against us. We petted her, and she put her head in my lap. It helped a little.

"I need to call Detective Hunt and tell him what's happened. And I need to get in touch with Reese and tell him I can't go to the prom with him."

Francie breathed in and out. "I guess this is really happening, isn't it? Do you want to use our phone?"

"Yeah. Thanks." I went into Francie's parents' bedroom, where there was a second phone. Detective Hunt was my first priority. When I dialed the police station's number, a bored male voice answered. "Valencia police. How can I help you?"

"Uh, can I speak with Detective Hunt? It's important."

"Sorry, miss, but he's gone for the evening. Can I have him call you in the morning?"

I took a deep breath. Of course he'd gone home. It was late. "No. I don't know where I'll be in the morning. I'll try to call him again when I get a chance."

"Are you sure? I could give him a message. Or maybe somebody else could help you."

I thought about it. At that point, nobody could help me, not even Detective Hunt. I hung up.

Turning to Francie, I said, "I'll let you know my address and phone number as soon as we get to wherever we're going. Will you tell Detective Hunt where I am?"

"Sure. Oh, Faye." Her voice broke, and we hugged. After a little while, we separated. "What about Reese? Do you want to call him now, too? He's probably at home."

I couldn't imagine how I would be able to tell this story again tonight. "No. I'll write him a note. Maybe I could leave it in the clinic, and you could pick it up and give it to him sometime tomorrow."

"Okay. I'll do that. Anything else?"

My anger was like a forest fire burning up everything inside me. "My parents have moved me one too many times. I'm done playing by their rules. I don't know how I'll do it, but I'm going to Boston. North Carolina is closer to Boston than Florida. So look for me at the starting line. Will you look for me?"

"I will, and so will Jess. He's coming with me." She grabbed my hand. "And if you don't show up, we'll know it's because you can't. And I'll run the race for you."

My hour was nearly over. I stood up, wiping my nose, and went outside.

"Don't leave yet. Wait here. I'll be right back." Francie went inside.

I looked into their cozy kitchen and wished for the millionth time that I lived in this family instead of the one half a mile up the road. Francie's parents were somewhere else, and Kyle sat alone at the table. He turned and met my eyes, then he stood up and walked to the door.

My ravaged face must have gotten to him, because he reached up and brushed a tear off my cheek with the back of his hand. "I'm sorry for whatever's going on with you. My parents will be back in a minute, but I want to ask you something. You know I'm going into the marines, right?" When I nodded, he said, "Would it be all right if I write to you? Just as a friend," he quickly added. "I really like you, and I like talking to you."

I shrugged. "If you want. Francie will have my address. But we're moving tomorrow."

"I'm sorry to hear that." He glanced into the kitchen, which was still empty. "I've got to get back inside. But I've got something that might help." He reached into his jeans pocket and pulled out a crumpled joint. "Here. It looks like you need this worse than I do."

I stared at the joint then slapped his hand. The joint flew away into the yard. "Are you nuts? You think every bad thing can be solved by smoking *pot*? My dad smokes pot, when he's not drinking, and it hasn't solved one thing for him. He's worse than ever. And you think I'm going to do it, too? No way, not ever again. You shouldn't, either. Being stoned won't keep you from getting shot at."

We glared at each other for a few seconds, until he held up his hands. "All right, all right. I'm sorry. But I'll still write you, okay? You can write back if you want to."

I took a deep breath and gave him a small smile. "Stay safe, okay?"

"You, too." He headed back into the house.

He and Francie passed in the doorway. Francie pushed an envelope into my hand. "This is for you. It's all I could come up with right now. As soon as you let me know where you're living, I'll try to send you some more."

I looked in the envelope and saw the green of paper money. "Oh, Francie." We hugged again. "I love you." I had rarely said those words, even to my parents. But I had never had a friend like Francie before, and I might never have one again.

"I love you, too."

We shared a sad smile, and I whirled around and headed back home.

WE PACKED ALL THAT night, just as I'd done many times before. Because we had been in Valencia so long, I had more possessions than usual. Not everything fit into the boxes we saved from move to move, or into my tiny suitcase, so I had to leave some things behind. Among them was my beautiful prom dress. I hoped Francie would rescue it after we left. If she didn't want to wear it, she could sell it back to the resale shop.

I emptied out all of the notes and folded pieces of paper that had been stuck into my textbooks, because I'd be turning in all the books in the morning. A bunch of envelopes fell out of my geometry textbook. Letters. I couldn't remember where they came from, so I opened a couple. One was from a man who wanted me to model athletic footwear. Another was from a man in Massachusetts who thought I was his long-lost daughter.

I was puzzled at first, but then I remembered that Coach Lopez had given them to me right after I'd run in the track meet. A million years before. They were letters from some of the kooks who'd come out of the woodwork when I'd been on the news. I had planned on reading them with Francie and laughing about them one day. Instead, I crumpled them up and threw them in the trash, along with the little love notes from Reese, asking me to meet him for a quick kiss before I went running.

Useless. Everything that had happened to me in Valencia was going into the trash. I would have to start again somewhere else. I didn't know if I was up to it.

A couple of hours later, I remembered the letter from the Massachusetts man who thought I was his daughter. What if he wasn't a kook, and I really was his daughter? I pawed through all the trash cans I could find but didn't see it anywhere. I went into the kitchen, where Mom was still packing dishes.

"Mom, I had some trash in my room. Do you know what happened to it?"

"Oh, your father took it out and burned it a while ago. Why? Are you missing something?"

What were the odds that this letter had something to do with my parents' adopting me? Pretty slim. "No. I guess not." I went back into my room.

That night, while I packed up my belongings, I stopped being a teenager who was bruised and battered by the world's unfairness and became a woman who was going to take charge of her life. I resolved to no longer be a victim. I was finished with whining and complaining that my parents were doing me wrong. I'd sounded like a tired country song, the kind my dad liked to play. But no more. As Bob Dylan had sung, the times were a-changing. And I was changing with them—into somebody strong and determined. Somebody grown up.

I stood up straighter when I realized I was in charge of my life. And I felt my breath deepening, my shoulders relaxing. I felt my mind working in a different way.

My parents, or whoever they were, had messed me up as much as I was going to allow. Yes, Bud and Sue could make me move to a new place. But they couldn't make me think that what they were doing was right. And they couldn't keep me from coming back to Valencia the minute I turned eighteen. Above all, however these next two weeks played out, I was going to run the Boston Marathon—or die trying.

In the early-morning hours, I wrote: "Dear Reese, I'm sorry, but my parents are moving me to North Carolina. By the time you read this, I'll be gone. I'll miss going to the prom with you, and I'll think of you next Saturday night. I don't know whether I want you to take someone else or spend the evening pining over me. But I'll be pining over you. I'll write to Francie as soon as I find out my new address, so she can give it to you. I hope you'll write to me when you can. I'm already missing you. Sincerely, Faye."

I couldn't say, "I love you" to him. I liked him, but I didn't think I loved him. He really was more of a friend than a boyfriend. But "Sincerely" didn't seem to cover it, so I added hearts and Xs and Os all around the page. Then I wrote brief notes to Jess, Laney, and Stan, thanking them for all they had done for me.

As we packed the car, Mr. and Mrs. Barrett came out to say good-bye. They shook hands with Mom and Dad. Mr. Barrett hugged me and whispered, "I wish you were my granddaughter." I wished it, too, but wishing didn't make it so. Hopefully, I would see him again one day. He rubbed his eyes, and they walked slowly back into their house.

Mom and I went in to the school office, and she withdrew me from school. I handed in my books, and that was that. The school secretary said she was sorry to see me go, that I had been a valuable addition to Valencia High, and she wished me well. I nodded, trying to keep my anger from showing.

I took a minute and ran down to Laney's clinic. She wasn't in, so I slid the notes under her door and hoped they would get to the proper people. It was a terrible way to say goodbye to friends who'd meant so much to me, but that was the way it was.

It wasn't really goodbye, because I would see these people again. I didn't know when or how, but I would.

Chapter 26
"Runaway"

My dad's new job was on a tobacco farm on the outskirts of a small town in eastern North Carolina. We moved into a shack that was nothing like our pretty cottage in Valencia. For one thing, the house hadn't been painted in this century, and roaches crawled on every surface. Mom and I cleaned and sprayed for two days before we could even put away the dishes. The sweet, clingy smell of tobacco saturated everything and made me sick to my stomach. The view from my bedroom window was bleak. There were no beautiful oak trees and no lovely smell of citrus. Just acres of tobacco plants.

My school was full of country hicks, kids who hated me on sight because I was new and had seen more of the world than they probably ever would. The only good news was that I was ahead of most of the other kids in the easy classes that were offered in that school. Of course, there was no girls' track team. There were no sports of any kind for girls. No matter. I still ran every day. Eight to ten miles up and down the twisting two-lane roads was my regular routine, just as I'd done back in Valencia, with a longer run on the weekend. Farmers in battered pickups looked at me curiously as they passed, but nobody tried to run me off the road.

I carried my container of mace to protect myself if I needed it, but I wasn't afraid. I didn't know if I would ever be afraid of anything again. And I slept well, with no nightmares.

At the new house, I tried to pretend I was resigned to being in North Carolina. Dad was outside in the fields most of the time, but he didn't drink when he got home at night. Mom must have made a deal with him to stop his wicked ways if she agreed to move. I didn't care what they did or didn't do. I no longer expected them to act like decent, responsible people. They were not my parents, no matter what they or anyone else said. Someday, I would find my real parents or at least create a family of my own.

I wrote to Francie right away, and she wrote back immediately, as did Reese. So did three other girls. One of them was the girl who had bloodied my nose in PE class when I was new at Valencia High. LaVonda had heard about how I'd stood up to those rednecks who'd beat up Jess, and she thanked me. She also told me she had joined the track team, and Coach Lopez said she was pretty good—not as good as I was yet, but she could be, with coaching.

I cried when the letters came in, one or two every day. Kyle even wrote me a friendly letter, wishing me well and telling me how excited he was to finally be out on his own. I did my best to convince Mom that I would be fine going to visit Francie for a week during the summer. I didn't let her see how sad I was when the prom came and went or show her the daily letters I wrote to Reese and Francie and mailed from a mailbox at the high school. Every day, my plans to escape became firmer.

THE BOSTON MARATHON was held every year on April 19, to commemorate the battles of Lexington and Concord in the American Revolutionary War. April 19 was on a Friday this year. On Wednesday night, after Mom and Dad were in bed, I got up and quietly packed my suitcase, the only one I owned. It was a child's case, heavy cardboard with brass corners and a frayed handle that my hand, no longer tiny, barely fit through. I'd carried this suitcase during every move I'd made with Bud and Sue, but this would probably be its last trip.

I'd thought of running away when I was in Valencia, but I hadn't had the nerve. Now I had nothing to lose. If the police caught me, I would say that my parents abused me. Social workers would look into my story. Meanwhile, they would send me somewhere else to live. A foster home would undoubtedly be better than here.

I packed lightly. First into the suitcase were the trusty sweatpants and sweatshirt I'd worn all winter, which I folded carefully, because they were going on their last run. They'd looked brand new when I'd bought them at Goodwill, but after many washings, they were faded and bedraggled. I'd start the race wearing them, when their bagginess would hopefully obscure my girl curves, and then toss them after a few miles. By Friday evening, they'd belong to someone else. I hoped it would be a girl who'd wear them for running.

Shorts and a T-shirt, for under the sweats, came next. In Valencia—in another life—I'd bought a white tank top just for that purpose, and beneath it I would wear a sturdy bra that Francie had given me. The special shoes from Germany took up almost half of the case, but they were essential. They were well broken in and ready to carry me 26.2 miles. Socks were a problem. Many runners chose not to wear socks because they got damp and caused blisters. But I always wore thick cotton socks, white with red stripes around the top. So socks went into the suitcase.

Vaseline was another essential. I'd smear it anyplace on my body that might chafe. Upper arms, where the soft skin rubbed against my T-shirt, inner thighs, between my toes, and a few other places I didn't want to mention. Vaseline was the runner's friend.

I added a change of clothes and a few toiletries, and I was done. The little suitcase was stacked so high I feared it either wouldn't close or would explode. On the very top, I added my birth certificate and my sketchbook. Those were the most meaningful things from my life with the Smiths. I smashed the lid shut with one hand while the other snapped the latches, and then I stood back, eyeing it carefully. The latches would likely hold. But it looked sad, lying on my bed—so small and brave, like something a refugee might carry.

Come to think of it, the suitcase was absolutely appropriate. I was a refugee in my own life. I slipped out of the house, not bothering to leave a note, and walked three miles to the bus station in town. Whatever had to happen would happen. Thanks to Francie, I had enough money to get myself to Boston. Earlier that day, I had bought a ticket to Hopkinton, Massachusetts. The trip would take almost thirty-six hours, and if things went well, I would arrive a couple of hours before the race began.

I would need a miracle to find the right bus and not get caught before I even started my journey. As a juvenile, I should have had my parents' written permission to board a bus, so I tried to look older. I had wound my shoulder-length hair into a bun on top of my head, and I wore a University of Florida cap, along with a slouchy sweatshirt and jeans. I hoped I looked like a young man instead of a teenage girl.

Apparently, some angel was looking out for me, because the bus left at two in the morning with me on it.

I TRANSFERRED IN RICHMOND, Virginia, then Washington, DC, and again in Boston. I slept as much as I could, ate at greasy-spoon restaurants when the bus stopped, and minded my own business. Finally, miraculously, the bus pulled into the Hopkinton station. I got off and asked someone to point me toward the high school, where the race was being staged. It was less than a mile away.

The parking lot at the high school was crowded with cars and runners. It took nearly twenty minutes to locate my friends. When Francie saw me, she whooped and ran to give me a hug. We were both dressed as males, but nobody paid any attention to our shrieks.

"I knew you'd get here. I just knew it," she said, a smile filling her face.

"Me, too." I wore a similar smile. It had been ten days since we'd seen each other, but it felt like much longer.

Jess hugged me and held me tightly. "I was so worried about you, girl. It's great to see you. Sometime, you can tell me how you managed to get here."

Laney hugged me. "Listen, let me say that I don't approve of you running away from home. After the race, we'll need to talk about that. And some other things. But it can wait until afterward. For today, you do the best you can, and don't worry about anything. I have faith in you."

All these people had faith in me. I wasn't sure I had as much faith in myself. I might not be able to finish the race, having had only spotty sleep for the past two nights, but I was going to give it my all.

I changed into my running clothes in the high school's restroom. Months before, Jess had preregistered Francie and me, using names that didn't automatically signal that we were females. Part of the registration process included getting a physical, but there wasn't a place on the form to indicate my gender, so the doctor hadn't mentioned it. After I moved away, Jess had added his name to our team so Francie wouldn't have to run alone.

As team captain, Jess had to pick up our bibs. He waved as he headed into the high school, and Francie and I hunched down in Laney's rental car, trying to be invisible.

After a few minutes, Jess came out carrying our bibs, a relieved smile on his face. The bibs resembled cardboard car-license tags, with individual ones for each runner's front and back. I smiled happily at the number 303. It wasn't a special number for me, or hadn't been in the past, but it would be now. Laney helped us pin the bibs over our sweats. We'd have to stop and repin them when we removed the sweats, a few miles into the race. It would take time away from running, but at that point, I might welcome the delay.

Laney kissed us all, wished us good luck, then left. We watched her drive away, my suitcase in the back of her rental car. She would be waiting at the finish line, prepared to take our photographs and drive us to our hotel. Whatever happened in the meantime, we were on our own.

Jess frowned. "They seem to be checking people more carefully than I remember from the past. Looking for females, I guess. Keep your caps on, and don't make eye contact with the officials if you can help it."

The three of us stretched and jogged a little to loosen our muscles. Just before entering the pen that led to the funnel and the starting area, Jess gave us one last pep talk. "This day is for you ladies." He touched the number on his chest. "I've already run the race. But it's a big deal for women to run this far." He smiled at Francie and me. "If either of you has to stop, we'll decide whether all three of us will stop. We're a team. We've come this far together, and I believe we'll cross the finish line together. We'll run at the pace of the slowest of us. It's not about winning, but finishing. Hopefully, we'll do it in less than four and a half hours, but however long it takes, we'll do the best we can."

I was as ready as I would ever be.

Chapter 27
"I Get Around"

At eleven forty-five, we made our way toward the officials who were checking bibs, and we tried to get lost in the crowd of excited runners. The smell of liniment was so strong it stung my eyes.

With a pounding heart and sweat streaming down my face, I went first, the hood of my sweat jacket pulled up and my trembling hands inside the pockets. The official, a middle-aged man with a clipboard and a scowl, noted the number, checked it off on his list, and nodded for me to move through the gate. Jess was next. And finally, it was time for Francie—or *Frank*, as her registration packet said. The official noted her number, checked it off, then raised his head to examine her more closely.

His eyes took in her face, and his gaze traveled down her body, lingering longer than necessary on her chest. "Hey, you're a girl," he blurted. "You can't have a number."

She drew herself up to her full height of five feet four. "I'm a woman. And you can plainly see that I do have a number."

He studied the determination on her face. "I'm sorry, but you can't run with a bib. You'll have to take it off." He shook his head. "Those are the rules, and I'll get in big trouble if I let you through."

The two stared at each other while runners behind muttered, "Aw, buddy, let her through. The race is about to start."

He shook his head and said more forcefully, "Stand over there, and take off that bib, or I'll have to call security."

I could tell by how she gathered herself that Francie was thinking of pushing through and taking her chances with security, but she hesitated. The hesitation was her undoing. She took a deep breath and let it out with a whoosh then nodded, about to cry. She deliberately didn't glance in our direction. Turning away, she said to the official, in a loud voice, "I'll do what you say, but it won't be long until women will be welcomed in this race."

He shrugged. "Maybe. Or maybe not. Either way, it won't be today."

Jess and I had been waiting on the other side of the fence. I wasn't proud of it, but part of me wanted to join the pack and run the race with that precious number on my back. But of course, we had prepared for this possibility, and so I held back my tears, knowing what I had to do. Jess and I nodded in agreement, and he stepped back toward the official. "I can't believe I've lived to see the day when a black man can do something that a white woman can't. If she can't run, then I won't run, either." He started to unpin his bib. I pushed back my hood and shook my long hair out loose. The official's eyes got big.

"Look, I never said she couldn't run. She can run, along with your other friend here." He gestured toward me. "But they can't have bibs. The two women will have to leave them with me."

The three of us unpinned our bibs and handed them to the official. I held onto mine a little longer than necessary, and the official had to pull it out of my hands. I was going to have to say goodbye to number 303, and it wasn't right. It wasn't right. *It wasn't right.* It took all of my restraint to keep from punching that man in the nose, but eventually, I opened my fingers and allowed him to take the bib. My shoulders slumped in defeat.

The official looked uneasy. "And, uh, without bibs, you can't be in this section. You'll have to wait until all the numbered runners have started, and then you can run as bandits. If you want, you can wait over by that telephone pole." He pointed to his left. "There's already a girl over there."

Crushed and holding back tears, the three of us shuffled off the course. A pretty young woman smiled at us. "Good try."

Francie rubbed her eyes. "All our work, for nothing. We've been training for this day ever since we read about that girl getting assaulted last year. It's not fair to keep us out."

The young woman nodded, an expression of disgust on her face. "I know. It's not fair. But you can still run the race. It's my third time."

I examined her more closely. "I've heard about you. I even saw your picture in a magazine. Aren't you Bobbi Gibb?"

She laughed. "Well, there you are. I got a lot of publicity in 1966 as the first woman ever to run the entire race. But the press forgot about me last year when Kathy and Jock tussled." She shrugged. "I just like to run. I'd rather do it with a number, but what's a number, really? Can a number make you an official person or the lack of one take away your satisfaction in running?"

We pondered this. Francie said, "No, of course not. But I want to be counted as official and not kept out. I'm tired of being treated as a lesser being."

Bobbi squinted at me. "Did I see you on television last fall, running the mile on your high school track team? That was groovy. You were great."

"Thanks. But I didn't win."

"Who cares? You competed, and that's what matters."

I started to reply that winning was important, but before I could, we heard the pop of the gun that signaled the beginning of the race. We watched as the mass of runners began to move, slowly at first.

When nearly everyone was past, the stranger said, "Showtime. Nice to meet you. See you at the finish line." She took off from where we stood, nearly a hundred feet in front of the starting line.

I started to follow her, but Francie held out her hand like a traffic cop. "Wait. Let's go back and begin at the starting line. I want to run the whole thing."

Jess laughed. "You won't care in a few miles if you miss out on a few yards. But you're the boss. Let's do it."

The three of us backtracked and held hands as we ran over the starting line. I threw a nasty glance back at the official who still held our bibs. He watched us, his face impassive, as we passed him. I was going to have to let go of my anger or channel it into my feet, because even without numbers, we were running the Boston Marathon. Only a couple of other women could say that. Despite the anger and disappointment, I did a hop and a skip when I crossed that starting line.

WE DROPPED HANDS AND concentrated on finding a pace among the river of runners. Even though we were at the back of the pack, we actually passed a few men with bibs as they tried to keep their feet from running too fast. Well-wishers lined the road, shouting encouragement. I'd never run in a crowd before, and I definitely hadn't been the object of so much attention. People screamed at me, smiling, holding out their hands for a high five. I tried to smile back.

The three of us talked and laughed as we found our pace. In spite of the past few days, I felt good, strong. *Alive.* I strutted with pride, responding to the encouragement from bystanders. Many people yelled, "Go, girls!"

A woman with tears streaming down her face and a radiant smile waved to us. "It'll be me next year!" she shouted. I smiled and flashed a peace sign.

Most people seemed to welcome our presence in the race, but a few guys booed when we passed by. One man holding a beer bottle even yelled, "Get back in the kitchen, girls." And then he laughed and laughed until we'd passed him by. What a creep.

We ran out of Hopkinton and into Ashland. By that time, the field had spread out, and the runners were finding their paces. My breathing slowed, and my arms swung low. The road was flat and the running easy.

Exhilaration rose in me like a bubble, and I felt as if I could run forever. I sped up just to feel my legs run fast, but Jess grabbed my elbow. "Slow down, tiger. There's lots of road up ahead. Our splits are right at ten minutes a mile."

By the third mile, I was thirsty. I angled over toward the bystanders, many of whom held out paper cups of water. I grabbed one as I ran by and drank it without stopping, dropping the cup behind me. The road was littered with paper cups and orange peels.

"What's with the orange peels?" I asked Jess.

"Those are for the elite runners, not for slowpokes like us." He laughed. "Maybe somebody up ahead will hand us one. Are you hungry?"

I scanned my body and realized, no, I wasn't hungry. I'd eaten a big breakfast at a restaurant when the bus had stopped for a break. And I wasn't thirsty now that I'd drunk a little water.

Somewhere in mile five, we heard horns honking, and someone shouted, "Runners, move to your right." We dutifully moved to the side of the narrow road. A flatbed truck rumbled past, the smell of diesel fuel fouling the air. It was the press truck, filled with cameramen aiming their cameras at the runners.

Jess groaned. "They see us now. You may as well smile."

He was right. The truck slowed to our pace and hovered a few feet away. A journalist yelled at us to say something. Francie said hi to her mom, and I looked into the closest camera and said, "Hi, Reese."

The man gave me a thumbs-up.

Another man yelled at me, "Why are you running the race since you don't have a number?"

"Because I can," I yelled back. "One day, women will be allowed to have numbers."

The runners around me cheered, as did most of the spectators.

"When are you going to quit?" the reporter fired at me.

"I'm not going to quit. When are you going to start?" I snapped.

He nodded, pleased at the banter. Finally, the truck rumbled past.

The temperature was in the seventies, and I was warm. I moved to the side of the road and quickly stepped out of my sweatpants, flinging them into the crowd. Then I pulled off my jacket and threw it behind me. Francie and Jess did the same. Within a few seconds, we were running again. I felt much freer in my T-shirt and shorts.

"On the one hand, we have an advantage," said Jess as he loped along. "We've been training in hot weather all this time, and most of the rest of the runners haven't. We'll do fine as it warms up."

"But what's the other hand?"

"We haven't trained on hills. There aren't many in our part of Florida. Not that the hills on the course are huge," he hurried to add after seeing the expression on our faces. "But there are several hills. And they go up as well as down. We'll take it one step at a time."

I nodded. I was starting to feel a little tired. This was the sixth mile, less than one quarter of the way through. The euphoria I'd felt at first had disappeared like smoke, and in its wake was depression. I'd gone to so much trouble over the past year, merely to run down the road with a horde of men who couldn't care less that I was there. I thought about the hours and hours that I'd invested in running. All to pound my feet along this course without even being a legal contestant—and without having the slightest idea what the consequences would be for running away from home.

I asked Francie, "Do you know what your mom wants to talk to me about?"

She shook her head. "Nope."

"Is it about what happened with my dad?"

"I don't think so. It's probably about you running away from home. She doesn't like that."

There was nothing I could do about it at that point. After a few minutes, I said, "Is Kyle all right?"

"Far as I know. He's toughing it out in boot camp and wishing he was still in college, I think. But he makes an effort to sound happy in his letters to Mom and Dad."

I tried to imagine what boot camp would be like. Would Kyle have to run a long way, maybe with a pack on his back? I had no idea, so I just said, "Huh."

By mile ten, we were running smoothly. Jess told us about some of the students he'd coached over the years. There were hundreds of them. Some of them had even run the Boston Marathon. "They were all boys, but if I were to go back to it now, I'd make sure there were girls, too."

Francie said, "It sounds like you miss it."

"I do. I surely do. Coaching you two has reminded me of how much. And speaking of which, I've been offered a job coaching track at Bethune-Cookman University."

"Jess, that's great." I slapped him on his sweaty shoulder.

"Wait a second. I haven't said yes yet. My wife and I are considering it. I make more money selling real estate, so we need to think on it some more."

"Sure. It's your life. But you're a great coach. We wouldn't be here without you."

Soon we came into Natick, where the crowds were even bigger than the ones we'd seen so far. We passed fans who shouted encouragement with a beer in one hand and a pretzel in the other. I tried to ignore the increasing pain in my ankle and the blister on my left heel. Another blister was forming on the outside of my right foot. My knees were also beginning to ache. The asphalt seemed harder than what I was used to.

I heard faint echoes of a faraway din. "What's that noise?"

"Oh, you're going to like this. It's the Wellesley girls. When you see them, maintain your pace. It's easy to speed up, but don't."

"Yes, boss. Whatever you say."

We laughed, but our laughter ended when we heard someone yell, "Amby Burfoot has just won the race with a time of two hours and twenty-two minutes."

My heart sank. "Oh my God. The leaders are already finishing, and we're only halfway."

"Yeah, but don't let your concentration slip. All we've got to do is finish."

I listened to the *slap, slap* of our feet hitting the ground and asked hesitantly, "Jess?"

"Hmmm?"

"Do you hurt anywhere?"

After a while, he answered. "Yeah. My left knee is killing me. I think I've got arthritis in it. And my left big toe hurts when I bend it. Which is with every step. But I'm handling it. You?"

"My ankle feels like an elephant's kicking it. And I've got blisters."

"Oh, the blisters. I didn't count them. I've got at least three of them. Do you need to stop?"

"No, of course not. I just wondered if you hurt, or if it was just me." I gave a self-conscious laugh.

"Child, every person on this course is suffering right now. You don't have a monopoly on pain."

"That's good. I guess."

Francie said, "Just about every joint in my body is screaming at me. I'm trying to ignore the pain, so don't remind me."

The noise had gotten louder and sounded like screeching. We ran over a small hill and to the gates of Wellesley College, where coeds lined the street on both sides, screaming their guts out. I heard shouts of, "It's two girls!" I wanted to hold my hands over my ears to block out the racket. But that wouldn't have been friendly. They meant their screams to be encouragement, so I ran through the tunnel of screeches with a smile plastered on my face.

"We've passed the halfway mark," said Jess, sounding grim. "Now it gets hard."

A little voice in my head said that I could quit anytime. I'd run half of a marathon, and that might be enough to get me a scholarship. But what if it wasn't? What if, for lack of determination, I was doomed to be a farm laborer for the rest of my life? That was the worst fate I could imagine.

I ignored the voice and ran on. I saw a sign that read, "Route 16 East–Cambridge/Boston." Taking that left fork gave me a lift.

The three of us weren't talking so much anymore. The route was getting hillier. In spite of myself, my pace slowed. Picking up my legs over and over required more effort than I thought I could muster. I was just plain tired. Beside me, Jess was huffing like an asthmatic steam engine. Francie's face was beet red, and her breath was louder than I'd ever heard it. We couldn't help but slow even more when we reached the Newton Hills.

"There are three of them," Jess reminded us between breaths. "The last one is called Heartbreak Hill. But the first two are just as hard."

Going up the first hill, I struggled to catch my breath and slowed even more. Looking down at my feet, I realized I was running just a tiny bit faster than a walking pace. It felt totally ridiculous to be going so slowly, but it was the best I could do. I looked over at my friends. Francie's mouth had dropped open as she gasped for breath, and her tongue stuck out a little, but otherwise, she seemed to be doing all right. Sweat poured down Jess's face, and his shirt stuck to his chest. He was moving at about the same speed as we were. If I'd had enough energy to be amused at our glacial pace, I would have laughed. But it wasn't possible.

Glancing around, I noticed that a number of the other runners had slowed to a walk. As slowly as I was moving, I was still able to pass them one by one, and I gave them a grin and a thumbs-up. My legs wobbled like Jell-O, though, and some very big blisters were just about to burst.

After the first hill, the course leveled out, and my pulse slowed. Jess was limping a little, but otherwise, he seemed all right.

"I told you this is where it gets hard," he said after gulping down a cup of water. "But we're on mile twenty. We got this far. We can finish."

"Six more miles," Francie said, gasping. "I don't know..." But she kept running.

The second hill was another lesson in suffering but not essentially different from the first. To take my mind off the pain, I asked Jess, "Why are marathons more than twenty-six miles long? Why not twenty?"

"They were never twenty, but for a while, they were twenty-four miles. But the King of England wanted the marathon to start at Windsor Castle and end in front of his box in the Olympic Stadium. So he issued a proclamation making it twenty-six miles and three hundred eighty-five yards, and it stuck. Stupid, lazy king."

I laughed, although it came out more like a croak. "I agree." We were silent while we struggled down the second hill. Nothing mattered except that next step.

Next was Heartbreak Hill. The spectators were especially thick there, watching the runners battle with personal demons. I ran to the top with my teeth gritted and fists clenched. My blisters had burst, and something was sloshing around in my shoe. I didn't dare look. At the summit, the crowd welcomed us like conquering heroes.

Toward the bottom of the hill, we were greeted with the street sign: "Boston." Just seeing that sign gave me the energy I needed to keep putting one foot in front of the other. Eventually, we turned from Commonwealth Avenue onto Beacon Street. We made our way through cheering crowds that opened like a flower for us to pass through and then closed behind us.

After what seemed like an eternity, we rounded the corner onto Boylston Street and saw the long slope down to the front of the Prudential Building and a line painted on the road with the word, "Finish."

Jess held back so Francie and I could limp over the line first. I felt nothing, not even relief, when I crossed the line. I was so depleted that I didn't even feel human—more like an overtaxed machine that was close to falling apart. I had expected to be thrilled when I crossed that finish line. I'd thought about little else for the past six months and had pictured myself pumping my arms in the air and dancing a little jig when I finished, but none of that happened. All finishing meant was that I could finally stop running.

Our time was four hours and twenty-three minutes—almost exactly on schedule, with an average of ten-minute miles throughout. Somebody threw an army blanket over my shoulders, and a volunteer told Francie and me to report to the ladies' locker room. There was a ladies' locker room for a race that was limited to men? In spite of my exhaustion, I had to laugh. The volunteer pointed us to the Prudential Building's garage. Inside, we got Band-Aids for our bloody feet and were pronounced otherwise healthy.

"How many women have you seen today?" I asked the doctor who examined me.

"Five," he said, "counting the two of you."

"Do you know who they were?"

"Nope. I didn't ask."

Francie and I shuffled back to the finish line to meet Jess. Laney waved from the bleachers, so the three of us climbed up to meet her. She hugged and kissed us all as though we were heroes.

I actually felt like a hero when she did that, and I was able to stand up straight and smile. Against all odds, I had made my dream come true. If the UF coach's promise could be believed, I would be going to college.

Chapter 28
"The Dark End of the Street"

The next morning, Francie and I lay on our beds and compared complaints. We both had blisters and other aches and pains, but we would live.

The day before, all I'd thought about was finishing the race, but now I started to worry about what was next. Mom had probably called the police about me running away, and they would pick me up and take me to a facility of some sort. Maybe, if I was lucky, it would be a foster home with nice people in it. I packed my suitcase so I would be ready to leave at a moment's notice.

After a long shower, we headed down to the hotel's restaurant for breakfast. Jess and Laney were already there, looking tired and worried. I wasn't worried, though. Whatever was going to happen would happen. I was starving, so I ordered a giant omelet, bacon, and toast.

After we finished eating, Jess said, "Uh, Faye, I need to tell you something." He looked sad, as if he were going to tell me I'd broken his heart in some way. But then his sad look turned to a happy smile. "Just playing with you. I've got good news. I called Coach Peters this morning to tell her you finished the race within her time frame. She said there's a scholarship waiting for you if you get decent grades." He lifted his coffee cup. "Here's to you, Faye."

I grinned and clinked my coffee cup with everybody else's. Some days in my life were like the best movies I'd ever seen. I could almost hear the soundtrack of happy music in the background.

Then the whole thing fell apart.

"I'm sorry to have to wreck the mood, but there's something I need to talk to you about, Faye, and it's not so good," said Laney, her voice thick with emotion. "Yesterday, I called Sue to tell her you'd arrived safely. She figured you might be coming here, so she hadn't reported you missing. But she was worried out of her mind. I assured her you were fine. She's coming up here on the early flight tomorrow to take you back to Raleigh with her. You've got a reservation. We'll meet her at the airport."

I felt as if the top of my head were going to fly off. "That won't work," I said, trying to keep my voice even. "I didn't run away. I left home. There's a difference. And I'm not going back there. Can't I come home with you? Kyle's room is available, isn't it?"

Francie looked hopeful, but Laney said, "No, honey. Richard and I would be happy for you to live with us. You're like our own daughter. I asked Sue, begged her even. But she wouldn't budge. Remember back at your birthday party when she thought I was trying to take you away from her? Well, she thinks that even more now. And she's mad at me, I think, that your dad got fired from his band. She thought all that was my fault, even though it wasn't. She said she would have me arrested if I tried to take you home with me." She wiped away tears with a napkin. "I'm so sorry, Faye. You can come and visit us whenever you want. Maybe Sue will let you spend the summer." I shook my head, but she continued. "I wish things were different, but you're only sixteen, so I don't have any say in the matter."

"I'll run away again if you make me go back there." I started to slide out of the booth, but Francie was in the way. I punched her to make her move, but she rubbed her arm and shook her head. I couldn't believe she was siding with her mother instead of me, her best friend.

I flopped back on the seat. My voice rose. "I don't care what you say. I will not go back to those people who aren't my real parents."

Laney sighed. "We've been over this and over it. We don't know for sure they aren't your parents. I'm sure Detective Hunt will be in touch soon. Until then, you'll need to go back. And be patient."

"Nooo," I howled, not caring that everyone in the restaurant turned to look at me. The thought of going back to those people was unbearable. Francie wrapped her arms around me and made soothing noises. It didn't help.

Laney quickly paid the bill and guided me out of the restaurant. My mind was filled with a dreary chant I must have heard somewhere: *I have to go back. I have to go back. I have to go back in the morning.* Every cell in my body screamed, but according to the law, I was too young to make my own decisions in life. No matter how many marathons I ran or how awful my parents were, it seemed that they could keep their tentacles in me until I was eighteen. I was so exhausted from fighting all the time that I wasn't sure I could hold myself upright for much longer.

"I've got to get out of here," I said when we reached the lobby. I wasn't sure what I was going to do. Running away again seemed like the best option, but I needed to figure out where to go. I did my best thinking when my body was in motion.

Laney shook her head, but I ignored her. She gave me a small, sad smile. "I know you're mad at me. I hope one day you'll see that I'm on your side."

If that was what being on my side looked like, I'd have hated to see her working against me. The doorman held open the door, and I was about to walk through it when Laney caught up with me. "Here," she said, placing some money in my hand. "Be careful. I'll see you when you get back."

I stormed outside and stood on the sidewalk, looking around at the tall buildings. Whatever had possessed me to think I wanted to live in a city? I could barely see the sky. There were people all around. A group of hippies at the corner played guitars and begged for money, men in suits carried briefcases and looked straight ahead, and cars honked. This was more people than I'd ever seen in one place, not counting the crowd at the race.

If I ran away again, where would I go? I had no idea, but I thought I knew who would. I walked to the corner where three girls and two boys, not much older than I was, stood chanting. They had long hair and wore tie-dyed clothes. I'd heard about hippies but had never actually talked to one before.

A girl with long blond hair parted in the middle smiled when I got closer. "Hi. How are you?" She tried to hand me a wilted daisy, but I shook my head.

I pulled out a dollar from the money Laney had given me and placed it in the tambourine she held out. "Hi. Could I ask you some questions?"

She nodded and walked a little away from her friends. "Sure. What's up?"

"Uh, where would a person go who wanted to...?" I didn't know how to finish my sentence.

She smiled. "Score some dope?" When I shook my head she said, "Live on the streets?"

I breathed out. "Yeah. That's it."

"A bunch of us have an encampment a couple of miles away, down by the river. You're welcome if you want to join us. Come back here around seven tonight, and I'll take you there. But we won't be here long. We'll be heading to San Francisco next week. It's a little cold here at night, so bring a coat if you've got one."

I bit my lip. "But what's it like on the street? Do you go to school?"

She laughed. "No way. Listen, we've all left home for one reason or another. School isn't part of our scene. We get by fine. What's your name?"

"Faye."

"Mine's Moondust. You'll get another name pretty quick. I'll be thinking of something that might work." She looked at her friends, and an expression passed over her face that might have been fear or something like it. Then she smiled at me. "Hey, I gotta get back. See you tonight if you want."

I nodded and walked back to the hotel. I had seven hours before I needed to decide. I rode the elevator up to our room, trying to figure out if I should take my suitcase with me if I left. When I opened the door, I saw Francie sitting on her bed. She broke into a big smile. "I'm so glad you're back. And I'm sorry about Mom making you go home. She didn't tell me about any of this beforehand." Spreading her arms wide, she said, "We've still got a day before we all leave, so what would you like to do?"

I didn't want to tell Francie what I was considering. I didn't trust her not to tell her mom. I plopped down on my twin bed. "Every time I hear the word *Boston*, I feel like there's something about it I ought to remember. Even though I don't recognize anything, I think I've been here before. I'd like to spend this day figuring out why it's so familiar when my so-called parents said we never lived here."

"Okay," she said, drawing out the word. "How do you want to go about doing that?"

My shoulders sagged. "I'm not sure. Let me think for a while."

She lay back, and we stayed quiet for a long time. Eventually, I reached into the drawer in the bedside table and pulled out the city phone book. It was three or four inches thick. Opening it to the *S* section, I saw that there were probably thousands of Smiths. My dad's real first name was Walter, and there were dozens of Walter Smiths. Looking in the phone book was not going to work. I dumped it back in the drawer.

Now what? Suddenly, I remembered the strange letter about the Boston Marathon that I had pulled out of my mom's metal box and stashed inside the envelope with my birth certificate. I jumped off the bed and found the envelope at the bottom of my suitcase. Inside was the letter. The name and address on the back were:

Ronald Lafferty

1008 Eustis St.

Boston, Massachusetts

Francie and I stared at each other. "Do you know where this is?"

"Maybe there's a map in the phone book." I pulled the phone book out of the drawer again, and sure enough, one of the front pages held a map. "Here it is. Not too far. A couple of miles, maybe?"

She looked at me and shrugged. "I'm not sure I can walk a couple of miles today."

"Me neither. But your mom gave me some money. Maybe it's enough for a bus. Or a taxi." I pulled a ten-dollar bill out of my pocket. "This should be plenty, don't you think?"

Francie scrunched up her nose. "Have you ever taken a taxi before?"

I snorted and shook my head. "Have you?"

"No. I'm not even sure how to do it."

"In the movies, the doorman at the hotel calls a taxi for people. Do you think that would work?"

She nodded. We headed downstairs. Before long, we were in a taxi, headed for Eustis Street. The car let us out in front of a tall two-story house with five windows on the street side and a short set of stairs up to the door. The only way it resembled the house I'd drawn so many times was that they both had two stories. There was no tree or swing, and worst of all, there were no dormer windows. Maybe Mom had been right and I'd mixed up several houses where my babysitters had lived.

We glanced at each other. I took a deep breath, walked up the stairs, and knocked on the door. A young woman with a toddler wrapped around her waist peered at us from behind the glass door.

She smiled and opened it a crack. "Tell me you're here to babysit, and I'll pay you fifty bucks."

"Uh..." I said.

She laughed. "A girl can dream, can't she?" She paused. "How can I help you?"

I pulled out the paper. "I'm looking for the man listed here. Ronald Lafferty. Do you know him?"

She took the paper from me. "This is what the city sends out every year to warn us how to get around on race day. But this is from 1956. You've got the right address, but we just moved here three years ago, and I've never heard of this man. Why are you looking for him?"

"It's a long story." I didn't feel like going into it with a stranger.

"Sorry. I can't help you." She started to close the door and then opened it again. "I do remember the people we bought the house from telling us that a family who lived here during the '50s had some tragedy. I don't have any idea what it was. Good luck to you." She closed the door and locked it.

"A tragedy, huh? I wonder what kind of tragedy and if it involved you." Francie gave me a look of concern.

We knocked on other doors in the neighborhood, but nobody knew anything about the Laffertys or their tragedy. Eventually, we gave up. No taxis came by, so we trudged back to the hotel, guiding ourselves by the map I'd torn out of the phone book.

Back at the room, Francie decided to take a nap. I lay on my bed, determined to think through my situation. Was I willing to be a hippie and chant on the street while I begged for money? I would be free, but I would be alone, except for the other hippies. I was down to less than twenty dollars, and that would go fast in a city. I had lived my whole life in small towns and farms. Boston felt huge and impossible.

And then there was the problem of college. Running away would wreck that dream, which was now, finally, within shouting distance.

Sighing, I admitted what I had to do.

MY FLIGHT TO RALEIGH-Durham was at ten in the morning, an hour before Laney and Francie and Jess's flight to Orlando. They walked me to my gate, which was filled with arriving passengers who had just gotten off the plane. Those people all headed off to pick up their luggage—except for my mom, who looked around until she saw us. Her face was fixed in a scowl that appeared to have been etched into her features. She nodded when she saw me, but she didn't smile or act happy to see me. I assumed she had gone to the trouble and expense of flying all the way to Boston to get me because she didn't believe that Laney would really send me back. Or that I would really go. She was right.

Her eyes moved around our group. She ignored Francie and Laney and narrowed her eyes when she saw Jess. We moved toward her. She made no effort to embrace me or even to speak.

I introduced her to Jess, and she nodded briefly then reached up and slapped him in the face. He touched his cheek but didn't say a word. He sent me a questioning look.

In a life full of bad moments, that was one of my worst. I was responsible for humiliating my friend, and I didn't think I would ever forgive myself or forget the sadness in his eyes. As for Mom, her expression could have peeled the paint right off the floor. Boy, was I in for it.

The airline staff called for the passengers to board our flight. Mom walked ahead of me, out the door to the tarmac, and up the stairs that would take us onto the airplane.

Trying to cheer me up, Jess said, "It's only a little more than a year until you can leave. You can do it. And then your own life will start, and it'll be great." It was nice to hear the words of encouragement. I had said them to myself more than once. But I wasn't sure I believed them anymore.

"I'm so sorry, Jess. I should have..."

He gave me a hug. "Hush, child. You did the best you could. You've got other things to think about."

I broke down then, and Francie and Laney hugged me between them like a sandwich. We stayed that way for a few minutes. But at the next call for the flight, I had to go. I rubbed my eyes with a handkerchief that Laney had given me and followed my mom onto the plane.

My seat was a few rows behind her, so we didn't have to talk to each other. After we were airborne, I stared at the clouds and thought about how different this trip was from the one a few days earlier. Riding the bus north, I'd been excited and confident that my life was about to change for the better. Flying south, I was as depressed and frustrated as I'd ever been. The fact that I'd run the Boston Marathon wouldn't make the slightest difference to my so-called parents. Although I would have a scholarship to college, I had to live with these people until I finished high school. And they were going to be so mad that I couldn't be sure I would live to finish high school.

Needless to say, I wasn't in the best of moods when the plane landed. Sue waited for me, and together we walked to baggage claim. She didn't have any luggage, but I'd checked my little suitcase. I watched the suitcases travel around and around on the carousel, hoping mine had gotten lost and we would have an excuse to stay at the airport for a while. But no, it finally slid down the ramp. Mom grabbed it, and I followed her outside.

In the truck, she turned to me. "All right, missy. Now you're going to tell me why you ran away."

She knew I'd left to run the Boston Marathon, because Laney had told her. What more was there to say? She didn't need to know that I hadn't intended to come back or that I hated the life they made me live. I could feel her eyes stab into me, but I stared at the floorboard and didn't respond. There was nothing to gain by feeding the flames of Mount Vesuvius.

She made a loud huffing noise and started the truck. As soon as we were on the open road and heading east, she let me have it. "What were you thinking of, running away in the middle of the night and not even leaving me a note? Didn't you know I would worry? Your dad is out of his mind. He's been drinking ever since we discovered you were gone, and he hasn't done a lick of work. He's going to be fired from this job before we're even here a month, and it's your fault. And I used all of our savings to come and get you."

She went on and on. I thought about turning on the radio and tuning her out, but I didn't dare. Mainly, I just watched the fields rush by and wished the minutes would pass as quickly as the fields. But of course, time dragged. I wondered how I would stand it for another year.

An hour and a half later, we pulled into the driveway of our shack. When we walked inside, Dad was sitting at the kitchen table, a six-pack of unopened beers in front of him and a trash can full of empties on the floor.

When he saw me, he slammed his palm down on the table. "Well, if it isn't Little Miss Sunshine. Get in here. Sit." He pointed at the chair in front of him.

I dropped my suitcase and pocketbook and sat down, keeping my legs tensed, ready to run if necessary. Mom sat in the other chair, a grim look on her face.

"You scared your mama to death, you know. I ought to tan your hide for doing that, and maybe I will. But right now, we've got some news for you." He took a swig of beer then rubbed his forearm over his mouth and nodded toward Mom.

"First, you're grounded at least until Christmas," she said. "If you do everything we tell you and don't cause any trouble, we'll reconsider it after Christmas. And second, there will be no visit to Valencia this summer. Those people have been a bad influence on you. We never should have let you start running in the first place. Believe me, it won't happen again. No more running for you." She wrung her hands and licked her lips. I'd expected this, but it seemed that more was coming. A tingle of fear ran down my spine.

Mom and Dad exchanged a look. He took over. "You think you're an adult, so we're going to give you a taste of what it's like to be an adult. Tomorrow, your mama is going to withdraw you from school. And I got you a job weeding the tobacco. Doing that for thirty acres should give you enough time to think about what you've done to your mama and me."

It took a second for his words to sink in. They were making me quit school? Being grounded wasn't so bad, but even this country school was better than nothing. I'd never get to college if I didn't graduate from high school. And I might as well be dead if I had to work in the tobacco fields. The smell would probably kill me if I had to weed them for more than a day.

"You can't make me quit school."

"Oh, yes, we can," said Dad. "Lots of kids in this area have to quit school to go to work. You think you're special, but you're not. The law says you can quit when you're sixteen, and that's what's going to happen. Go to your room now. We'll call you when supper's ready."

I was too stunned to move. This punishment was far worse than anything I'd imagined. Dad glared at me, his hand on his belt buckle. "Do what I said."

It seemed that every day, I reached a new level of low. I'd thought I had nothing to lose before, but now I understood that I'd had a lot to lose. I might as well have stayed on the streets of Boston.

"No. I'm not a slave, and I won't quit school." I stood up and faced Dad, braced for whatever might come next.

He stood up, too, and leaned on the table for support. "That's it, then," he said, slurring his words. He unbuckled his belt and pulled it out. Doubling it over, he held it over his head. "Lean over that table." He walked toward me.

"I won't." I was not going to let him beat me with that belt, but I wasn't sure what to do. I glanced at Mom, who sat like a statue with her hand over her mouth. No help there. I had a clear path to the front door. I would pick up my pocketbook and... then it dawned on me. My canister of mace was still in my pocketbook.

But was any of the precious liquid still left in it? I couldn't remember how many shots I'd fired at those rednecks. Whatever. It was worth a try. While Dad stumbled toward me, I raced to my pocketbook and pulled out the canister, cocked it, and aimed it at him. "Stop!" I yelled. "Put that belt down, or I'll shoot you with this."

"I gave that to you, ungrateful bitch." He was standing right in front of me now, his arm raised, ready to hit my shoulders. I held my breath and pushed down on the button.

Nothing happened. I pushed down again. This time a few drops dribbled out. Not nearly enough to stop him.

He laughed. "Now get over there and bend over that table, unless you want me to hit you on your pretty face."

I let out my breath and threw the canister on the floor. I backed up until my foot hit my suitcase. Turning around, I grabbed it and my pocketbook and raced out the front door, down the stairs, and into the driveway. I started walking down the road, wondering where to go. I didn't dare call Laney, since she'd sent me back there. Maybe I could call Mr. Barrett and beg him to send me money for a bus ticket. He might take me in.

Better yet, I could call Detective Hunt. He'd told me to call him if I started feeling unsafe at home. I definitely felt unsafe. Maybe he could help, even from so far away. But I'd have to find a phone booth somewhere. The only phone booths I could remember were in town, three miles away.

I could easily run three miles. I stashed my suitcase behind a pine tree and hoped it would be there when I came back for it. Then, slinging the strap of my pocketbook over my shoulders, I started running.

In comparison to what I was doing now, the Boston Marathon two days earlier seemed like a joke. This time, I was running for my life. Bud's temper was out of control. I knew he would come after me, and I didn't think for a minute he would let me leave again. No, he would beat me within an inch of my life. Maybe even kill me. So every time I got to the top of a small rise, I turned around to make sure his truck wasn't chasing me. I didn't see it, but there were lots of trees in the way. I ran as fast as I could toward town.

And then, on the edge of the commercial district, I saw a phone booth. *Please, please don't be broken,* I thought as I opened the door. It slammed shut behind me as I laid my pocketbook on the shelf and searched for Detective Hunt's card. There it was, stuck in a pocket. I pulled it out and checked to make sure the truck wasn't in sight. All clear.

I dumped out my change on the shelf. Putting a dime in the slot got me an operator. I gave her the number. She said, "That'll be a dollar and twenty cents for the first three minutes." Fortunately, I had four quarters and another dime. Only two quarters and two dimes left, though.

Someone at the Valencia police station answered.

"Detective Hunt, please," I said.

The lady on the other end said, "Just a minute, hon. I'll see if I can find him." Before I could blurt out that I only had a few coins left, she put me on hold. I waited, sweat pouring from my forehead. Finally, when at least a minute had passed, he came on the line.

"Detective Hunt, this is Faye Smith. I..."

"Faye, I'm so glad you called. I have some news for you."

I didn't have time to hear it now. "You said to call if I felt unsafe. Well, I do. My dad tried to whip me with a belt a few minutes ago. I ran away. But I'm afraid he's going to find me and take me back. He might kill me this time."

"All right, Faye, you don't need to say any more. Are you still in Greenville, North Carolina?"

"Yes."

"Where, specifically? Do you know?"

"Yes, I'm at a phone booth at..." I craned my neck to see a street sign. "The corner of Darden Street and Fifth."

"All right. Stay right there. I'll send somebody to get you."

Frantically, I checked behind me. And saw Dad's truck. A block behind me. Dad was driving. Maybe he hadn't seen me yet.

Neon spots danced in front of my eyes, and I felt ready to throw up. I made my voice as steady as possible and said to Detective Hunt, "He's there. I see him."

"All right, Faye. Do you know which direction is toward town?"

"Yes."

"Then run toward town. Now. You'll probably find a police station soon, or at least an open business. Go in there and wait. I'll send a car for you."

I dropped the phone, picked up my pocketbook, and tried to run like a cheetah or a gazelle—or any animal that could outrun a predator. I didn't see a police station, and because it was Sunday, all the stores I passed were closed. I could hear the truck rumbling behind me, but I kept running.

Unless Dad was willing to run me over, I was safe enough. But this felt eerily like the time that Benny had run me off the road. For Benny, it had probably been a joke, but Dad was serious. I had to keep running until a police car found me.

A block went by. No police station. No open businesses.

Two blocks. Nothing.

And then I heard a siren coming toward me. I stopped running and stood on the sidewalk while I waited for the police car to find me.

The truck behind me stopped, too.

And then it began backing up.

I waved my arms over my head. The police car screeched to a stop. An officer rolled down his window. "Can I help you, young lady?"

"My dad. He was going to beat me with his belt. I ran away. He's behind me in a truck."

The officer glanced behind me and then turned his gaze back to me. "Are you Faye Smith?"

"Yes."

"Please get in the car. We'll take care of you. You're safe now."

As soon as I was settled in the back seat, I started to cry. An official-looking woman sitting beside me patted my hand. "Don't worry, honey. We were on our way to get you anyway."

Before I could ask any questions, the police car blocked the truck. The two officers in the front got out and headed toward Dad, their hands on their guns.

"What's going on?" I asked the woman.

She hesitated. "A detective from Florida called us a few minutes ago and said to bring you in right away. We were on our way when he called again and told us where you were." She hesitated and then patted my hand. "We've got some news for you."

Chapter 29
"I Shall Be Released"

A second police car pulled up, and the officers put Bud in the back of that car. They parked the truck, and we all drove to the house, stopping close to the front door. I watched from the back seat and rolled my window down so I could hear what would be said.

The officers knocked on the door. Mom answered, looking scared.

The taller officer said, "Are you Sue Smith?" When she nodded, he cleared his throat and said, "We're arresting you and Walter Smith for the kidnapping of Violet Anne Lafferty." He pulled a set of hand-cuffs from his back pocket. "Ma'am, please turn around and place your hands behind your back."

Suddenly, everything was chaos. More police cars pulled into the driveway. I watched while the only parents I knew were handcuffed and taken away. It all happened so quickly that neither of them so much as glanced in my direction.

The woman I was sitting beside introduced herself as a social worker. She took me inside the house. "Sit down, honey, before you fall down. Everything's going to be all right now."

I turned a blank gaze to her. "Kidnapping?"

She nodded. "They called you Faye? Do you remember when these people took you?"

I shook my head. The police officer had said my name was Violet, not Pilot. Maybe I'd been too young to correctly say my own name.

A man in street clothes came inside and said gently, "I'm Detective Willis. Detective Hunt called us from Florida because your fingerprints match those of Violet Anne Lafferty, who disappeared from her family's wrecked car in 1956. It took him a while to get the final confirmation from the police in Massachusetts, but when he called us, we got to you as soon as we could. Is there somebody I can call for you?"

I didn't hesitate. "Laney. Call Laney. She'll come." I could barely feel my lips, but I gave him her phone number.

I must have fainted then. The next thing I knew, I was lying on the couch. The man was kneeling beside me, holding my hand. When he saw I was awake, he offered me a glass of water. "I know this is a terrible shock, but you're safe now. The Smiths will never bother you again. Your friend Laney will be here in the morning, and your real father will also come tomorrow." He cleared his throat. "For now, if you're able, I'd like to take you back to the police station to answer a few questions. And I can tell you more about what happened to you. When you've had enough, we've arranged for you to stay in a foster home. It's a nice family who'll be happy to welcome you for tonight or as long as it takes to get everything settled."

At last—a foster home with a nice family. Hysteria was close to the surface, and I almost giggled. But with an effort, I stopped myself. The detective wouldn't understand. And then my mind kicked in. My real father. Real father. *Father*. What about my real mother?

Things became a little hazy after that. The police found my suitcase and took me to the station, where I met with the social worker and several officers. They told me the outline of the story. My parents—Ron and Marie Lafferty—and I had been in a terrible car accident on our way home from my grandparents' house in Springfield, Massachusetts, in April 1956. My mother was killed and my father knocked unconscious. Sitting in the back seat, I apparently hadn't been hurt badly. I wasn't at the scene of the accident when the car was discovered. The police figured that I'd spent the night in the car by myself before either wandering away and being eaten by an animal or being kidnapped.

Somewhere in the bowels of the Greenville police station, Sue had confessed everything. The officers told me the gist of it. According to her story, she and Bud had stopped to investigate the accident when they came upon it the next morning. Their own daughter had been about my age. She had died some time back, so they took me and gave me her name.

Now I understood why I'd had the dark dream. It must have been beyond horrible, shaking my parents over and over and not being able to wake them up, seeing their blood everywhere, being afraid of the long, dark night, and having to pee so badly that I wet my pants. In the years since then, my mind had given me a wonderful gift of only allowing me to remember the details in my dreams.

When working with Terry, I had remembered seeing Sue's face in the car window. At first, she'd looked like a monster. Which, of course, she really was. If I had known that, I would have fought to stay with my real parents, even if they weren't responding. But I didn't know. I was only four years old. I was probably so happy to see anybody alive that I didn't even complain when she took me away. And look where it led me. I felt like a plant that had been uprooted and stomped on until it lay in shreds on the ground.

The social worker took me to the foster home for the night. The people seemed nice enough, but I barely noticed that my fondest dream of being safe had been realized. At that point, not much mattered except becoming unconscious. I ate a few bites then fell into bed and slept for twelve hours.

BACK AT THE POLICE station the next morning, Laney raced in. I'd never been so happy to see anyone. She enveloped me in a hug.

"I'm so sorry, Faye. I shouldn't have let Sue take you back, no matter what she said. I was wrong. Will you forgive me?"

That had happened a lifetime ago. I cleared my throat and croaked out, "It's okay. You didn't think this would happen. You're here now, and that's what matters." I stepped back and looked around her. "Where's Francie?"

"She's at school. It's just me. But we can call her later."

I nodded and clasped her hand like a drowning person holding onto a life preserver. She held my hand just as tightly. Her hand was strong and warm, and she was the only adult I trusted. I couldn't remember the last time an adult had held my hand like that, and I wasn't about to let her go.

Soon, a man walked in who introduced himself as a police psychologist. He asked what I remembered about my early life, and I described the drawings I'd made of my real mother. He showed me a photograph of both parents that was taken with Violet—me—just before the accident. We were standing in front of a big car with gull wings. The mother in the photograph looked a lot like my drawings, except her chin was more pointed than I remembered. I didn't remember my father very well. He did look a bit familiar but not as much as my mother. I must not have spent as much time with him as with her.

And the little girl—she was me. I was wearing the white dress I'd remembered, with the embroidered rose on the front. On my feet were black patent leather shoes and white socks with ruffles.

Wait a second. That car was exactly like the one that Benny drove. I shivered when I recognized it. No wonder I had been so freaked out when he ran me off the road. I'd spent the most terrible night of my life in that car.

"This was taken the day before the accident," the psychologist said, keeping a sharp eye on me. "Just after your fourth birthday party. Do you remember that?"

"I do remember a birthday party, but... wait a minute. My birthday is in January. You said the accident happened in April?"

He glanced down at a file. "Yes. April 8. Your birthday is April 7, 1952."

So not only was I not who I thought I was, but I had a different birthday. *Different parents, different name, and now a different birthday.* It was too much to endure. I teared up.

Laney patted my hand. "It's okay. You're still the same person inside that you've always been. You'll have to get used to some new things about yourself, but you'll always be the girl who runs like a gazelle. Don't forget that."

"All right," I whispered.

He talked to me about flashbacks. Parts of my old life had flooded back into my consciousness from time to time. Benny running me off the road had probably been the trigger that started it all. But my real parents had been runners, and my dad had hoped to run the Boston Marathon one day. I might have heard him talking about it at home or run around the yard with him and my mom. Maybe Francie's talk about the marathon had jolted my memories. The psychologist said that I might never understand why those early memories were triggered, but it was a good thing they had been, because they had led to me being safe.

Safe. What a reassuring word that was. Only four letters, but they made the difference between paralyzing terror and peaceful comfort. I wondered when the last time was that I had felt really, truly safe.

The psychologist smiled and stood up. "You can meet your father now."

All kinds of thoughts raced through my mind before I saw him. What if he was disappointed in the girl I'd become and decided he didn't want me after all? What if he took one look and decided he'd made a mistake and I wasn't really his daughter? Laney rubbed my back and told me how brave I was, and that helped a little.

The psychologist stepped outside and came back a few minutes later, followed by a man I didn't recognize. I knew it could only be my dad, but seeing him in person was different from viewing photographs. I stood up, and we stared at each other.

He was more than six feet tall. And slim, like me. Our hair was the same color, but his was starting to turn white at the temples. And we had the same freckles covering our faces. It hit me that, for the first time in my memory, there was someone who looked like me. I didn't have to make up excuses for why nobody in my family had red hair and freckles. Anybody could tell we were related. I stared at him and let amazement wash over me.

He bit his lip, and I recognized the gesture. I did it all the time. Suddenly, a flash of red-hot anger ran through my body. If he hadn't wrecked the car that day, we wouldn't be meeting like this after twelve long years.

He said, "Violet," and grinned with his whole body. "You look just like I've pictured you. I thought I was dreaming when I saw you on TV last year, running so proud in that race."

I tried to contain myself, but I couldn't keep the outrage from seeping out. "You saw me? Why didn't you come and get me then? Why wait for six months until the police found me?" Laney clasped my fingers, encouraging me to calm down. I shook my head. I needed to know.

He flushed bright crimson. "I wrote a letter to your coach, but I never got an answer. And I'd had so many disappointments, so many times when I thought it was you but it wasn't, that I didn't dare drive all the way down to Florida if I wasn't sure. I kept waiting to hear back before I did anything. I'm sorry, sweetheart. I should have come and gotten you right away."

My heart sank. So it really had been him writing to Coach Lopez about me possibly being his long-lost daughter. We'd thought he was a crank, but if I'd written back, everything might have been different.

And if I hadn't thrown the letter away the night before we moved, I might have known, before I was nearly killed, that I had a real dad who wanted me. But I hadn't known. I hadn't known.

After that, my anger dissolved. He held out his arms, and I walked into them. We hugged for a long time. I heard sniffles behind me—Laney, probably, and maybe even the psychologist.

But neither my dad nor I cried. Tears weren't strong enough for how I felt. I basked in the feel of his arms around me. I even thought I recognized his smell—a mixture of talcum powder and Aqua Velva aftershave. It felt safe.

After a while, with his arm still around my shoulders, we sat down. The police officers went on to other duties, and only Laney and the psychologist remained.

My dad told me about my family. My mother, Marie, was from Montreal, and her first language was French. That was why she had an accent. He held back a sob. "She loved you so much, Violet. More than anything in the world. We hoped for more children, but it hadn't happened yet." He said that both sets of grandparents were still alive. I also had an uncle and two cousins. Ron had called them the previous night, before boarding the plane to North Carolina, and told them the wonderful news. They were eager to meet me whenever I was ready.

Of course I wanted to meet them, but I needed some time to get used to all this. If I had ever had epilepsy, all this change would have surely set off a seizure. I found myself wishing I had one of the pills my mom—Sue—had made me take. In spite of them being aspirin, I could have used the sheer familiarity of something soothing. Right then, the only thing in my world that was familiar was Laney. I didn't let go of her hand.

I asked him about the accident. His eyes grew sad. "It was completely my fault. We'd gone to your grandparents' house on Saturday for your birthday party and spent the night. We were slow to get started back to Boston on Sunday afternoon."

He was quiet for a while, and when he finally spoke, his words came slowly, as if they hurt his throat. "It started snowing as we crossed the mountains. I can't recall everything, but I think I lost control of the car when I swerved to miss a deer. I should have been more careful. I grew up in the mountains, and I knew how bad the deer are at sunset. Anyway, we smashed into a tree, hard enough to demolish the front of the car. I woke up three days later in the hospital. The doctor told me that your mother was dead and you were missing. It was a terrible time." He stopped to take some breaths. "You must have been terrified all alone in the back seat. I'm so sorry, Violet."

Violet. That didn't seem like my name, but I nodded. We sat for a while, thinking our own thoughts. I had so many questions and no idea where to start.

"Uh, did you ever call me Pilot?"

He laughed. "Sure. It was my pet nickname for you. It sounded a little like Violet, and when you were tiny you couldn't say your *V*s. Why?"

"I had a wreck a couple of months ago, and when I woke up, I thought my name was Pilot. Everybody thought it was a joke."

Shaking his head, he said, "No. No joke."

We sat for another few minutes in silence. Eventually, I told him about finding the letter about the race and going to visit our house in Boston. "It didn't look at all familiar." I showed him the drawing I'd made of a house. "Do you recognize it?"

He stared at my drawing. "I'm not sure, but it might be your grandparents' house in Springfield. We lived around the corner from there before we moved to Boston. We'd only been on Eustis Street for about six months before the accident. After a couple of years, I moved back to Springfield and spent most of my time searching for you."

"Do you know why Sue and Bud had the letter in their metal box?"

"Not at all. But it might have been in your mom's pocketbook that day."

The psychologist said, "We can ask Mr. and Mrs. Smith about it if you want."

I nodded. And then a wave of exhaustion washed over me. Too much emotion. I couldn't cope. I made a face at Laney. *Help me out here.*

She looked at her watch. "I hate to break up the party, but Faye needs to make some phone calls right now. We'll have to finish this later."

Thank God for Laney. I felt like a shirt that had gone through a wringer washer—flat and dry. Before we left, I asked if it would be all right if I called him "Ron" instead of "Dad," at least for a while.

"Call me anything," he said with a smile, "as long as you call me."

An old joke, but he meant it. And I hoped I would never be without him again. I just needed to take a break and talk to Francie and Reese to get my bearings.

As Laney and I walked out of the police station, I stopped the psychologist who had introduced me to my dad. I knew I shouldn't be thinking this way, but I couldn't help myself. "Uh... I hate to ask this, but how is my mom... Sue... doing?"

He took a long inhalation before answering. "She's in a cell now. I've talked to her. She's sad and remorseful. She knew what she did was wrong, and she feels terrible about it. But her main thoughts are with you, that you're all right. She asked me to apologize to you if I saw you. But I didn't want to bring it up unless you asked, and now you have." He leaned in toward me. "Faye, it's going to take some time for everybody to get used to the new situation. I think it's best that you not see her right now but focus on getting to know your real dad instead. You and Sue can write letters to each other later if you want."

"No," I said as forcefully as I could. "I hate her, and I especially hate him. I don't want to see either of them ever again." I turned away.

"That's your choice, of course," I heard him say as Laney and I walked out the door.

Chapter 30
"Piece of My Heart"

I spent three days talking to the police and getting to know my dad before going home with Laney for the rest of the school year. I wasn't ready to move to a strange house with a strange man, even if he was my real father. The social worker and judge agreed. Ron understood and promised that we would visit each other often. I could stay with Laney until I felt comfortable going back to Massachusetts to live with him. I felt like a zombie, doing what people told me to do—*go here, talk about this, feel this way*. Certainly, I was happy that my life was changing for the better.

I still didn't want to see Bud or Sue again. They were extradited to Massachusetts to stand trial for kidnapping and a host of other charges. Relief washed over me in waves every time I realized I didn't even have to be in the same state as they were.

After much thought and many talks with Ron, I decided to keep the name Faye—I didn't feel like a Violet. I wasn't a fragile flower but a strong young woman who needed a simple, straightforward first name. I became Faye Lafferty, a combination of my two identities.

Before we left for Florida, Laney and I went through Bud and Sue's belongings. I boxed up almost everything and took it to Goodwill. It was ironic to be donating to Goodwill instead of shopping there. My real dad owned a Cadillac dealership and had enough money that I would never have to enter a Goodwill store again unless I wanted to. The only things I kept from that part of my life were the family photo album and the pelican I had carved for them for Christmas.

Back in Valencia, I stayed in Kyle's room under the eaves. The walls were filled with posters of near-naked women and baseball trophies, and I wasn't entirely comfortable among such male belongings. But Kyle wrote that it gave him a lift to think of me as safe and happy in his room. It was going to take me a long while to feel *safe and happy* anywhere, but he didn't need to know that.

I finally understood that although Kyle liked me, he was in love with Linda. Whatever happened with the two of them, he and I would only ever be friends. It hurt a little bit to give up the fantasy of being with this handsome older guy, but the ache was minor compared to the major pain of having my life turned upside down.

At school, everyone was extra nice to me. They must have known what had happened, because it was all over the newspapers, but hardly anyone mentioned it. I didn't know if it was because they didn't care or because somebody had warned them to give me a break. Most likely, Laney had told my friends to handle me with care. And amazingly, they listened. Every day, I was filled with gratitude that I was able to be a regular teenager attending high school in Valencia instead of having to work in the tobacco fields of North Carolina.

Reese came to the house most afternoons, and we played board games and listened to record albums. He tried hard to make me laugh, reciting his Romeo lines in a silly way that I would probably have thought was hilarious at another time. Unfortunately, I was too exhausted to do more than occasionally crack a smile. He was a sweet guy, but I didn't feel anything but friendship when I saw him. He didn't press the issue.

That must have been when I stopped laughing, stopped being the lighthearted girl who was willing to risk everything to run in a race. My mind felt frozen. It seemed that the words people said to me had to pass through a wall of ice before they penetrated into my brain.

And then it took me a while to process whatever it was they said. After that, for the most part, it was just too much trouble to try to break through the icy wall to respond. So most of the time, I was silent.

I don't think I would have survived without Francie. She made me run around the track every day, although it took me a while to manage more than a lap or two. A toddler could have run faster than I did. But Francie didn't mention our slow pace. She'd always preferred running slowly anyway.

Thanks to Francie's tutoring, I made it through the year with halfway decent grades. At the final assembly for the year, the principal presented Francie and me with roses for running the Boston Marathon. Even though we'd run without bibs, we were heroes for finishing the race. He said he hoped we would be willing to cocaptain the girls' track team he was going to start the next year. Everyone gave us a standing ovation. I wouldn't be there to captain anything, of course. The principal pretended not to know that.

IN JUNE, AFTER SCHOOL was out for the summer, I was ready to start my new life. Ron arrived in Valencia to drive me back to Massachusetts. I had my last date with Reese, and we agreed to just be friends. I could tell that Francie had a crush on him, and I didn't want to stand in their way. Besides, I wanted to be free to go out with boys in my new school.

One of my last acts was to walk over to the cottage where I'd spent almost eight months living with Bud and Sue. It looked much the same. A new family had moved in, and a boy's bicycle leaned against the wall. An old car was parked in the driveway. Nobody came outside to speak to me, so I turned and walked away. It was the last home I'd had with my faux parents, other than the few weeks we'd spent in North Carolina, and things hadn't turned out well there. I hoped the new family would be happier than we had been.

I was going to a new home, and I had no idea what I would encounter. Really, I would have stayed with Laney and Richard if I could have. But of course, I needed to move on into my new life. It was actually an old life I would be returning to, but I didn't remember anything about it—except for that swing in my grandparents' yard. Ron said it was still there. I would get to be part of a real family with grandparents and cousins. Something I'd always wanted. Still, I dragged my feet as we were getting ready.

When the car was packed and I couldn't put it off any longer, I hugged Richard and Laney goodbye and thanked them for everything.

"You're family," Laney said. "Come back anytime."

I turned to Francie and hugged her as hard as I could.

"I'll miss you. Write me, okay?" she said.

"Of course. And I'll see you in August."

Francie was going to visit me in Massachusetts in two months, before we began our senior year. I would be attending Springfield High, where there was an active girls' track team.

She sighed. "That seems like such a long time." She smiled and said, "Guess what? LaVonda's going to start running with me. So I won't have to run alone."

"That's great. When I come back to visit at Christmas, maybe we can all run together."

Ron came into the kitchen. "All right, we need to get on the road."

Thanks to Laney, I had finally gotten my driver's license, so Ron let me drive at the start of the trip. I backed out of the driveway in our new Cadillac, into my new life.

Chapter 31
"Turn! Turn! Turn! (To Everything There Is a Season)"

My first day at Springfield High was completely different from my first day at Valencia, or any of the other schools I'd attended. For one thing, Ron drove me to school and got me registered. I carried my real birth certificate and all my transcripts and presented them to the secretary with a smile. Registration didn't take long.

When Ron left me, he hugged me goodbye. "Now, you be sure to call me if you have any problems. I'll be right there." I believed him.

Since I was starting at the beginning of the school year, there were plenty of other transfer students, and maps to the classrooms were included in my registration packet. I didn't get lost once. My cousin Connor, who was also a senior, looked out for me. I wasn't used to having a cousin, but I liked him.

I understood right away that my classes were going to be harder than the ones in Valencia. With Ron and Connor to help me catch up, I thought I would do all right. That first day was really long, though. I missed my friends at Valencia High, especially Francie and Reese, and I struggled not to cry.

I got through it, though, and things got better. It helped that I signed up for the girls' cross-country team after school that first day. I was sort of a celebrity among that group. I hoped it was more because I had run the Boston Marathon than that the story of the kidnapping was on the cover of the local newspaper every day.

That evening, Ron introduced me to his girlfriend, Rose. We met at a local pizza place. I could tell he was nervous, because he talked nonstop all the way to the restaurant. Rose was the bookkeeper for Ron's car dealership, so they saw each other every day. They had been dating for five years, but Ron hadn't wanted to get married until he found me. When he introduced us, instead of shaking my hand, Rose enfolded me in a hug that reminded me of the hugs Laney gave. I'd missed knowing my real mom, but I could tell right away that Rose was going to work out fine.

Rose was my savior those first months. She hadn't known me before, so I didn't have to worry that I had forgotten something I should have remembered. She didn't try to be a mom to me, but she was a better mom than anybody I could remember, other than Laney. Rose and Ron set their wedding date for after I was in college so he could dedicate all his time to me in my last year of high school.

SINCE MOVING IN WITH Ron, I rarely thought about Bud. I was glad that his dangerous presence was gone from my life, but I felt sick to my stomach every time I thought about Sue. I often dreamed I heard her voice calling, "Faye, are you all right?" I tried hard to answer, but for some reason, I couldn't get the words out. And then I would wake up, knowing that I hadn't really heard a thing.

I didn't read any of the letters she sent me, and I forced my mind away when I found myself wondering what she would think of whatever I was doing. I couldn't get past the fact that she had kidnapped me from a good life and forced me into a shit one, and the shit one had eaten my entire childhood.

Beneath the fury about the kidnapping, however, part of me was enraged that she had abandoned me to my real dad. She'd forced me to come home from Boston. If she had really loved me, wouldn't she have fought for me again? I knew that was crazy thinking, so I tried to banish her from my mind.

One evening in October, Ron answered a phone call. I was in the living room, writing an essay on the French Revolution. Ron's strained tone made my ears perk up. He was talking quietly, but I could tell the call had something to do with me.

Please, I thought. *Please don't let it be anything bad. I can't take another bad thing.*

Eventually, Ron came into the room. His serious expression made me put down my pen and prepare myself for the worst. "Faye," he said. "I have some news about Sue and Bud. Do you want to hear it?"

I nodded, my heart thumping hard.

He reached over to hold my hand. "They decided to plead guilty. You won't have to testify in court." He smiled. "Honey, it's over. We can get on with our lives now."

Guilty. Of course they were guilty. Everyone knew it. Sue had given a full confession when she was first arrested, though later she'd claimed that her confession had been coerced. Our lawyer had warned us to be prepared for a *not guilty* plea. In that case, I would be the star witness against them.

Ron cleared his throat. "Sue sent you a message. She said to tell you that they were pleading guilty because they didn't want to put you through any more pain. And that she was sorry."

Writing my essay was impossible after that. Ron probably wanted me to say that I forgave them, but I didn't say a word. I couldn't speak either of their names out loud without wanting to spit. And I couldn't think about forgiveness.

Ron must have had some inkling of what was going on with me, because he insisted that I visit Sue at least once to hear her story. He didn't say a word about visiting Bud, though, and I didn't, either. To get it over with, just after Thanksgiving, we drove over to the women's prison in Framingham. It was strange to return to one of the towns

I'd run through the previous spring. I tried to think about the race and not about what was going to happen in the next few hours.

SUE WAITED FOR ME IN the prison's visiting room, dressed in a red prison jumpsuit. I hardly recognized her. She'd lost a lot of weight and was rail thin. Her once-brown hair had turned gray. My mother for a dozen years, and I might not have known her walking down the street. I tried to think of her as a stranger and myself as a volunteer do-gooder.

But she recognized me and beamed when I walked in. A light hug was as much as I could tolerate. I introduced her to my dad, and we all chatted for a while. I'd come prepared with a list of questions.

"Why did you take me?" The question had never left my mind since the day they'd been arrested.

Sue glanced down at the table and rubbed tears from her eyes. When she looked up, she said, "I need to tell you this story for both our sakes. Will you allow me to tell it in my own way?"

I nodded, feeling as if my heart had been replaced by granite.

"Bud and I moved around a lot in those days. You know about our Faye?" She didn't wait for me to reply but talked over her own words. "Of course you do. She'd died two years before, when she was eighteen months old. I was at work, and Bud accidentally left her alone in the bathtub for just a few seconds. She drowned."

Her voice was flat, a monotone. "I was a weak woman. I wanted to turn him in to the police, but I knew it was my fault for leaving her in his care when he'd been drinking. After she died, he promised to never take another drink if I would stay with him. And I did, against my better judgment. Of course, eventually he started drinking again, and you know how that turned out. Anyway, we buried Faye in the woods behind the house where we were living in Arkansas, and we headed out. I was so depressed, so sad, that I could barely talk or think. Bud took care of me, worked steadily, and didn't drink. But I felt like my life was over."

She stopped and asked me to bring her a drink from the fountain on the other side of the room. I carried a cup of water to her, and she took a sip.

"We'd stop at a place long enough to get a little money together and then move on. That April, we were in western Massachusetts, heading to upstate New York. We'd camped alongside the road the night before, but we didn't sleep well because it was so cold. It had snowed, so we started out before dawn. Within a couple of miles, we came upon a wreck."

She cleared her throat. "The fancy new Cadillac was smashed into a tree. We didn't see any other cars, so we figured it had slid on the ice during the storm. We jumped out to look in the windows. The driver's face was covered in blood, and he was slumped over the steering wheel." She glanced at Ron and shuddered. "And there was a pretty woman sprawled in an odd position across the front seat. Neither of them appeared to be breathing."

She took a sip of water and gave me a sad look. "In the back seat, a child was crying. Her face was bruised, and she had a small cut on her forehead, but mostly she looked scared and lonely. When she called out, 'Mama,' and held out her arms to me, I opened the door and grabbed her up, and I fell in love. That little girl was you, of course." Her eyes squinched up as she tried to keep herself from crying. I knew that look so well.

I didn't remember any of this, except in the way it had haunted my nightmares for so many years. "Is that when you decided to keep me?"

She shook her head. "I knew right then I wanted you, because I could feel the hurt in my chest start to ease up when I held you on my lap. I was convinced that God had led you to me. But Bud argued with me. He said your parents might not be dead, and even if they were, you probably had relatives who would want you. He took that letter about the Boston Marathon so we could get in touch with your family if we needed to."

I grunted. "Or if you wanted to collect a ransom." I wasn't going to be taken in by this fake emotion. No way.

She glanced at Ron and shook her head. "That was never the plan, although we might have asked for a reward for rescuing you. We decided to drive into town and call the law so somebody would come and check on your parents. And we would leave you somewhere that you'd be safe." She paused, probably hoping for a kind word from me. When one didn't come, she continued. "So anyway, we took you to a restaurant to get you some breakfast, and we were going to leave you there. But after you ate a few bites, you fell sound asleep, curled up in my lap. I was in heaven."

I bit my lip, holding back the angry words I wanted to spew at her. I needed to hear her story through to the end before I said any more.

"Honey, I just couldn't leave you. I thought I heard God's voice telling me to take you, so I grabbed you up and carried you to our truck." Her tone held satisfaction as well as pain.

She paused and then continued in a soft voice. "I know now it wasn't really God's voice, but mine. I wanted you, so I pretended it was God speaking to me."

I wasn't sure what to say. She sounded proud of what she'd done, not ashamed. But I didn't want to get into it with her. We only had an hour, and I had more questions.

"Why did you tell me I had epilepsy?"

I watched her face crumple. She turned toward the wall, and harsh sobs came from deep inside. I reached out to pat her leg to try and soothe her, but then I remembered who she was and where I was, and I dropped my arm. Whatever was going on for her, she deserved it. Ron and I glanced at each other, but we let her cry.

When she had calmed down a little, I repeated, in a hard voice, "Why did you do it?"

"We had just gotten you, and—"

"Just kidnapped me, you mean."

She sighed. "Yes, that's right. We'd only had you for a week or so, and I needed you to call me Mommy so people wouldn't be suspicious. You wouldn't do it. You kept screaming for your real mom, saying, 'You're not my mommy,' over and over, and I was afraid the neighbors would call the police. So I had to make up some reason for you being so out of control."

She rubbed her nose with a handkerchief. "I had a cousin with epilepsy, and she got away with anything even when she wasn't falling down with fits. So I took you to a doctor and told him you were having seizures. He was just a country doctor and couldn't imagine that anybody would make up something like that. He gave me a prescription for phenobarbital." She smiled at me. "I knew you didn't really have epilepsy, so I didn't give you that medicine except for a short while. It made you really sleepy, and that was helpful, because you weren't screaming all the time. But after a while, when you were willing to call me Mommy, I switched it to aspirin. I didn't think it would do you any harm."

"But why did you keep telling me I had epilepsy, even after I started calling you Mommy?"

She shrugged. "You kept remembering things for a long time, and I needed to have some reason for your memories. So I told people you had epilepsy and had an overactive imagination."

I stood up on legs that wouldn't bend and staggered to the other side of the room. I wasn't sure I could breathe the same air as that woman. I wanted to kick the wall until I broke my foot, or slam my fist through the window over and over until I was cut and bleeding and my outside matched my insides. Pacing up and down, I realized that, beneath my anger, there was a sliver of relief at finally knowing the truth. And then a bigger wave of realization crashed over me—I knew why lying came so naturally. If I didn't lie, someone might give me medicine that would make me so sleepy I would forget who I was. Because of that, I had become a liar, and a good one.

I resolved, right then, never to lie again, at least not consciously. Either I would tell the truth, or I would keep what I was feeling inside where it wouldn't hurt anybody. That might not be a great thing, but it would be better than lying. At least something good would come from this horrible visit.

After a few minutes, I returned to the table where Sue and Ron sat in stone silence, not looking at each other. I burst out, "You were a bigger liar than I ever was."

She met my eyes and nodded, anguish filling her face. "Sometimes your teachers would call me to ask if the outlandish stories you made up were true. I remember once you told your teacher that we'd just moved there from the West Indies, where your father was a diplomat and women carried water in pots on their heads. You were such a creative little thing." She chuckled, but when I didn't join her, she stopped. "I never mentioned those calls to you. Lying wasn't such a big deal, considering what could have happened."

She continued, looking miserable. "I'm sorry about the aspirin. Along with everything else. Sorry, sorry, sorry. I'll never forget the way you glared at me when I insisted you call me Mommy. Your eyes were knives, stabbing me over and over. It took weeks before you finally gave up and said, 'Okay... Mommy,' in your baby voice. I knew then that my first days as a mother were a failure. But I thought you'd forgotten your old life, because you seemed so happy after that."

Happy? She'd thought I was happy? Had I been? Suddenly, I wasn't sure which of our memories was correct.

We sat in silence for a few minutes and listened to the clock ticking on the wall above us. Sue said, "You brought me back to life. Not that it's any excuse for what we did, but I loved being your mother.

I thought your real parents were dead and that you were an orphan. It didn't seem right to leave an orphaned girl by the side of the road when we had so much love to give."

I had one more question. "Why didn't you want me to run?"

"Why do you think? There was that paper in the back of the wrecked car that talked about the Boston Marathon. I was terrified that something bad would happen if you started running. Either you'd remember your previous life, or you'd want to go to the Boston Marathon and then we'd lose you." She sounded miserable. "It was my worst fear. And it came true."

"And yet you didn't absolutely forbid me from running."

"No. You're right. I guess there was a part of me that needed the lying to be over. Bud was furious at me for taking you, so he took your side against me, at least until the end. But I never meant to hurt you. I did the best I could for you." She blew her nose. "If you blame anybody, blame me. Everything's my fault."

I took a deep breath as something dawned on me. I burst out, "*You* took my money. Not Bud."

She jumped, startled, then sank down in her chair. "I knew you were saving for the marathon, and I couldn't stand the thought of you leaving us. I meant to give it back to you after the race, but I never got the chance."

"And you blamed Bud."

She nodded and took a deep breath. "He knew he hadn't stolen your money, and he couldn't stand it that I didn't believe him." Tears streamed down her face. "Honey, that's what I'm most ashamed of. It's the one thing I did on purpose. I'm so sorry."

Part of me wanted to forgive her. I wasn't used to being so hard on people. But I wasn't ready to do that right then and probably wouldn't be for years. I asked, "Did you steal the money in Kentucky, too?"

"No, I didn't. Maybe Bud did, but I never knew."

We were quiet while I tried to think if I had other questions. Nothing came to me. Finally, she said, as cheerfully as if nothing had happened between us, "You seem to be doing real good. Do you like living in Massachusetts?"

She was talking to me as if nothing had happened—as if she were still my mother and just making sure I was doing well. I wasn't going to give her the pleasure of thinking I was okay with everything she'd told me, so I just said, "Yeah."

"And I guess you'll get to go to college after all. I'm glad."

I could have said something spiteful or just plain nasty. But the truth was, I was glad, too. I still had the possibility of a scholarship to the University of Florida, but Ron had enough money to send me wherever I wanted to go, and he had asked me to stay in New England, near him. I had applied to several colleges, and I would see who accepted me before making my decision.

The murmur of other conversations reminded me we weren't alone in the room. Sue said, "I have no reason to believe that you'll do it, but I have to ask. I've asked God to forgive me, and I think He has. But could you find it in your heart to ever forgive me? You don't have to do it now, but if you think there might be a time when you could look kindly on me again, it would make the years I have to spend in here go faster."

I didn't answer right away, just watched a woman at another table dangle a toddler on her knee and kiss the top of his head as if she'd discovered the world's greatest treasure. Finally, I said, "You took me away from my life and moved me all over the country for a dozen years. The truth is, you weren't such a great mother. But you tried—I'll give you that. It may be a while, but I'll try to forgive you. I can't ever forget, though."

"That's good enough for me." She closed her eyes.

The bell rang to signal the end of the visiting hour. This time, I gave Sue a lingering hug. Part of me hated to leave her in that prison.

Another part of me wanted to get out of there and away from that crazy woman as quickly as I could. But the biggest part was just plain tired. I wanted to be in my own bed, in the house I shared with Ron, and think about everything I had learned in my own time. And I wanted to be a normal teenager thinking about cross-country and boys.

Before the guards took her out, Sue reached over to pat my cheek. "You know," she murmured, "you'll always be my Faye."

No, I won't, I thought with a shudder. I'd never been her Faye, no matter how much she tried to convince me I was. But I didn't bother answering. She was the one in prison, after all, and I was free.

Epilogue
"The End"
October 3, 2015

I sit on what used to be my favorite bench and watch the sun set over Valencia Lake. The bright-orange disc slowly sinks from view and spreads pinks, golds, and deep reds across the clouds and over the lake. A more beautiful sight, I cannot remember seeing. It's funny that I remember so much about my time in this town but don't recall the amazing sunsets. Go figure.

My phone rings. I look at the readout and groan. Tom. My husband. Actually, my estranged husband. He wants a divorce, but so far, I have refused to grant it. He usually only calls when he wants to get into the house to pack up more of his clothes so that he can take them to his new girlfriend's apartment. I press Decline.

I stand and stretch. I can feel the ache from arthritis that has settled in my spine. Maybe I need to cut back my running. That's a surprising thought. Whenever my doctor has told me that, I've replied, "I'm nothing if I can't run." What an extreme thought, that running would define me as a person. I do love to run, but I'm much more than that. And I'm never, ever *nothing*.

I've been sitting on the bench for hours, but now it's time to go to Francie's retirement party. As I walk to my car, I remember all the years of our friendship. Even though I never returned to Valencia, Francie visited me many times. She and I even ran the Boston Marathon again in 1972, the first year that females were officially allowed to register. My bib is framed on my living room wall, along with the ribbon from that first race at Valencia High. Jess didn't run Boston with us, but he came and watched us finish, and that was wonderful. He died not too long after that, and we attended his funeral. He was a great man. I owe my career to him, and maybe even my life.

At the B and B, I change into my formal gown. It's yellow, which has always been a good color for me, and it reminds me of the one I bought for my junior prom and never wore. I'll have to ask Francie if she ever picked up that dress from the cottage where I left it.

I arrive at the country club a few minutes late. Francie is standing at the door, greeting people. Her face lights up when she sees me. We hug for a long time. There's nothing like seeing someone in person and touching them. Francie and I are Facebook friends, and we Skype every Sunday afternoon. We've remained close even though it's been several years since we met in person.

I let go of her reluctantly.

She can probably see the tiredness in my face. "How are you, sweetie?"

Remembering everything that happened in Valencia has exhausted me, but I've emptied all the garbage from my soul, and surprisingly, I feel better. Refreshed. Ready to start again. "I'm okay. Really. It's nice to be back. I'll tell you about my afternoon later. But this is not about me. How are you?"

She smiles and gestures to the room filled with people. Her smile is still the same as it has always been. I can remember when her enthusiasm exasperated me. That was a long time ago. Now I appreciate her smile as I do a sunrise—it's fresh and welcoming every day.

She says, "I'm so happy I might burst."

As a teenager, she was kind of mousy, but she matured into herself and has become more beautiful every year. Now she resembles one of those women in the movie *Steel Magnolias*, maybe an aging Julia Roberts, except with heavy eye makeup and short highlighted hair. I feel like the mousy one now. My hair has turned white, and I wear it short and curly. I never did get the hang of applying makeup.

Reese comes over for a hug. He became a banker and is rotund and bald. But Francie loves him. I always knew I did the right thing by giving him up, but when I see them so happy together, I feel a pang of jealousy. Tom and I were never close like that. I wonder if the breakup really was my fault, as he insists, or if I could blame part of our demise on him. Maybe he didn't try hard enough to be close to me.

And then it hits me that the atmosphere in my marriage was full of tension, much like that of Bud and Sue's. Ron and Rose, on the other hand, are lighthearted and enjoy each other's company even after all these years. Maybe because I lived with tension for so long in my early life, I didn't even notice it in my own marriage. I contributed to it, of course, and may even have played the biggest part. But Tom must have contributed, too.

For the first time, I accept that my marriage is really over. Surprisingly, I feel lighter than I have in years. In his willingness to end it, Tom set us both free. If I have another opportunity, I will use Ron and Rose as my models instead of Bud and Sue.

But that's for later. Right now, I'm at a party with my oldest friends, and I intend to have a good time. Francie introduces me to the other people in the room—her children, grandchildren, and friends. I'm happy to meet them, even if I can't remember all their names.

Then a man approaches me, and I know him immediately. Kyle. I haven't seen him since I left Valencia. He's wearing a perfectly tailored suit with a red tie and one of those little flag pins. We hug, and I ask him to catch me up on his life.

"Let's see," he says. "After Vietnam, I went back to college. You were right about Vietnam, by the way. We shouldn't have been over there, and I realized that after a while. So I majored in political science and even participated in some protests. After I graduated, I came home. I didn't want to be a realtor like my dad, so I ran for office." He flashes me that movie-star smile, and I understand how he got elected.

"City council to begin with. And then I ran for congress and served there for a while. But I got tired of being harassed by people who weren't happy with how I voted, so I became a lobbyist. I live in Washington now." He pauses and shrugs. "That's about it."

I must look amazed, because he laughs. "I know. I'm a surprise to me, too. I think it helped having all those talks with you when we were young. Arguing with you was so much fun that I decided to argue for a living."

"Uh, what about your personal life, or do I dare ask?" Francie has kept me informed about his romances, but I'm enjoying this conversation. I realize I'm flirting a little, and it feels good. It's hard to believe that I still know how to do it.

"Ah, of course you can ask. I know what you're asking. If I'm still with Linda, right?"

I grin and waggle my eyebrows.

"We were married for five years, long ago. But she still didn't want to commit, so we ended up splitting up." He makes a face. "I married twice more, but neither of them took. I've been single for years now." He pauses. "And you?"

I sigh. "My husband of forty years left me a few months ago." I try to keep my tone light and unaffected, but I don't think I'm successful.

He nods, and I see compassion in his eyes. Francie must have kept him informed about me, too. "You'll get past it. I remember how strong you always were. I hate to say it because it's such a cliché, but it's his loss." He hugs me again.

We sit together at the dinner and toast Francie's retirement. It feels oddly familiar and very pleasant to be around him again. It's the biggest surprise of my evening.

Across from me sits LaVonda, whom I haven't seen since high school. If it hadn't been for her elbowing me in the nose, I might not have ever gotten to be friends with Francie. After I left town, we exchanged letters for a while, and then we lost touch.

"Did you become a PE teacher like you wanted?" she asks before taking a bite of fresh-caught grouper.

"Yes, I did." I feel warmth rising in my chest. Despite all my failures, I managed to achieve my goal. "I went to Syracuse University and majored in physical education. Then I got a job teaching and coaching at the same high school in Massachusetts where I graduated. I'm still there. Two of my students set state records."

"Wow. That's wonderful, Faye, after all the trouble you had."

Nobody has mentioned that to me in years. It feels strange to be around people who know my story. "Yeah, but that's long behind me."

We're silent for a few minutes as we eat. Eventually, La Vonda asks, "Whatever happened to the Smiths? I heard they went to prison, but I don't know after that."

"Oh. Well, Bud was killed in a fight shortly after he went to prison. And Sue died from cancer a couple of years into her sentence." Sadness prickles around the edges of my memory, but it's old news now. I visited Sue's grave in Kansas once. I forgave her long ago.

"Huh," she says, looking down at her plate.

This type of conversation is always awkward. Nobody knows whether to express relief or regret that the Smiths are dead. I don't know, either. I clear my throat and make my voice light. "What about you? Did you make it to college?"

She smiles. "I got a scholarship to the University of Florida, maybe the one that you turned down. And I went on to set some records of my own. I ended up as an accountant, though. More job stability. And I got married and have four kids and six grandchildren. You marry?"

"Yeah. I met my husband, Tom, at Syracuse. We ran together on the track team for a while. But he eventually switched to tennis."

Hmm. Maybe that was when we started drifting apart. "We have two girls, Sophia and Marie. Only one grandchild so far." I don't need to tell her that Tom has filed for divorce. This is a night for celebrating our successes, not our failures.

We finish our wonderful meal. Francie and Reese went all out for this celebration. They've got it to spend, though. Francie's dad made big bucks by brokering some of the land sales for the big theme parks, back in the day, and she's continued his real estate dynasty. I'm proud of what she's made of her life, even if she did stay in this small town for the whole of it. She and Reese plan on traveling to every continent now that they're both retired.

Laney is wheeled in after dinner and receives a round of applause. She was always the most popular mother in our group. She's in a wheelchair now, weak from the cancer that is no longer treatable. Not able to eat much, she has saved her limited energy for after the dinner. She smiles and shakes hands with all thirty or so guests. I'm the last in line.

She's too fragile to hug, but she holds my hands and gives me a huge smile. "So good to see you, honey," she says, patting my cheek. "My other daughter."

"I'm so sorry, Laney. Please forgive me." I start to sob. Her nurse sees what's happening and wheels her into a small room. I follow, and the nurse leaves us alone.

"Oh, sweetie. There's nothing to forgive."

"But I didn't come and visit you."

She's quiet for a few minutes. I start to get concerned, wondering if she's all right. Then she sighs. "We both made some mistakes. I never should have sent you back to those people. And even worse, I never should have flirted with Bud when you all first moved here. If he hadn't gotten into a fight with Richard, you might not have had to move away. And some of the terrible things might not have happened. I was an awful flirt when I was younger. I didn't mean anything by it, but it had some bad consequences. So please forgive me, too."

We had worked this out years ago. I can't believe it still bothers her. "Laney..."

She shakes her head to stop me then pats my hand again. Her body is failing, but it's obvious her mind is crystal clear. She speaks slowly and carefully. "I understood how painful it would have been for you to come back here. You had more courage than anybody I ever met. It took all of it for you to get to know Ron and the rest of your family and to get over losing Sue and Bud like that. I never held your lack of visiting against you. But I'm happy to see you now."

Everybody keeps telling me how much courage I had or how strong I was. I never thought about it that way. I just did what was in front of me and hoped it would work out. I should not have neglected this woman. But I don't argue with her. We're past that.

We spend a half hour together, talking and catching up. Then she says, "I'm sorry, Faye, but I'm all tuckered out. It's been wonderful to see you. Come and see me tomorrow if you can. Would you get my nurse now?"

After she leaves, I cry for a few minutes in the small room by myself. And then I rejoin Francie's party. I've done everything I needed to do. Tomorrow I can go back and face the rest of my life.

It's time I think about retiring, too. I'll soon be sixty-five, after all. Maybe I'll take a class in drawing. Or wood carving. I haven't done that in years. Just thinking about it brings a smile to my face.

We drink and dance until the wee hours. In a way, it's like a second prom—I went to my first prom at Springfield High—but with a live band instead of someone in the corner, spinning records. The band even plays the '60s music I love so much. I dance with all the men, and then the women, and then by myself until my feet won't hold me up any longer.

At the end, Kyle walks me to my car. He gives me another hug and touches my cheek. "I can't believe how great it is to see you again. Uh, can I ask you something?"

I nod. I want to raise my hand and touch my cheek where it's still warm from his touch, but I don't. Later maybe.

He blushes, and I can see the young man still in him. "Uh, would it be all right if I called you sometime? I like talking to you."

Hearing that, I laugh so hard I nearly wet my pants. How many times did he say that to me when we were teenagers? Over and over and over. He looks startled at first, but then he remembers, and we laugh together.

Maybe I will let him call. I like talking to him, too.

Author's Note

On April 19, 1966, Bobbi Gibb became the first woman to run the Boston Marathon. Women weren't allowed to officially enter the marathon (which was the only one in the country at that time) until 1972. But Bobbi was a strong runner and thought she could finish. Also, she didn't think it was fair that women were not allowed in the race. So, she hid in the bushes near the start line and joined the male runners. She finished in the top quarter of the entrants, which was an amazing feat for someone who was self-trained.

Bobbi ran again, unofficially, for the next two years. In 1967, another woman—Kathrine Switzer—also ran. She had managed to get an official bib by registering using her initials, and ran the race with her trainer and her boyfriend in the middle of a snowstorm. During the race, the race manager saw a woman running with a bib, and he was furious. He ran up to her with the intention of pulling the bibs off her chest and back. He pounced on her, but her friends pulled the race director off her and told her to "Run like hell." She did—dazed and confused, but determined—and she finished the marathon. Her refusal to stop running made history and played a major role in bolstering the growing women's movement.

I have tried to honor these courageous pioneers with my novel, and to think about how their actions might have influenced other women and girls who heard about them. Somewhere in my research for this novel, I read that five women ran in the 1968 Boston Marathon. I only know the name of one of them—Bobbi Gibb. Although Faye and Francie are figments of my imagination, I like to think that the other four women were similar to them.

If you want to read more about the women pioneers of distance running, I've listed some books on my website to get you started. Check it out on www.dianebyington.com[1].

Thank you for reading my book. Happy trails!

Diane Byington

January 2018

---

1.   http://www.dianebyington.com

Acknowledgments

Writing a book is like running a marathon. You write, revise, revise some more, and wonder if you'll ever get to the finish line. It took me seven years to make this novel come close to matching the vision I had for it in the beginning. Many people helped along the way.

The most important person was my husband, Daniel Booth. Daniel encouraged me to write when it wasn't at all clear I could do it. He read draft after draft and listened to me rattle on about the book pretty much every day, including when we first woke up in the morning. And he never once complained. Talk about going above and beyond the wedding vows!

Judy Wise, my friend and writing partner, also read numerous drafts and gave me a pile of sweet-natured edits. We spent many afternoons eating chocolate and talking about the book's character arcs, plot holes, and themes. She wrote "Applause! Applause!" on every draft. Thank you for everything.

Because I was determined to write this book but didn't really know how to go about telling the story, I enrolled in Stanford's two-year certificate program in novel writing. It was a great experience. I have so many people to thank, among them teachers Wendy Nelson Tokunaga and Malena Watrous, and fellow students Joanne Godley, Katherine Kleespies Christenson, Melanie Denman, Susan Shott Karr, Molly Goodman, Anne Walsh Kelly, and Douglass Seaver. I am grateful to you and to all the others in my classes who read and commented on chapters of this book, over and over. Thank you for your help and support. You are all amazing writers.

Many friends and family were kind enough to read drafts over the years. Thank you, Roy Benjamin, Alea Blum, Domenica Blum, Nancy Butts, Marty Dick, Kathy Dolan, Linda Goerner, Annie Kauffman, Kim Kluger-Bell, Jenn Perez, and Jim Zander. You were wonderful. If I forgot anyone, please forgive me. It's been a long haul, and sometimes important memories get lost in the mist of time.

Last but definitely not least, thanks to the fantastic people at Red Adept Publishing who had faith in this book and worked with me to make it its best self: Lynn McNamee, Jessica Anderegg, Sarah Carleton—and Traci Borum, mentor extraordinaire.

Finally, thanks to Bobbi Gibb and Kathrine Switzer, who were my inspirations.

About the Author

Diane Byington has been a tenured college professor, yoga teacher, psychotherapist, and executive coach. Also, she raised goats for fiber and once took a job cooking hot dogs for a NASCAR event. She still enjoys spinning and weaving, but she hasn't eaten a hot dog or watched a car race since.

Besides reading and writing, Diane loves to hike, kayak, and photograph sunsets. She and her husband divide their time between Boulder, Colorado, and the small Central Florida town they discovered while doing research for her novel.

CPSIA information can be obtained
at www.ICGtesting.com
Printed in the USA
FSHW01n1056090718
50300FS